TENTACLES

The Baron Blasko Mysteries
Book 4

A. E. Howe

Books in the Baron Blasko Mysteries Series:

FANGS (Book 1)

KNIVES (Book 2)

CLAWS (Book 3)

TENTACLES (Book 4)

DUST (Book 5)

Copyright © 2020 A. E Howe

ISBN-13: 978-1-7346541-1-0

This book is a work of fiction. Names, characters, places and incidents are the product of the author's imagination or are used fictitiously. Any resemblance to actual events, locales, business establishments, persons or animals, living or dead, is entirely coincidental.

PROLOGUE

Peter Nicolson's lifeless body drifted slowly over the sandy bottom of a small tidal pool on the coast of the Gulf of Mexico. His pallid, water-logged limbs never flinched as the occasional crab scuttled across his chest, nor did he hear the screech of horror from the young woman who found him.

Soon others came and dragged the body higher onto the beach. One person recognized him as the stranger who'd come to Cedar Island a month earlier. The sheriff arrived within the hour and quickly realized that the marks on the back of Peter's head were the result of an attack. But he also accepted that this was going to be one more in a long line of events on Cedar Island that he would have to gloss over. He'd vowed years ago to come out to the island only when he absolutely had to, and to get back on the mainland as soon as he could.

The body was loaded into the back of a truck and covered with a tarp. The sheriff then hauled it back to the mainland, where he made sure the coroner certified the cause of death as drowning before the man's body was shipped back to his family in Alabama.

CHAPTER ONE

Twenty years later...

"This heat is unbearable!" Baron Dragomir Blasko growled.

"It's southern Alabama in June. What do you expect?" Josephine Nicolson responded without looking up from the book she was reading.

"I didn't even close the lid of my coffin this morning. Do you know how vulnerable that makes me feel?"

"We're just having a little heat wave. It will pass soon enough." Josephine wiped a drop of sweat from the end of her nose. "You know what I've found? The heat isn't as bad if you don't talk about it all the time."

"Bah!"

"It couldn't be no hotter if we were on the sun itself," Grace Dunn said, bringing in a tray of iced tea. "Dinner is ready whenever you want to eat," the maid told Josephine.

Josephine had asked Anna Durand, her cook, to stick to cold dinners until the weather cooled off a little. Though, in an Alabama summer, cooler only meant highs in the low nineties instead of the hundred-degree temperatures they'd lived with for the last few days.

"I'll come eat in the kitchen. No sense in you setting the

table for sandwiches."

"I thank you for that small mercy," Grace said with sincerity as she wiped the sweat from her dark brown cheeks.

Josephine stood up and her eyes fell on a book lying on an end table: *The Complete Works of Edgar Allan Poe*. It wasn't the book that caught her attention, but the memory of a letter she'd found inside of it when a supposed spiritualist had channeled her late uncle.

Josephine turned to Blasko. "I want to know what happened to Uncle Petey."

"Ah, the letter." Blasko knew that it had been on her mind for months. "Your uncle is buried in the cemetery here in Sumter, yes?"

"He's there next to my mother and father. I was sixteen when he died in 1914 and I'm afraid I was a bit self-absorbed at the time. I can only vaguely remember the funeral. It wasn't that I didn't care about Uncle Petey, but before his death he wasn't around much. He'd come to town whenever the whim took him, or when he needed money. It's funny, though. I have such clear memories of him. He'd do crazy things to make me laugh, like somersaulting across the backyard. One time when I was very young, he challenged me to a tree-climbing contest in the big ol' oak out back. My mother yelled at him good for that one."

"He died in Florida?"

"That's right, on Cedar Island."

Blasko walked over to her and took her hand. "I know that letter stirred something in you which you need to put to rest."

"Maybe it's guilt. I don't think I grieved much when he died. Not like I should have. He was always kind to me, and there was a gentleness in him. He cared too much and was too hard on himself."

"You did make it sound like he took advantage of your father."

"Papa groused about it, but he didn't mind. Uncle Petey

was a decade younger and, besides, he meant well and he never took much. Just enough to get started on his next adventure. I think the letter shows how much he disliked begging from the family."

"So how are you going to investigate his death?" Blasko asked, putting a light emphasis on the word "investigate." He had come to embrace his role as a singularly unconventional sleuth.

"I think I need to find someone who remembers the funeral better than I do. Tomorrow I'll go down to the newspaper. Maybe there will be an article about his death or, if not, the obituary might tell me something," Josephine said as she and Blasko went into the kitchen.

"Who else could you talk to?"

Josephine put off his question until she was sitting at the table with a plate of ham sandwiches and coleslaw. A metal fan whirred in the corner of the kitchen, pushing the humid air around. Blasko leaned back against the counter and watched her. He could eat, but he derived no value from the food so he only participated in the ritual when it suited him.

"I've been thinking about that," Josephine finally said. "Colonel Etheridge was my father's best friend. Papa might have said something to him."

Grace joined Josephine at the table. Since she had become Josephine's co-conspirator in hiding the baron's true nature, their relationship had changed to be more than that of mistress and maid. After casting a quick glance at Blasko, Grace turned her gaze on Josephine, who quickly lowered her head. Grace nodded and bowed her own.

"Lord, thank you for this meal, but please could you make it a little cooler tomorrow? Amen." Grace spent a good part of her time at church and now, whenever she felt that Blasko brought a whiff of brimstone into the house, she'd been putting a little pressure on her employer. Josephine held a neutral stance where the church was concerned, but she was willing to be more observant if it kept the peace in the house.

"Who else might remember the funeral?" Blasko asked after the women raised their heads and began to eat.

"I'm not sure. I can't even remember if my father went down to Florida to bring the body back."

"Maybe they sent it back on the train," Grace said before taking another bite of her sandwich. "I remember my uncle's body being sent back from the war on the train."

"That's possible."

"Wouldn't there be a record of it if the body was shipped up here?" Blasko asked.

"Probably, and my father kept meticulous records." Josephine stood up.

"You need to finish your dinner," Grace said sternly.

"It's too hot to eat anyway." Josephine ignored Grace and headed for the library. "Why didn't I do this months ago? That letter's been under my skin since I found it," she muttered to herself as she walked.

Blasko followed her into the library and watched her sort through shelves of account ledgers before taking one down.

"The date on his gravestone is June 28, 1914."

Josephine had taken note of the date the last time she'd visited her parents' graves. She opened the ledger and flipped through it with an ease that came from years of working with the accounts at her father's bank.

"Here's the purchase of the gravestone. Also a donation to the church, care of Father O'Hanlon, who passed away just after the war."

Blasko was looking over her shoulder and she pointed to an entry. "This is probably it. Paid to the freight office in Montgomery four days before he paid the church. Papa must have driven over there to collect the body."

"What is that notation?" Blasko pointed to another line in the ledger.

"A payment to Utley's Ice House. That would have been for storing the body for a few days. Utley has a room toward the back where bodies can be kept in the summer."

Blasko nodded, thinking of the many differences between

Alabama and his home in the Carpathian Mountains of Romania. There they'd had the opposite problem. Bodies would sometimes have to be stored for months in the winter when a family was too poor to afford a crypt and the ground was frozen too hard to dig a grave.

"Do you think the colonel knows anything about your uncle's funeral?"

"Maybe, though he was often out of the country during the war." She closed the ledger thoughtfully. "But it won't hurt to ask him."

"No time like the present," Blasko said, then shouted, "Anton!"

Anton Lacob stepped into the room as though he had been standing just around the corner, waiting to be summoned. The grey-haired gnome of a man with a shaggy beard and deep-set eyes had arrived that spring, along with two crates that Blasko had sent for from Romania. Ever since, he had acted as a kind of butler-slash-henchman for Blasko.

"You are going out, Baron?" Anton asked with a slight bow.

"Yes. My hat and coat, please," Blasko told him.

Before Josephine and Blasko got to the back door, Anton had returned from the baron's basement apartment with the requested items

Once outside, Josephine climbed into the driver's seat of her car. It was understood that she drove whenever possible, though the baron had his own car. She wasn't sure if it was because of Blasko's near immortality or just a general recklessness, but his driving always left her feeling like she'd had a near-death experience… or two.

"We really should have called before coming over," Josephine said.

"He is still the acting sheriff. I'm sure he is used to being interrupted of an evening by now," Blasko said, waving away her concerns.

The colonel's house wasn't that far from Josephine's. If

the weather hadn't been so stifling, she would have suggested that they walk. As it was, she went several blocks out of her way just so she could enjoy the air coming through the car windows. But soon enough she was pulling up in front of the little brick cottage with its turret and bay windows that had always reminded her of something out of a fairytale.

Colonel Samuel Etheridge answered her knock wearing a large smile.

"Well! To what do I owe the honor of this call?" he said, brushing back his unruly grey hair. The portly man wore only a shirt and pants held up by suspenders. Sweat dripped off his lavish mustache. "I hope you'll excuse my state of undress. Damnable heat. Come on in."

"I'm sorry to bother you," Josephine said as she and Blasko walked through the door.

"Baron," the colonel said, shaking Blasko's hand. "It's no bother at all, Josie. I just got back from the office. Fine mess you've gotten me into," he said good-naturedly. Josephine had talked him into accepting the governor's appointment as interim sheriff of Semmes County after Sheriff Logan had suffered a stroke.

"I want to ask you some questions about my uncle," Josephine told him when they were all seated in the colonel's study.

"Your uncle? As you know, I was good friends with your father, but I'm not sure I ever met your uncle. What was his name?"

"Peter, but everyone in the family called him Petey. He died in June of 1914."

"1914? I was in the Belgian Congo in '14. Diplomatic work," he said, making it sound like it was anything but diplomatic work.

"Did Papa ever mention Uncle Petey or how he died?"

"No, I can't say that he did."

"He died in Florida, but he's buried in our family plot in Pine Grove Cemetery."

"I remember seeing his gravestone not far from your father and mother."

"I'm just curious about the circumstances of his death."

"Did you check the paper's archives?'

"I'm going there tomorrow."

"Old Man Connelly would have been the mortician back then," the colonel said thoughtfully. "He passed away during the Spanish flu epidemic after the war, but his son Jerry should remember. He's worked at the funeral home from the time he was old enough to see into a coffin."

"That's a good idea."

"Why are you so interested in this now?" Etheridge asked, taking out a handkerchief to wipe the sweat from his brow.

Josephine explained about the letter she had found.

"Do you think you can trust the letter? After all, the man who told you where to find it was a monster."

"I've thought about that, but I believe that the letter truly was written by Uncle Petey and that he hid it in the book where I found it. I don't know if the séance was real or just some trick of LeSauvage's, but that doesn't matter to me because I'm sure the letter is real."

"Be careful. I don't trust anything connected to LeSauvage," the colonel told her.

"That's why I want to find out everything I can."

"Failing to look into the letter could be dangerous too. Inaction has its own risks," Blasko said. With everyone drowsing in the summer heat, Sumter had been a quiet little town and he'd been bored for weeks. He was seeing this as an interesting puzzle to solve.

"Ha! As a military man, I'd have to agree," Etheridge said, nodding.

"I don't want to go home," Josephine said as she drove down the brick street away from the colonel's house. The thought of going back to the warm, stale air of her own house wasn't appealing in the least.

"Drive down to the river," Blasko suggested and Josephine smiled.

Once they left the town behind, the air seemed fresher and perhaps a little cooler. Here and there they passed farmhouses with windows wide open, soft yellow light spilling out into the night. Though the throaty roar of the car made it impossible to hear them, Josephine imagined the sounds of radio programs drifting out into the night.

As they got closer to the small community of Cotton Dock, they could hear the sound of rhythm and blues coming from The Dock, a small juke joint on the banks of the river. Josephine parked down by an old cotton warehouse and they got out of the car.

"It's so peaceful here," Josephine said as they walked toward the river. "I can't believe that it's been less than a year since someone tried to kill both of us on this very spot."

"We've had some… interesting times." Blasko took her hand and they strolled out onto the dock. A light breeze sent the water lapping against the rough wooden pilings.

"The river is beautiful in the moonlight." Josephine followed the baron's gaze across the water. "What's it like?"

"What?" He turned to look at her.

"Having enhanced senses, or whatever you call them?"

Blasko was quiet for a long while. Then he squeezed her hand and led her to an old bench on the edge of the dock.

"Sit with me. It's time that I told you a story."

CHAPTER TWO

When I first turned, it might have been considered a great gift. It was at a time when we were besieged by enemies. Every year we would find ourselves fighting invading armies or neighboring warlords. My family was exhausted. I'd lost a brother, several uncles and dozens of cousins. Our knights were worn out and the peasants were starving.

I was sent to what is now Budapest to gather arms and hire mercenaries. The journey was long and arduous, the roads little more than opportunities for highwaymen. Eventually I made it to a small village about one hundred miles from the Danube. I spent the night and was assured that the rest of my journey would be safe from bandits. The innkeeper told me that hardly a man had been held up in the last ten years. Incredulous, I pressed him on the matter. His explanation was that the local magistrate had done an excellent job ridding the woods of bandits. Several patrons of the inn told me it was far more likely that the night riders had simply found better hunting grounds.

I should have been more skeptical, but I was anxious to be on my way. My family's situation back home in the Carpathians was desperate. With the moon almost full and the way clear of highwaymen, I decided that I would ride night and day until I reached the city.

On the second night out from the village, I was riding half asleep through dense woods. In the darkness I could see nothing, so I was letting my horse choose the path. Halfway through a copse of trees, someone dropped from above onto the back of the horse. Before I could turn to fight them off, I felt fangs sink into my neck. In desperation, I threw both of us onto the ground.

The fall didn't break my attacker's hold on me, nor dislodge the teeth sucking blood from my neck. So I plunged my dagger into my assailant's stomach, but this did no more than the fall to free me from the monster's grip. As we struggled, I felt the life draining from me and then I blacked out.

When I came to, I was on my back and so weak that I was unable to open my eyes. The place where I lay was cold and damp. At last I heard two voices. They were speaking in a dialect that was unfamiliar, yet I could understand most of what they said.

"You disobeyed me," a man's voice said sharply.

"I thought he was a highwayman," a young woman's voice answered.

"Around here? Nonsense. We chased away the ones we didn't kill years ago. Look at his clothes. Do they look like the clothes of a bandit? Shame on you, Edda!"

"I'm sorry, Papa. What are you going to do with him?"

"He would be dead already if I hadn't followed you. I must save him. And to do so will be at great risk to our family. Do you understand me?"

"Yes, Papa."

"Get your mother. We must do this together."

I blacked out again, but soon woke to find the man's wrist pressed against my mouth and his warm blood running down my throat. I choked and tried to fight him off, but I was too weak to resist.

"You must drink it," he told me firmly. "It is the only way for you to survive."

After a while he pulled his wrist away and I surprised myself by trying to grab it back, only to discover that my hands were bound.

"No more from me. Vitaliya, give him some of your blood."

"Yes, Thanases."

I opened my eyes to see a woman stretch out her arm to me. Blood was dripping from her wrist and I suckled at it hungrily.

"That's enough," the man said after a few minutes. I struggled to hold on as the woman pulled her arm away and the man placed a hand *firmly on my chest. "Settle. Edda, you now."*

A younger woman knelt beside me and held her bloody arm to my mouth. When she had determined that I'd had enough, she pulled her arm away and I heard a strange voice cry, "No!" Only later did I realize that the voice was my own.

"The change will happen soon," Thanases said to me. "It will be painful, but we won't leave you."

I passed out again. When I regained consciousness, pain doesn't even begin to describe what I felt. It was a physical torture unlike anything I'd ever known. But the worst was an intense craving for more blood that maddened me. It seemed to stretch on for weeks, though Thanases told me later that the transformation only took two days.

Eventually, I heard him whisper softly to me, though the words rang in my ears like gunshots: "It is over. I should warn you that you will be especially sensitive to light, sounds and smells. The sensations will overwhelm you at first, but you'll slowly get used to it."

He removed a cloth from my eyes and helped me to sit up. I groaned and tried to cover my eyes from the harsh light that surrounded me, only to feel the ropes that still bound my hands. More ropes secured my legs. Squinting, I realized that I was in a cave and that the only light came from the dim glow of a single candle, though to me it illuminated the room like the brightest sun.

"What have you done to me?" I croaked.

"We've done you a great wrong. All I can do now is try to make it right. I pray that I've done the right thing."

Over the next two days, I gradually adjusted to the increased strength of my senses, though I was still very weak. Edda, young and vibrant, and Vitaliya, mature and strong, sometimes came to sit with me in my part of the cave, sometimes giving me more blood. But when I tried to get them to talk, they would only shake their heads and tell me that Thanases would explain everything.

On the third day, Thanases came and sat on a rock a few feet away from me.

"What is happening to me?" I begged him, fighting against the ropes holding my arms. For a long time I thought he wasn't going to answer me; then I stopped struggling and studied my captor for the first time.

"Good. I see that you are beginning to think," he said, watching my face as I made note of his gentleman's clothes, clean but worn. His square, hard face was framed by blond hair that was long and wild.

"Damn you!" I swore.

"Yes, I believe that I am damned. And I fear that we have damned you too."

"Don't talk in riddles. Turn me loose."

"For your own good, I can't do that."

"My people will be hunting for me."

"No, they won't. Not yet. I went through your papers. You're on a mission to raise troops to help defend your family's lands. They won't think you overdue for another month. Even then, where would they start looking for you?" He shrugged.

"If you know all of that, then you will understand how important it is that I leave this place. Give me my horse and belongings and I'll be on my way."

"For your own safety, I can't let you go until you understand what has happened to you," he said solemnly.

"I know that someone dropped from a tree onto my horse," I said, and only then remembered the searing bite on my neck.

"That was Edda. She disobeyed my orders."

"Is she your daughter?"

"In a manner of speaking."

"You all live here?" I had heard them talking in other parts of the cave during my days of convalescence. "Why?"

"Because we are not quite human anymore." After a pause he added, "And neither are you."

"Don't talk rubbish!" I barked as fear crept into my heart. Not just fear for my safety, but for my very soul. I knew that something dramatic had happened to me, but to not be human? What could he mean?

"You will be burned by the rays of the sun if they touch you."

"You are mad!"

"That is why you are bound. If I let you run out into the daylight, you would die."

"I don't believe you," I said flatly.

"I knew you wouldn't. I didn't believe it either."

"Who are you?"

"I was a priest."

"Yet you have a wife?" I scoffed.

"She came after," he said with a depth of melancholy that made me shiver.

"What happened to you?"

"I crossed paths with the wrong demon. I was at an inn one night where Vitaliya was serving food while her husband poured drinks. A stranger came in and tried to grab Vitaliya. When I challenged the man, he released her and gave me an evil smile as he left the inn. When I went outside later, the creature attacked me and dragged me off to a crypt where he'd made his home. He turned me and a nightmare began."

"If Vitaliya was married to—" I started to say, but the former priest held up his hand to stop me.

"After the demon turned me, I went a bit mad. I went back to the inn, killed Vitaliya's husband, then changed her. Crazed, she also changed her daughter, Edda. We all went berserk for a while before I realized that we must come back to God. Forty years ago, we came to live in these caves. Since then, we have tried to take blood only from those who do harm to others. But Edda…"

"This is all ridiculous," I said, though I could feel the truth of his story in my veins.

"I will have to prove it to you. I regret what we've done to you and perhaps I should have let you die." He reached down and pulled on my legs, dragging me toward the entrance to the cave. With my hands bound and still weak from the transformation, there was nothing I could do to stop him.

Vitaliya met him with several blankets in her hands. She helped Thanases to wrap one completely around my lower body, then she knelt beside me as he pulled another large blanket over his head and wrapped it securely around himself.

"You need to stay under here," Vitaliya told me as she placed a third blanket over my head.

"Are you as insane as he is?" I snapped.

"You will find out soon enough," she said grimly.

Again Thanases grabbed my feet. I skidded over the rough ground, *clutching at the heavy woolen blanket with my bound hands. I was tempted to twist and turn until I could see where I was going, but I hesitated. Their attitudes had not suggested they were lying. Suddenly a little light came through the blanket and my eyes watered, even though I knew it was only a tiny amount of daylight.*

Thanases dropped my legs. "I am going to free your hands. But remember—if you uncover yourself, you will die."

I felt his hands searching for mine and he poked me once or twice with his knife as he cut through the ropes that held me. Finally free, I flexed my hands. Part of me wanted to untie my legs and run away, but the strangeness of the situation made me hesitate. I didn't dare ignore the warnings.

"Move your hand to the edge of the blanket, then I suggest you try extending a finger outside. It is twilight. The sun is weaker now."

I did what he suggested and lifted a small edge of the blanket to expose my smallest finger to the rays of the setting sun. To this day I can still feel the searing pain that burned through my flesh.

I screamed. Screamed from the pain and the knowledge that they had transformed me into a monster.

"Drag me back inside!" I yelled, fearing that he might have left me alone outside the cave.

"Wait," he said calmly from a short distance away.

Huddled like a child inside my blanket, I saw the light fade. A little time passed, then Thanases jerked the blanket off of me. I cringed, not knowing what to expect. Through squinting eyes, I could see a blue line of light along the western horizon where the sun had set.

"You are now a creature of darkness," Thanases proclaimed, untying my legs. "May God have mercy upon your soul."

I struggled to my feet, stiff and sore from all the time spent lying on the cave floor. We were standing on the ledge of a cliff, the forested ground more than one hundred feet below us.

"What are you?" I asked.

"Vampir. As are you," he answered sadly. "From this day forward, you will derive all of your sustenance from the blood of others. You can never go out in the sunlight again. To cross running water, you must protect yourself with gold and the soil of your native land. During the day, you should sleep in a coffin, for you are dead to the diurnal

world."

"You are insane."

"You know better!" he said, thumping me on the chest.

Days of pent-up rage at being kept as a prisoner erupted from me as he touched me. I grabbed at him and hurled him over the edge of the cliff, surprised at my own strength. The last thing I heard before he disappeared into the abyss was his laughter.

I screamed in fury, my voice echoing across the dark valley. What do I do now? *I wondered. I turned back toward the cave, but before I reached the entrance I heard a sound behind me. Turning, I found Thanases climbing back onto the ledge, his clothes torn and dirty.*

"You, like me, are also invulnerable to most dangers," he said, panting a little. "Things that would have killed you no longer can. But hunters will come with stakes to drive through your heart and swords to sever your head. Those you must still be careful of," he said with a strange laugh.

I'd called him mad and now I knew it was true. No wonder. At that moment, I knew that my own *sanity was at very grave risk.*

CHAPTER THREE

Blasko grew suddenly quiet. As Josephine held his hand, she realized that she could feel the rough scar on his small finger.

"What did you do? What became of Thanases and the rest?" Josephine asked softly.

Blasko brought her hand to his lips and kissed it. "We'll save that for another time."

He stood up and she followed him back toward the car, thinking that his usual mask of calm reserve hid some frighteningly dark memories.

As they walked, they could hear that the rhythm and blues from The Dock had given way to a local mix of jazz and Dixieland.

"I have an idea," Josephine said, encouraging Blasko to get into the car.

She drove to The Dock and parked under a spreading live oak that was draped in Spanish moss, its branches unmoving in the still heat. There was another car parked on the opposite side of the oak. Josephine cast a furtive look at it and saw a young couple slouched together in the front seat, the smoke from their cigarettes drifting out through the windows.

"Are we going in?" Blasko asked.

"No. But this is where white folk come to park and—" Before the words were out of her mouth, a short dark man in overalls cautiously approached the side of the car.

"Pardon, ma'am. I got the good stuff and the cheap stuff," he said with a tip of his hat.

"A pint of your best."

"Yes, ma'am!" The man hustled over to a couple of boxes hidden under an azalea bush. In a moment, he was back with a bottle.

"Five dollars," he said, holding out his hat for Josephine to drop the money in. "Thank you, ma'am."

After the man had returned to sit on a stool by his boxes, Blasko turned to Josephine and watched as she tipped the bottle up and drank an ounce of the clear liquid. "You have no idea what you're drinking," he said, astounded.

"The man who sold it to me is Martin Telford. His son was killed in France. Everyone in the county respects that man's ability to build a still. If Alabama ever goes wet again, I'd be proud if our bank loaned him the money to open a proper distillery." She didn't bother to offer Blasko a drink, as his condition prevented him from experiencing the effects of alcohol.

They sat in amiable silence for a while, listening to the jovial sounds from The Dock.

"The music is… wild," Blasko observed. "In an odd way, it reminds me of the mountains and the villagers of my homeland."

"Working people around the world share a common culture." Josephine rolled her head on her neck, feeling the alcohol loosen her muscles and her mind. "I'm going to Florida and I want to go now," she said, surprised by her own determination. "Uncle Petey's letter said that he would leave another note at the post office on Cedar Island. If he did, then maybe that will explain why he went there."

"Of course," Blasko said as he tried not to look at the other car where the two people were engaged in some rather intimate… wrestling. "I will have to make some preparations for the trip."

"You don't have to go," she told him, receiving a narrow-eyed glare in return. She took another pull from the bottle, then replaced the cork. "Okay, fine. That will give me time to visit the paper tomorrow. Anything we can find out might help," she said as she started the car.

Josephine had slept for about four hours when she was awakened by someone softly calling her name. She barely resisted the urge to jump when she saw Blasko standing over her bed.

"I believe I can be ready to leave tomorrow night," he said. "I'm sorry. Were you still asleep?"

"What time is it?" she asked, squinting to see him in the darkness. "And haven't we talked about you barging into my bedroom in the middle of the night?" She reached out to turn on the bedside lamp.

"I only have ten minutes before the sun comes up. I wanted to tell you that Anton is preparing our supplies for the trip. Of course, we will have to take both cars."

"I hadn't thought it all through yet, but if Anton is going… Don't you think he should stay here and watch over your rooms?" Josephine still found Anton a bit odd and she wasn't sure how he'd be received on the roads of the Deep South.

"When I've traveled I've always had a… watchman on duty during daylight hours. I sleep more securely."

"You didn't have one when you came to this country," Josephine said lightly, receiving a certain amount of pleasure from the heat that flashed in Blasko's eyes.

"You know very well that you kidnapped me," Blasko said with passion before realizing that she was goading him. "It is precisely because of persons like yourself that I need protection," he said, his eyebrows raised.

"Okay, Anton goes. I want Grace to go too. There's me

and you, all of our luggage. By the way, how are you going to transport your… bed?"

"Ah, ha!" Blasko said with delight. "Anton is quite skilled as a carpenter. He's made me a coffin that breaks into three parts that fold into the approximate shape of a suitcase. They are weighty, but can be handled easily."

"He did this tonight?"

"Certainly not! I thought of it months ago. We acquired the wood and he's been working on it steadily. The last section still has to be assembled and we will have to forego the final coat of varnish, but I think it will serve its purpose."

"Bully for Anton." Josephine paused, considering all she'd need to do. "Sure, why not? We can leave as soon as you wake tonight."

"We will be ready," Blasko said, then cast a nervous glance at the window. "I must go."

Before Josephine could say a word, he'd disappeared back into the hall. As she heard him hurry down the stairs, she fell back onto the bed. *This is crazy*, she thought, but then realized, *I don't care*. She rolled out of bed to start her busy morning.

"Here's the list of items to pack," Josephine told Grace, after informing her of their plans to leave that night.

"I know how to pack for a trip to the coast," Grace told her, sounding affronted as she took the note.

"This trip is going to be a bit different with Blasko and Anton along for the ride."

"He's going to the beach?"

"We aren't necessarily going to the beach, just the coast."

"As long as there's a breeze, I guess I don't care," Grace said, scanning the list.

"I've packed my own bags and Anton can help us load up the cars. In fact, he can go ahead and carry my cases down to the hall. Now I've got to run to the bank and do a few chores."

"This about your uncle?" Grace asked. She had long since stopped pretending that she didn't eavesdrop.

"Yes." Josephine took a deep breath, then gave Grace the details.

"Seems that anything that came from that monster can't be any good," Grace pronounced.

"The letter came from my uncle. You wouldn't judge the worth of a letter by the quality of the mailman."

"I wouldn't be taking any mail from a minion of the devil," Grace argued.

"I'm taking the source of the discovery into account," Josephine assured her. "Would you ask Ronnie to check on the house and feed the cat while we're gone?" she asked, referring to Grace's brother who lived with his family in Grace's little shotgun house on the street behind Josephine's.

"He'll be happy to," Grace said.

"I can't blame you for going down to the Gulf. At least it should be a little cooler than here," said Daniel Robertson, the bank's manager and a long-time friend, after Josephine had explained her plans to him.

"Sorry you and Alice can't go with us," Josephine said, only half seriously.

"Alice hasn't quite recovered from the… incident," Daniel confided. His wife had been witness to a rampaging werewolf earlier that year and, ever since, Josephine had noticed that Alice had been avoiding her. "Besides, someone has to stay and keep the bank running."

"I don't know exactly how long I'll be gone. Maybe just a week. However, it could be longer. I'll keep in touch." Josephine was the bank's majority shareholder and, while the economy seemed to have stabilized, no one was giving any guarantees. Even almost five years after the crash, people still felt shell-shocked.

Josephine withdrew what she judged to be enough cash for their journey and was on her way out of the bank when

Deputy Robert Tucker walked through the front door. Josephine had dated Bobby for years before deciding that they couldn't be more than friends. Bobby had accepted the new terms of their relationship reluctantly.

"Josie," he said with a smile. The sweat stains on his shirt reached almost all the way down to the .45 revolver on his hip. He swept off his hat and planted himself in front of her.

"Bobby! It's good to see you." In truth, Josephine had hoped to get out of town without running into the deputy. Lately he had become very protective of her. Of course, the horror-filled experiences they'd shared since Blasko's arrival had given him some reason to be concerned for her safety.

"I was hoping I'd run into you. Can we talk?"

"Now?" Josephine knew that the longer they spoke, the more likely it was that her plans would come out.

"Only if you have time. If not, tonight would be fine."

Hell's bells, Josephine thought. "Now's fine. Let's go into my office."

Bobby followed her and stepped around her in time to open the door where her name was stenciled on the glass in gold. Just then, Daniel came out of his office.

"Hi, Bobby!" he said before turning to Josephine. "I'm glad I caught you. I realized that if you're going to be gone for a couple of weeks, there are a few items I'd like to get your approval on."

Josephine saw the look on Bobby's face and knew that she was going to have to tell him about her trip. *A postcard would have been easier*, she thought.

"I'll come see you when I'm done talking to Bobby," she told Daniel.

"A trip?" Bobby said once they were in her office with the door shut. Josephine tried to ignore the hurt in his voice.

"We're just going down to the coast. A little summer break, that's all," Josephine said dismissively.

"I guess the baron is going with you?" Bobby wasn't really jealous. He understood that Josephine's relationship with Blasko was complicated. Still, he seemed to hold on to some faint hope.

"Yes, along with Grace and Anton."

"How long will you be gone?"

"A week or two," she fudged.

"Where are you staying?"

"Is this an interrogation?" She didn't want to tell him that they were going down to Cedar Island, as it would only open up another round of questions.

"Is it a secret?"

"No."

"I'm your friend, and I'm also a deputy who knows that bad things often happen around you and the baron. Besides, what if I need to get ahold of you?"

"The Cedar Island Hotel," Josephine said reluctantly. She'd sent a telegram to the hotel that morning to confirm their reservations.

"Cedar Island? That's not exactly a tourist spot. You usually go to St. George."

"Dragomir wants to see what Florida's fishing industry is like," she lied. Fishing was the only thing that Josephine knew they did on the island.

"He's never struck me as a fisherman," Bobby said, looking unconvinced. "Why are you really going down there?"

Josephine chewed on her lip.

"I'm your friend, Josie. After all we've been through in the last year, I'd think you'd trust me," he pressed.

"Of course I trust you, and I know you have my best interests at heart. That's the problem. I don't want you trying to talk me out of this trip." Josephine went on to explain the reason for it.

Bobby frowned. "I don't feel any better about this knowing that LeSauvage was the one who told you about that letter."

"You aren't the first person to point that out. Believe me, I've taken it into consideration. But I can't see any other way to get answers without going to Cedar Island."

"I could probably get some time off."

"You can't leave the colonel right now. There isn't anyone else he can lean on. You know that." Josephine wasn't overstating the case. The Semmes County Sheriff's Office was small and, while the other deputies were good men, they weren't the type who could be trusted to make the right decisions in a crisis.

"Promise me you'll call if you need me," Bobby continued to pressure her.

Josephine found it hard to look at the obvious love in his eyes. "You have my solemn word on it." If there was real trouble, then Bobby would be the first person she'd call. "Now, what did you want to talk to me about?"

Bobby smiled boyishly. "Nothing really. I just wanted to see you."

Josephine could only shake her head in exasperation.

Having dealt with Bobby and reviewed the papers that Daniel needed her to sign, Josephine headed for Connelly's Funeral Home. She'd decided she was more likely to find Jerry Connelly up and about before noon than Emmett Wolfe, the editor of the *Sumter Times*. Emmett spent most of the night editing stories and running the presses.

The Connelly family had served as the county's morticians since the War Between the States. When she pulled into the driveway of the large Victorian that doubled as the family home, she saw one of their drivers washing a hearse under the side portico. The man looked content, polishing the car in his vest. His hat and coat hung over one of the stone lions that flanked the steps up to the side entrance.

"Morning, Calvin," Josephine said.

"Why, good morning, Miss Josephine," the middle-aged man said, doffing a hat he wasn't wearing. He was a cousin of the Connellys; when they could, they hired family. "If you're looking for Jerry, he's having his coffee on the back porch."

"Quiet around here today?"

"Yes, ma'am. Always have mixed emotions about that. Good for the county, but bad for business," he said in a conspiratorial whisper.

"I'm afraid you never have to worry about the long-term prospects."

"Aye, the Lord will call us all home one day, as my sainted grandmother used to say."

Josephine went inside. She'd always thought of funeral homes as the dark stepchildren of churches. They had all of the somber atmosphere with none of the hope. No one else was around, so she found her own way back to the screened-in porch at the rear of the house. She found Jerry reading the morning paper with his coffee and toast. A ceiling fan moved the warm air around him.

"Miss Josephine," he said, standing up abruptly. "To what do I owe the pleasure?" He looked embarrassed to be caught in his shirtsleeves.

"Please sit down. I just came by to ask you a few questions about my uncle's funeral," she said, taking the wrought-iron chair across from him. She knew he'd never sit back down until she did herself.

"Your uncle?" he asked, puzzled.

"This was years ago. 1914."

"My father was still doing most of the embalming back then. I can't say that I remember an uncle of yours."

"He drowned down in Florida."

"Wait… Now I do remember. Oh my, yes! My father asked for my assistance on that one. It was… I'm sorry, I don't want to sound insensitive. Let's just say that he was a difficult client. There was no question that the casket would need to remain closed. In fact, we needed to perfume the body and kept it packed in ice until the burial."

"Was there an examination of the body? I mean, did the sheriff or a doctor look at it?"

Connelly looked surprised. "No, I can't imagine why they

would have."

"Was there anything about his body that struck you as odd?"

"Well, he came to us without any clothes. I found that surprising at the time, but looking back, there could have been any number of explanations for that."

"Such as?"

"He might have been examined by a coroner or the sheriff where his body was discovered. That would have been the ordinary course of events. The clothes might have been destroyed when they were removed. The condition of his body would almost certainly have necessitated cutting them off in order to remove them."

"What exactly do you mean?"

Connelly looked uncomfortable. "Miss Josephine, I don't think this is a topic that—"

"Tell me, Mr. Connelly."

He sighed deeply. "Very well. The body was bloated and the skin was... sloughing off." He turned away from Josephine as though wanting to avoid seeing any evidence of offense in her eyes.

While the image made her feel a bit green, Josephine wasn't going to let the gory details keep her from pursuing the truth. "I understand that nature is not always kind." She took a breath. "Do you remember any other... wounds on the body?"

"Honestly, Miss Josephine, I don't remember much about it. It was twenty years ago. The only reason I recall the preparations at all is because my father requested my help." Connelly paused, looking down at his coffee. "Though now that you mention it, I remember that the head was... damaged."

"Damaged how?"

"Even though there wasn't going to be an open coffin, my father always took pains to restore the body as best he could. I remember we had to stuff the head with newspapers to get the shape more... natural."

"So he'd been hit on the head?"

"From what I can remember, it's possible. Not to say that it wasn't an accident. We had a young man about ten years ago who was swimming with friends down at the river. They'd been climbing up on the railroad trestle and diving in. Well… he slipped and hit his head before going into the river. Anyway, I don't think there is anything else I can tell you about your uncle."

"I appreciate your time," Josephine said and stood up, causing Connelly to jump to his feet.

"If you don't mind me asking, why are you interested in your uncle's death now?" he asked.

Josephine thought she heard another question hidden between the lines. The county had been through a number of dramatic, even horrifying, events in the past year and Connelly himself had seen the remains of much of it. Josephine was tied in the minds of many of the townsfolk to these strange affairs. She'd noticed the occasional sideways glances from people on the street, so it wasn't surprising that Connelly might be nervous about her interest in a long-dead relative.

"I've recently found a letter that Uncle Petey wrote which caused me to wonder about his death." *Which is only the truth*, she thought.

"I see. Rest assured that nothing about his death seemed… sinister," Connelly said with a nervous smile.

"Of course not! I just want to understand what happened. I was so young when he died."

Connelly nodded and Josephine took the opportunity to maneuver around the chairs and make her way toward the door. The mortician walked her to her car past the now-gleaming hearse.

At her next stop, she found Emmett Wolfe in the back room of the newspaper office, trying to dislodge a small metal type block that had fallen down into the workings of the old press he used to print the *Sumter Times*. The typesetter, Jack, stood by with a frown on his face.

"I can't quite reach the damn thing!" Emmett grumbled from under the press.

"Language, Mr. Wolfe. There's a lady present," Jack said in his thick Bavarian accent. Jack's name was actually Johan Bauer, but the barrel-chested Bavarian had changed it during the Great War to the more American-sounding Jack in order to highlight his allegiance.

"What?" Emmett yelled, half crawling out from under the press. "Oh!" He scrambled to his feet. "Josephine. I didn't hear you come in."

"You were too busy cussing at your machine," she said, smiling. Emmett was usually a natty dresser, so she found it amusing to catch him with his hands and clothes covered in ink.

"I wouldn't have been down there if this moose of a man's hands weren't in proportion to the rest of his body," Emmett said as Jack held up his mutton-sized hands as evidence. "How you can set type as fast as you can, I'll never figure out."

"It is a wonder!" the big man said with a heartfelt belly laugh.

"We'll need a monkey, not a moose, to get at that piece of type. It's jammed in a tight spot. Go out and see if there are any street urchins you can recruit. I'll pay a dollar to anyone of them that can get that da… piece of type out of there," Emmett told Jack, trying to clean his hands with a rag that was probably putting more ink *on* than taking it off.

Jack nodded and headed toward the front of the building. Josephine and Emmett followed him. "We can go to my office," he told her. "I assume this isn't a social visit."

"We may as well go to the morgue," she said. He looked at her sharply. "Your newspaper morgue. Isn't that what you call it?"

"We call it the big musty room where we keep the old editions," Emmett laughed. "What are you looking for?"

"Information on an uncle who passed away twenty years ago." Remembering Connelly's questions, Josephine added,

"I'm doing some genealogy research."

"With your father passing away last year, I can understand the urge to find out as much as you can about your family." Emmett opened a door into a large room that he'd correctly described as musty. Bare light bulbs hung from the ceiling, illuminating a dozen or more rows of wooden shelves. Most of the shelves were full with wooden boxes, each labeled with the name of the paper and a range of dates.

"I didn't know there'd been this many editions of the *Times*," Josephine said in awe at the number of crates.

"We don't just store our own papers. We archive the Montgomery papers as well so that we have them for quick reference if we need background for a statewide story. Now, what are the dates you're looking for?"

"It would be around the end of June, first of July in 1914. He died on June 28 in Florida. I don't remember exactly when the funeral was held."

Emmett walked down one aisle, checking the dates on the various boxes before doubling back and heading down the next row of crates.

"Here we go." He pulled a box off a shelf, sending a cloud of dust into the air. "Let's take it up front where we can breathe."

After placing the box on his desk, Emmett pulled out a small stack of papers and handed them to Josephine before taking a stack for himself.

"Here," Emmett said a while later, pointing to an article on the second page of a paper dated: Sunday, July 5, 1914. The small headline read: *Local Banker Mourns Brother's Death.*

Josephine took the paper and quickly read the article. Other than noting the cause and location of Peter's death, and the plans for the funeral the following day, the article mainly spoke about Andre Nicolson and his accomplishments and connections in the county. There was very little about Peter himself.

"Not much here," Josephine said. She had hoped the

paper would have covered the return of the body, and maybe even have speculated on how he drowned.

"Tell me a little about your uncle," Emmett said.

Josephine gave him a quick rundown of Peter's roguish habits.

"Ah! There's the problem," Emmett said. "Your father was well thought of and important to the community. This Uncle Petey sounds like a black sheep. The paper wouldn't have wanted to rake up dirt that might stain your father or your family. Better just to stick to the most basic facts and let the matter go."

Josephine nodded. His explanation made a lot of sense. If she'd ever had any doubt about whether she needed to visit Cedar Island, it was gone now. There was a mystery here, benign or not, and she intended to solve it.

CHAPTER FOUR

Having done everything she could in town, Josephine went into high gear planning for their trip. As soon as she got home, she sat down with Anna in the kitchen to discuss preparing a basket of food to take with them. Traveling at night along rural roads, there would be few places to stop.

When she was through with Anna, she went down the stairs to the door leading into Blasko's basement apartment. It was too early for him to be awake, but she wanted to make sure that Anton was fully prepared. There was no answer to her first knock at the door, so she rapped more loudly.

"Yeeessss?" came a hesitant and suspicious voice from the other side of the door.

When he'd first shown up, Josephine had been unnerved by Anton's immunity to criticism and his habit of always hiding right outside any room where Blasko was. But he'd proven his loyalty and usefulness to the baron on several occasions since he'd assumed the role of manservant. *Lackey, more like it*, Josephine thought, glaring at the closed door.

"It's the owner of the house," Josephine said.

"Oh, Mistress." Anton opened the door, though he didn't move out of the way so that she could enter. "HE is resting," Anton said, and Josephine could hear the capital letters.

"I'm well aware of his schedule," she said. "I wanted to see if you've made all the necessary preparations for our trip to the coast."

Anton's eyes opened wide and a smile grew on his face. "Ah, yes, yes. Come in! I show you!" He backed away from the door and ushered her in with wide, sweeping motions of his arms.

Josephine followed him reluctantly, wary of getting caught up in a long conversation with the man. Between his wandering narratives and broken English, it could go well beyond the boundaries of her patience.

"Look!" Anton said, standing in the middle of Blasko's Victorian-inspired parlor and pointing at three square objects made of finely polished wood. They looked like collapsed folding tables with elaborate brass hinges.

"I should put one more coat of varnish on them, but no time. Here, here, I show."

Excitedly, Anton began to unfold the three objects, then connected them together by an intricate series of latches. When he was finished, the three pieces had been assembled into a single box that looked like what it was—a coffin.

"For the baron," Anton said proudly.

In spite of herself, Josephine was impressed. She stepped forward and ran her hand along the wood. "You did this?"

Anton bowed, then saw her looking at the hinges. "No, no, not the metalwork. I send back to my country. A friend, he is a great worker in metal. He make them from the baron's design."

"This is beautiful," Josephine told him.

"Too kind. I am but a woodworker. Now you don't worry, I will pack everything. The baron gave me very detailed instructions."

"Is your English getting better?"

"Yes. The baron will not let me speak our native tongue. He tells me that I am no use to him without I'm able to talk to people."

Josephine was sure that's *exactly* what he'd told Anton.

"You are doing very well."

"The baron said we will leave as soon as he wakes."

Josephine nodded and left to finish her own preparations.

The sun had been down less than an hour when two black automobiles rumbled out of Josephine's driveway and through the streets of Sumter toward the dark stretch of two-lane roads that led south toward Florida.

Josephine drove her '32 Chevrolet with determined skill, peering into the night and hoping that the headlamps would illuminate any cows or deer that might decide to stand in the middle of the road. She also checked the rearview mirror regularly to make sure that Blasko was keeping up. When she'd seen him don his black leather driving gloves and get behind the wheel of his enormous Daimler Double-Six, she'd felt a little queasy. Blasko loved to drive, but he wasn't that good at it.

Two hours into the trip, they had their first flat tire. The roads were rough and the tires were only somewhat reliable. Josephine had made sure they had several spares tied to the luggage racks before they'd left home. Now, as she watched Anton and Blasko work at changing the tire while getting in each other's way, she wondered if it had been a mistake to come on this journey.

"Too late to turn back now," Grace said, reading her thoughts. "'Course, with those two doing the work, we'll be lucky to get a foot farther from home."

"Is this crazy?"

"Was it crazy to go into those mountains and bring your baron home?" Grace asked. "I accepted long ago that you're going to do the unpredictable and take the path that leads through the darkest woods."

"I don't try to make life difficult."

"Sure you do. You're a rich woman who doesn't have to lift a finger, but the truth is, you can't stand being safe and warm. You got to go out and find trouble."

"That's taking it too far," Josephine protested.

"Who's sittin' right here beside you? So if you're loony, so am I," Grace said, fanning herself.

Finally, Josephine saw Blasko stand up and look at the wheel with satisfaction. "We can proceed," he told her.

In a short while they passed a metal sign that welcomed them to Florida, but they were all getting nervous when, five hours later, they were still seventy-five miles from Cedar Island. Josephine cursed herself for not making better plans. She hadn't considered just how bad the roads would be through the pine woods of North Florida, and traveling at night had slowed them down more than she'd planned.

"We're going to have to stop somewhere for the day," she told Grace, who had just woken up from a nap.

"Where we goin' to find a place?"

"It's not much farther to Apalachicola. We'll find something there," Josephine said as she slowed down and pulled off to the side of the road.

"The baron wants to know why we have stopped." Anton shuffled up to the window almost before Josephine made a complete stop. "He is very worried about the dawn."

"I'm going back to talk with him," she said, trying to open the door with Anton standing beside it. With a nudge of the door, he retreated to let her out.

"We must hurry." Blasko leaned out the window as she approached his car.

"We aren't going to make it to Cedar Island tonight."

"What do you mean, we aren't going to make it?!" Blasko's eyes blazed. "How could you—"

Josephine didn't let him finish. "There is a town just a few miles away where we should be able to find someplace to hole up for the day." As she said it, she wondered how easy it would be to find someone who'd let them take a room at five in the morning.

"Bah! You do realize that I will die in agonizing pain if I'm exposed to the sunlight?"

"We could bury you out here in the woods and come back for you tonight," Josephine offered sweetly.

"Go! Move!"

Josephine couldn't really blame him. She was worried herself.

Twenty minutes later, they reached the oystering town of Apalachicola and she saw a sign for the Gulf Waters Hotel. It was a large clapboard house with a number of added wings. There were lights on at the back of the building, where Josephine assumed the staff must have been preparing breakfast in the kitchen. They parked the cars and Josephine tried to convince Blasko to let her go in and make the arrangements.

"I will talk to the innkeeper," Blasko said, trying to push ahead of her.

"All you're likely to do is get us kicked out. Do you want to sleep in the swamp?" Josephine knew that in Blasko's current frame of mind, he might do or say anything if they weren't allowed to check in. And anything might include tossing the clerk through a window.

"Go then. But I'm going with you. Do not take 'no' for an answer," he hissed under his breath.

Josephine tread lightly up the steps to the expansive wooden porch that held a dozen rocking chairs. Her knocks at the front door brought no one. Behind her, Blasko was pacing back and forth.

"Knock louder," he told her.

"Let's go around back. There are people in the kitchen." She didn't wait for him to agree.

As they approached the back door, they could smell bacon frying and hear a couple of women speaking softly.

"Remember, I'll do the talking," Josephine said.

"Remember, they have to give us a room," Blasko growled.

"Can I help you?" said the young woman who answered the door. She wore an apron over a plain brown dress and swept her hair back from a sweaty forehead as she talked.

"We need to get a couple of rooms," Josephine said, trying to sound somewhere between desperate and exhausted, which she gauged would get them the most sympathy. Fortunately, it wasn't much of an act.

"Mr. Hanson isn't up yet. I can't check you in. Come back around ten and he'll be glad for the business." The woman started to close the door.

Josephine could feel Blasko tensing up behind her. "I'm afraid it's rather urgent. My father isn't feeling very well. He needs to lay down on a bed. We've been traveling all night…"

"Your father?" The woman sounded puzzled and Josephine saw her looking at Blasko.

"My father is in the car. This is my… cousin."

"I can't wake Mr. Hanson up. He'd fire me," the woman said plaintively.

Josephine felt time ticking away as she tried to think of the best way to break down the woman's resistance. Before she could say anything else, Blasko stepped in front of her.

"We need two rooms. I promise you that Mr. Hanson will be glad you woke him up," Blasko said, giving the woman a five-dollar bill and showing her the twenty that he intended to give to Mr. Hanson to expedite their check-in.

"Yes, sir!" the woman said, her eyes wide as she took the cash. She turned and disappeared into the building. Blasko and Josephine heard a brief discussion in the kitchen before it grew quiet again. Blasko went back to pacing as Josephine shifted from foot to foot, whispering a prayer.

The sound of heavy shoes clumping down a hallway signaled the approach of Mr. Hanson. A frumpy-looking man opened the door and stared down at them.

"Tess said you needed a room right away. Why?"

Blasko handed Hanson the twenty-dollar bill. "We've been driving all night and her father needs a place to rest."

"He's not sick, is he?" Hanson asked with a querulous tone, but his hand slipped the twenty into his pocket.

"No. Just tired from traveling," Josephine said, regretting

that she'd presented Anton as her father. She hoped that Hanson wouldn't want to meet him before checking them in.

"Good, good. We've had a few dead bodies in the last couple of years. Messy business. Fine. Come around front. I'll meet you there." He closed the door before they could say anything else.

They managed to get signed in and pay for the rooms just as the first pink streaks of dawn lightened the eastern sky. Blasko quickly grabbed two of the folded sections of his portable coffin and carried them upstairs, followed by Anton carrying the third, along with Blasko's suitcase.

Hanson looked at Anton struggling up the stairs behind Blasko and turned to Josephine. "That's your father?"

"He's very independent," Josephine said. Before he could ask any more questions, she grabbed her own suitcase and followed Grace up the stairs.

The rooms were satisfactory, if a bit musty. Josephine opened her window and turned on the electric fan. The room had a small adjoining alcove where Grace could sleep.

Before settling down, Josephine went across the hall to Blasko's room to make sure he had gotten safely settled in before the sun came up.

"The baron is resting," Anton said, peeking through the door.

"We told the innkeeper that you are my father." Anton looked amused. "Just in case anyone asks."

"Yes, I remember," he said and started to close the door.

"Get some rest. We'll continue on to Cedar Island as soon as the sun goes down."

"I will guard the baron," Anton said, sounding offended that she thought he would sleep with his master resting in a strange hotel.

CHAPTER FIVE

Josephine went back to her room and was getting ready to lie down when she heard the sound of heavy boots coming up the stairs and down the hallway, stopping outside her door. As she walked to the door, she heard several hard raps on Blasko's door across the hall. Quickly putting on a robe, she opened her door and stepped out into the hallway. Two men turned and stared at her.

"What's going on out here?" she asked, trying to sound like she'd been disturbed from her sleep.

A large man with grey hair and a neat beard swept off his hat. "Sorry, ma'am. Hanson here thought there might be some—"

"She's one of them," Hanson said, looking slightly embarrassed.

"Her?" The bearded man frowned at Hanson. Josephine took note of the badge pinned to the man's belt and the large revolver in his holster.

"I told you they rented two rooms," Hanson reminded him.

"What you said..." The man started to argue with Hanson, then said, "Oh, never mind." He turned to Josephine. "I'm Sheriff Luke Avery. Mr. Hanson here had some concerns about the… odd way you chose to arrive this morning."

"He didn't seem too concerned when he took our twenty dollars," Josephine said, giving Hanson a hard look. The man's face turned a dark crimson before he became very interested in the floor.

Sheriff Avery looked at Hanson, then continued, "Be that as it may, we've had some dangerous characters come through here headed south. Seems like gangsters prefer Florida vacations, just like everyone else."

"You think we're gangsters?" Josephine could hardly keep a straight face.

"Ma'am, you got to admit that showin' up here at the crack of dawn was a bit unorthodox. Bribes aside." He cast another hard look at Hanson, who'd obviously failed to mention the exchange of cash. "Seems your traveling companion cut a rather rakish figure."

"That's easily explained. He's from Romania. A baron, in fact."

"I see. Well, I'd like to meet this baron," Avery said, and it didn't escape Josephine's notice that he placed his hand on the butt of his revolver when he said it.

"I'm sure that he will be delighted to meet you. He's asleep right now, but plans on being up about sundown so that we can continue on our way," she said, trying to sound perky and good-humored.

"Now," the sheriff said.

Josephine could tell that he'd seen right through her stalling tactics. What could she do now? Finding Blasko in his coffin wasn't going to make the sheriff any more relaxed about their presence in town.

"I'm afraid the baron is very allergic to the sun."

"I've never heard of that." His manner toward her hardened.

"Nonetheless, it is a medical condition."

"Doesn't matter. I'm not going to take him for a walk down the pier. I just want to get my eyes on him and make sure he doesn't have a poster down at the post office, if you get my drift."

"I do. I guess it would be all right if he doesn't have to go outside," Josephine said, her voice raised. She hoped that Anton had been hearing all of this and was doing whatever he needed to wake Blasko and prepare him to meet the lawman.

"By the way, what is your relationship with… the baron?"

Josephine didn't mind the question if it gave Anton and Blasko more time to get ready. She even thought she heard a slight noise coming from Blasko's room.

"He's a distant cousin. I met him last year when I went to Romania to spread my grandfather's ashes. We got to know each other and I invited him to come to America for a visit. I live in Sumter, Alabama. Now that the heat is so atrocious, I thought it was the perfect time to come down to Florida and show him what a wonderful state y'all have," Josephine said, laying it on thick to give Blasko more time.

"I see. Let's meet this baron," Sheriff Avery said and abruptly turned back to the door. He brought his fist down with four sharp knocks.

"Yes?" said Anton from the other side.

"That's his… my father," Josephine said, barely remembering her earlier lie.

"I'm the sheriff. I'd like to have a word with you and the baron."

"Of course," Anton said, opening the door slowly. The sheriff became impatient and half pushed Anton out of the way. Behind him, Josephine could see the dark silhouette of the baron standing at the back of the room. The portable coffin had been disassembled and the curtains carefully pulled together so that no light shone into the room.

The sheriff clicked on the overhead light and squinted at Blasko, who stood silent in his silk dressing gown.

"You the baron?"

"I am," Blasko said politely. Josephine was glad to see

that he was on his best behavior. If for any reason the sheriff became irritated, he could drag Blasko out into the open, which would not end well. She suspected that Blasko would not allow himself to be pulled into the daylight without a fight. Josephine hoped she wouldn't get to see how such a confrontation played out.

"You got papers?" the sheriff asked suspiciously.

"As a matter of fact, I have my passport," Blasko said, pulling a small booklet out of his suitcase like a magician retrieving a rabbit from a hat.

Don't overdo it, Josephine thought. She also wondered where he'd gotten the passport. It was the first she'd heard of it. When they'd come to the States, he'd arrived traveling with the baggage.

Sheriff Avery inspected the document carefully.

"Did I hear you say that you thought we might be gangsters?" Blasko asked with a smile.

"We keep an eye on strangers these days." Sheriff Avery handed the passport back to Blasko. Josephine could tell by his expression that he wasn't happy. "Where are you all headed?"

"Cedar Island," Josephine said, glad that she could step in. She didn't trust Blasko not to do or say something stupid that could get them all in hot water… or bright sunlight, as the case may be.

Hearing their destination, Sheriff Avery clenched his teeth. "You might want to reconsider that plan."

"Why is that?" Blasko interjected. Josephine knew how much he hated to be left out of a conversation. She stared at him, trying to get him to understand that this was not the time to push the sheriff.

"'Cause there isn't anything worth seeing on that island. The cedar trees have all been cut down for pencils and the fishing… ain't the same."

"We heard that the beaches are quite nice," Blasko said, ignoring Josephine's hard look.

"You heard wrong. Aren't any beaches. Just sawgrass

around the island, mostly." Sheriff Avery looked at the three of them before going on in a more kindly tone. "I don't know what y'all are looking for, but I can tell you that you won't find anything you need down there. The place ain't been right for years. You get out there and need help, you'll be out of luck. There's no phone lines and my buddy who's the sheriff in Cedar County won't go out on the island unless he has to."

"What is so dangerous on the island?" Blasko asked. Josephine rolled her eyes behind the sheriff's back, wishing that Blasko would just shut up and let the man go.

Avery gave Blasko a hard look. "You questioning me?"

"No. I'm just curious what you think is wrong on Cedar Island."

Josephine didn't like the look on the sheriff's face and decided to give him an out. "If you don't want to talk about it, we understand."

The sheriff looked at her. "I don't know what you people think you're playing at, but I can tell you that if it involves Cedar Island, you're in for trouble. When the sun goes down, I want you people out of my county."

The sheriff spun on his heel and knocked Hanson out of the way as he stumped back toward the stairs. Hanson regained his footing and meekly followed, shutting the door to Blasko's room behind him.

"What were you thinking, asking him questions?" Josephine hissed at Blasko.

"There was no harm done."

"I'll give you a little advice. When a sheriff knocks on your door, he wants to be the only one asking questions." Josephine was still nervous after the close call.

"I needed to distract him. Anton didn't bring *his* passport with him," Blasko said with a wave of his hand toward Anton, who still stood by the door looking unconcerned.

"Speaking of passports, where'd you get yours?"

"You should get out more. A while ago, Matthew introduced me to a man with a contact in Birmingham who is very skilled at reproducing documents. I thought it might be… convenient to have a passport. It was easy with Anton's as an example for the man to—"

"Enough. I don't want to hear anything else about forged passports," Josephine said, exasperated at Blasko's cavalier attitude toward criminal offenses that could land a person in jail for decades. She made a mental note to give Matthew Hodge hell whenever he returned from New Orleans, where he was currently in residence learning how to live with being a werewolf.

"All's well that ends well. We even learned that there is something sinister taking place on Cedar Island." Blasko raised his eyebrows and smiled. "Now I really must rest. I hadn't expected this interruption to my routine."

Josephine wanted to say more, but as she calmed down she realized he was right. They'd escaped a tricky situation and been given warning of things to come, both of which should put them on their guard for the remainder of the trip.

"Get back in your coffin. I'll see you as soon as the sun goes down."

Across the hall, Grace was pacing the floor of Josephine's room. She had been in the adjoining bathroom when the sheriff knocked on Blasko's door and had known enough not to get involved in anything that had to do with the law.

"One time I'm glad to be the black woman. That sheriff probably didn't even give me a second thought."

By nine o'clock, they were motoring out of the county and were only an hour from Cedar Island. The air blowing through the cars was warm and moist as they approached the turnoff that would lead them through five miles of salt marsh and across the bridge to the island.

Josephine was glad Grace hadn't heard Sheriff Avery declare that Cedar Island held some unnamed danger. She would have preferred not to have heard it herself. Were the sheriff's concerns linked to her uncle's death, or were the two events separate and distinct?

As they crossed the steel bridge, they could see lights on in the homes scattered around the island. Some of the lights were brighter where the residents had electricity, while most were the soft yellow of oil lamps. Most of the houses near the water had docks jutting out into the Gulf. A full moon left a glittering trail on the waves.

The Cedar Island Hotel wasn't hard to find. It was one of only two buildings on the island with a second floor; the other was a dry goods store with living quarters above. All the rest of the businesses were simple one-story wooden structures, faded grey from years of wind and sand.

"Place looks dried up," Grace observed as they passed several store fronts with whitewash on the windows.

"What would you expect? Even the strongest towns are suffering with the Depression. A place like this out in the middle of nowhere is bound to be struggling."

Josephine parked her car at the curb in front of the hotel. Wide balconies wrapped around the first and second floors. Blasko pulled in behind her and got out of his car. Despite the heat, he was wearing a black coat, starched white shirt and a neatly knotted black silk tie. He joined Josephine and they entered through the hotel's double doors, which were propped open to catch the breeze.

The soft warm glow of the lights did little to brighten the lobby, which was paneled in dark wood. Only the brass bell on the counter seemed to pick up the light. Blasko stepped forward and was about to ring the bell when a gaunt woman in her fifties came out of the dining room, wiping her hands on the apron around her waist.

"Y'all must be the folks from Alabama. I got your reservation yesterday," she said as she stepped behind the desk and rooted around for a moment. "Here it is." She brought up the telegram that Josephine had sent. "Josephine Nicolson and… Baron Blasko. You a real live baron?"

Blasko gave her a crooked smile and a slight nod. "Yes, I am a Romanian baron," he said, not elaborating on whether he was alive or not.

"That's interesting. We seem to be getting our share of foreigners lately." She opened the guest register and turned it to face them. "Need you to fill out these two lines. The telegram said something about servants. We have quarters out back."

"I said that I would pay for them to have rooms alongside ours," Josephine reminded her.

"Not our usual policy and right now we got a pretty full house." The woman frowned. She looked past Blasko to Anton and Grace, who were each holding two pieces of luggage. "I suppose I can give you the four rooms on the west side. Each set of rooms has a bathroom between. Goin' to cost you. Those are the best rooms we have left. Can't do anything else. Our other guests wouldn't want to share a bathroom with the help." This was delivered with a slightly snooty upturn of her nose.

"We're fine sharing a bathroom with our employees… and friends." Josephine was rewarded with a sharp look from the owner.

"I'm Mrs. Lachlan. You're in luck. Our other guests are just sitting down to dinner, which we serve late most nights in the summer."

When Josephine was finished filling out the register, Mrs. Lachlan turned to the wall behind the desk and selected four keys. "I'll show you to your rooms. We don't have any bellhops or nothin' like that, so you'll need to carry your own luggage." She headed for the wide staircase.

At the landing, the hallway branched. Mrs. Lachlan went left and everyone followed. Their rooms took up the entire west side of the second floor of the hotel.

"Is there a post office in town?" Josephine asked as Mrs. Lachlan showed them the various features of their rooms and bathrooms.

"Of course there is. How primitive do you think we are? Two buildings down on the other side of the street."

"Shall we go down to dinner?" Blasko asked Josephine

once Mrs. Lachlan was gone. The woman had given them both a grumpy look when Blasko didn't retreat to his room, but stayed to talk to Josephine.

"I think she was about to give us a lecture on morals," Josephine said with amusement. "Dinner would be a good opportunity to meet the other guests. I'm curious why so many other people are here when Sheriff Avery made it plain that this island has nothing to offer a tourist."

"My thoughts exactly."

"I'll eat in the kitchen," Grace said.

"You don't have to." Josephine was already irritated with Mrs. Lachlan's attitude toward Grace and Anton.

"I, too, will eat in the kitchen," Anton said from the doorway.

"Certainly," Blasko said, receiving a frown from Josephine. "He is *my* servant," Blasko stated with a firm nod.

"Fine. Now you two get out and let us change."

"I will be ready shortly," Blasko said, bowing at the waist to Josephine. Anton kept his head down and scooted away behind his master.

"Why I'm changing to eat in the kitchen, I don't know," Grace said, heading for her own room while Josephine dug a light summer dress from her suitcase.

CHAPTER SIX

When Blasko and Josephine entered the dining room, they were surprised at the guests who were gathered there. Josephine didn't know what she'd expected, but she knew it wasn't this eclectic mix of sophisticates. It looked as if someone had grabbed a bunch of people milling about outside of a London opera house and transported them to Cedar Island.

The room was large, with a rectangular table that could hold twenty or more guests, and four smaller round tables. The six guests were seated at one end of the large table. The four men stood up when they saw Josephine.

"New guests! You've missed the cocktail hour; too bad for you," said an anemic-looking, red-faced man wearing a tan British military uniform. Even with his accent, it was clear that he was slurring some of his words. "Captain Reginald Hume, at your service."

"Baron Dragomir Blasko," he announced and gave a slight bow. "And my cousin, Josephine Nicolson." He took Josephine's hand and raised it in presentation.

"Well spoken. I'm Eric Donavan. It is very nice to meet you." A broad-shouldered man wearing a tweed jacket smiled at them. His accent spoke of a very cold upbringing, if not in Canada then within a short dogsled ride of the border. Like Hume's, his speech was a little slurred, suggesting more than a couple of drinks. "Should I presume to introduce the ladies?"

"If you must," muttered the dark-haired woman seated to his right.

"Then I'll start with you, my fiery Spanish maiden." He smiled down at her while she rolled her eyes, which were framed by the longest lashes Josephine had ever seen. "I present Jamila Molina."

"As he says. It is very good to have some more sophisticated dinner companions," she said, giving Donavan a sharp look.

"You wound me." He put his hand to his heart before extending his arm across the table in the direction of a starkly beautiful, dark-skinned woman. Her black hair was cut in a short bob and fine gold jewelry was liberally spread around her head and neck. "This rare Egyptian beauty is Neith Abubakar."

Neith made no acknowledgement of Donavan, but she turned and gave the slightest tilt of her head in the direction of Josephine and Blasko. Josephine couldn't help but notice that Neith's gaze lingered on Blasko.

"I'm Elliot Zhao," the third man said. There was a hint of China in his accent, but his features reflected parents born on two separate continents. "We are pleased to have you join us."

The man standing across from him said, "I'm Wallace Brock." In all ways he was unremarkable, yet Josephine thought his eyes held a cold darkness.

Josephine and Blasko joined the group at the table.

"I must say that I'm a little surprised to see such a… diverse group of guests," Josephine said, looking around at everyone.

"We didn't expect to meet a baron either," Donavan said. "Where do you hail from, Baron?"

"I am from the Carpathian Mountains, part of

Transylvania."

"You all fought on our side during the war," Hume said, more loudly than was necessary.

"Indeed. We had been living unhappily under the control of the Austro-Hungarian empire until Romania entered the war."

"Do we have to talk about the war?" Donavan grumbled.

"Too young. Feeble excuse," Hume pronounced.

Josephine guessed that Donavan was only a few years younger than herself. She figured that barely being a teenager was a reasonable excuse for staying out of the conflict.

"Here comes the food," Brock announced.

Josephine turned and saw Mrs. Lachlan and a young woman with odd facial features and barely discernable ears carrying in several platters and bowls.

"We got pork sausage and potatoes, corn, palm salad and cornbread," Mrs. Lachlan said as she placed the food onto the table. When the young woman put down the last bowl, it seemed to be the signal for the guests to start eagerly helping themselves. Only Neith seemed above the fray, watching all the others.

"I'm hoping to get some seafood while we're down here," Josephine said.

The words had hardly left her mouth when each of the guests suddenly stopped eating. Some looked down at their plates while others glanced up at the ceiling. Brock coughed uncontrollably for a moment. While Josephine tried to come up with a response to this odd reaction, she saw Blasko raise his eyebrows.

"Sorry, it seems the fisherman around here aren't the easiest to deal with," Hume said, waving the issue away. Josephine noticed that the odd young woman was watching them from the door to the kitchen, her unblinking eyes reminding Josephine of a frog.

The guests slowly went back to their food. Blasko looked ready to say something, but Josephine jumped in front of him, blurting, "This is a lovely old hotel." She was sure that

Blasko had been about to follow up on Hume's odd comment, but she decided it was best to keep the conversation non-confrontational.

"Built about fifty years ago, I understand," Hume said, taking a piece of cornbread from the plate as it passed him.

"My room smells moldy," Jamila said, wrinkling her nose.

"What brought all of you here?" Blasko asked, eyeing Josephine to see if she was going to interrupt him again.

The guests looked at one another for a moment before they took turns answering his question.

"I came down to find… a little peace of mind," Brock said, scooping potatoes onto his plate. "Chicago is a stressful town with all the gangsters."

"I came for my health. My doctor ordered me to find a warmer climate," Hume explained. He turned to Jamila.

"I paint. Audubon is a hero of mine," Jamila stated with a bland inflection, then turned to look at Elliot Zhao.

"I am on sabbatical from the University of Hong Kong. I just wanted to see different parts of the world." Zhao's gaze went back and forth between Blasko and Josephine as he spoke, then he nodded to Neith.

The woman shifted in her chair and looked uncomfortable. "I am here to study the ancient mounds of the Timucua Indians." She quickly returned her gaze to her plate and continued to pick at the food like a bird.

"You're from Egypt?" Blasko asked.

"Yes," Neith said without elaborating

"That leaves me." Donavan smiled. "I came down for some boating"

"Bravo for you," Josephine said, and Donavan gave her a smile and a slight nod.

"The baron is your cousin?" he asked with the slightest hint of flirtation. Jamila rolled her eyes.

"Yes, I met him on a trip to Romania."

"I'd like to hear about your trip sometime." Donavan's tone was even more suggestive.

"That might be arranged," Josephine said, and felt Blasko

tense up beside her. She gave him a small kick under the table.

For the next twenty minutes, everyone concentrated on eating until dessert was brought out. Josephine thought that the red velvet cake was almost as good as the ones Anna made.

"What do folks do in the evenings around here?" Josephine asked, noticing another exchange of looks.

"We've been having a game of bridge. Not much else to do, really," said Hume.

"I would think a walk down by the water would be very pleasant," Josephine said, looking at Donavan. She'd decided that if she was willing to flirt a little, he might tell her more about the island.

"I wouldn't recommend going out at night," Hume said.

"Night air isn't good for you," Brock agreed with a forced smile.

"I've always found the night air very refreshing," Blasko shot back. Josephine decided not to intervene this time.

"The island hasn't been very fortunate during these hard economic times. I think the captain was referring to some incidents where folks have been robbed at night walking home from the bar," Brock explained.

"Bar? I thought you said there wasn't anything to do around here at night," Josephine interjected, and this time she could clearly see the agitation in the others.

"You don't want to go to The Dragon," Mrs. Lachlan said, coming through the door from the kitchen. "That's a sailor's bar. Place is full of rough types. Even during Prohibition, the sheriff ain't had the guts to come on the island and close the place down."

Josephine again noticed the odd appearance of the young woman who was assisting Mrs. Lachlan with clearing the plates. When they returned to the kitchen, Josephine leaned close to Jamila. "Who is the woman helping Mrs. Lachlan?"

"Just a local girl. Skin problem. Very shy. Very sad." Jamila dismissed the woman as a topic worthy of conversation.

There was a little more small talk, punctuated by awkward silences. The other guests managed to deflect every effort by Josephine and Blasko to draw them out.

"Another meal done," Brock said when everyone finally stood.

"Bridge game in half an hour?" Hume asked. Josephine studied the man. He had a commanding air about him, even after an excessive amount of bourbon. Did he get it from arrogance or had he earned it?

"I'll grab a drink and meet you at the table," Brock said with little enthusiasm.

"Would either of you like to join us? We could always open another table," Hume said.

"One of them can have my spot," Donavan answered. "I'd play if it were poker, but I'm going to read for a while."

"I'll be glad to join you," Josephine told Hume. She was an average player and wasn't at all interested in winning or losing, but a card game could provide moments of unguarded conversation. She was curious to know more about this group. She didn't think it was mere coincidence that had brought them all to the island.

"Excellent. And you, Baron?" Hume asked.

"I think I will follow Mr. Donavan's example. I've got a new Ellery Queen mystery for my night's entertainment."

"I have letters to write," Zhao told Hume.

"Miss Molina?"

"But of course."

"She is a world-class player," Hume told Josephine. "We usually have to change partners during the evening."

"For two reasons. First, because whoever is partners with her, they're going to win. Secondly, because Jamila gets so angry with her partner that they have to be separated for the second game," Brock said with a small laugh.

"I wouldn't get angry if you all weren't such stupid card players," Jamila said without any trace of humor.

"You flatter me." Hume laughed.

Neith was headed toward the stairs, having completely ignored the invitation to play bridge. Blasko, with the excuse of fetching his book, followed her. She moved with purpose and entered her room across the open staircase from Blasko's just as he reached the second floor.

Blasko walked into his room and left the door open, watching Neith's door while pretending to look for his book. When she didn't come out after a reasonable interval, he closed his door and opened the French doors that led out onto the balcony. He walked around the balcony until he saw a figure leaning against the wall, her face illuminated by the ebbing glow of a cigarette.

Neith looked at him. Without a word, she seemed to extend an invitation to join her.

Standing at her side, Blasko looked out over the water sparkling in the moonlight. "The breeze off the water is invigorating."

"The smell of the salt reminds me of Alexandria."

"Do you miss Egypt?"

"Very much." For the first time, Blasko heard emotion in her voice.

"I would like to visit Egypt someday."

"I fear we have too much sun for you," she said with the smallest trace of humor.

Blasko looked at her. Was she hinting that she was aware of his true nature?

"Why don't you go home?" he asked, keeping his voice neutral. "Is your research so important?"

"This Timucua mound excavation will be the centerpiece of my doctoral dissertation."

"Which is?"

"A comparison of mound-building cultures."

"Of course. In your country, mound building culminated with the great pyramids," he said and saw fire in her eyes.

"Egyptian culture was and is far more advanced than these primitives."

Blasko bowed slightly, not wanting to start an argument

on a subject that was clearly dear to her heart. He was sure that if he riled her up, he'd never learn anything else from her. He didn't need great powers of observation to know that this was a woman who could hold a grudge.

"I've read with great interest about the excavations of King Tutankhamun's burial chamber."

Neith spat in disgust. "Howard Carter is nothing more than a grave robber," she hissed. "My country has been fought over for centuries. The invaders have always looted freely until stopped by the point of a sword." She seemed to mentally shake herself, then asked, "Why are you and that woman here?"

"Just a trip to the coast during a hot summer."

"Do not lie to me. There is more."

"What about your fellow guests? Are they all here for the reasons they say they are?"

"Who knows?" she snapped.

"I've angered you?"

"I am always angry," she said with a slight smile. "People anger me. You are no worse and no better."

"Do the other guests anger you?"

She took a deep drag of her cigarette. "I told you, everyone angers me." She dropped the cigarette on the floor and rubbed it out with her shoe. "I'm going in now. Enjoy the night." Again she seemed to hint that she knew his secrets.

This Egyptian is dangerous, Blasko thought as he watched her enter her room and close the door.

Downstairs, Josephine was sitting across the table from Captain Hume as he obsessively shuffled a deck of cards while they waited for Jamila and Brock to join them.

"I hope the southern climate has been good for your health," Josephine said.

"Doctor's idea. I do believe he just wanted to get me out of his hair." He was quiet for a moment, but before

Josephine could say anything else, he finally said, "I was with the Royal Marines at Gallipoli. We'd sustained massive casualties and were getting ready for another assault against the Turks when I went into our dugout for a box of ammunition for my Webley. Belcher had his old Victrola playing some daft song when I entered. Three days later, they dug me out of the rubble. Don't remember a thing. Got lucky when a support beam fell against another and held up part of the roof. Still enough debris fell on me to crush my chest. Six months' recovery. Pneumonia. Never should have lived, the doctors said. Anyhow, I got shipped to Cairo to recover. They wanted to send me home. Wouldn't let them. But they wouldn't send me to France; instead I served on staff during the invasion of Palestine. Only regret is I didn't get a chance to go toe to toe with the Jerrys." He had grown restive while he talked, shuffling the cards the entire time.

"I thought the marines served on ships?" Josephine watched the man closely.

"I did a bit of that too. Was on several different ships in the South Pacific." As Hume spoke, his eyes held an odd nostalgic gleam that hadn't been there when he was talking about his actions in Gallipoli.

"Is our hero telling you war stories?" Brock asked, walking up to the table with a tumbler full of amber whiskey.

Hume looked up at him with a frown. Josephine saw the hardness in his eyes and thought that Brock would do best to tread lightly.

"You will be my partner," Jamila told Brock as she joined them. "If no one objects?"

"Jolly good," answered Hume.

"Are you going to yell at me the whole time?" Brock asked before taking a deep drink from his glass.

"I will if you are playing like an idiot," Jamila challenged him.

"Ha! Let's do this then."

"Don't drink so much. It doesn't make you play any better."

"Makes you look better," Brock responded with an edge to his voice.

There are limits to how far Brock wants to be pushed, Josephine thought. She also noted that the barb got to Jamila, who looked down at the pile of cards she'd been dealt and ground her teeth.

"Our opponents are going to defeat themselves." Hume smiled at Josephine.

"A little tension at the table tightens up everyone's game," Josephine said and picked up her cards.

For the first dozen hands, there wasn't much talk as everyone tried to get a feel for how the other players were bidding and playing their cards. It was clear that Jamila was talented enough that she could pull along an average player like Brock, so that Hume and Josephine had to struggle to keep up.

During a break between games, Josephine stood up to stretch her legs. She saw Donavan sitting in a wingback chair near the bar and walked over to him. She noticed that he was reading a book on lost gold mines of the Southwest.

"What type of boat do you have?" she asked when he glanced up at her.

"I'm renting a local man's trawler while I'm here," he answered, his finger tapping the empty glass that he held in one hand. Josephine could sense an inner battle going on when he set the glass down on the table next to the chair. "I'd be happy to take you out on it." Then he added as an afterthought, "Your cousin the baron is welcome to join us, of course."

"Unfortunately, he is allergic to the sun," Josephine said, deciding to broach this subject as soon as possible and hoping she could head off any gossip once everyone noticed Blasko's odd behavior.

Brock and Jamila had walked over to the bar and seemed more interested in the conversation between Josephine and Donavan than in refilling their glasses.

"Really? I had a friend who burned just stepping out on a

sunny day, but I don't think he was actually allergic." Donavan sounded only a little bit skeptical.

"That must be… awkward," Jamila observed.

"I knew a fellow who was allergic to grass. Inconvenient for him," Brock said. Josephine was grateful for his comment, as it seemed to settle the matter.

"We should get back to the game," Jamila said, leading the way to the table.

Josephine would have preferred more time with Donavan. *I guess that will have to wait for the boat ride.*

"This is such an interesting group of folks," Josephine said a short while later as she sorted her cards and tried to decide what to bid. Her game was suffering as her attention was divided between play and finding ways to learn more about the other guests. "Jamila, you said you're an artist?"

Jamila glanced up from her cards.

"I do sketches of the natural world. But really, I am just like you and your cousin. I am a tourist." Josephine thought she detected a slight smirk.

Hume started the bidding, so everyone concentrated on the hand. The game absorbed most of Josephine's evening, and her efforts to learn anything more about her companions were met mostly with brief, unenlightening answers. It didn't help that Hume, Jamila and Brock all occasionally asked pointed questions of her, trying to learn what she and Blasko were doing on the island.

After four games, they agreed to call it a night. They had switched partners for the last two games, which resulted in Jamila and Josephine winning handily.

"You play very well," Jamila complimented her as they stood up from the table.

"Not as well as you."

"Several times in my life I've had to depend on my card skills to make a living," Jamila admitted.

"Were you born in Spain?"

"Yes," Jamila said, and Josephine thought this was going to be another in a series of one-word answers. To her surprise, however, Jamila continued, "But my family traveled around. The truth is I am Gitano… a gypsy."

"I guess that life wasn't easy for your family."

"Yes and no. Hard work and hard looks from the people in the towns. We traveled throughout Spain and Portugal. My father was killed in an accident and his brother wanted to marry my mother, but she despised him. It was not long before she took me and my sisters and fled. I was fourteen. That is when life truly became hard…"

Jamila stopped in front of the mahogany breakfront that took up half of one wall. She opened one of the cabinet doors to reveal numerous bottles of alcohol with people's names on them. "Mrs. Lachlan lets guests keep their own liquor. Would you care for some wine?" she asked, taking out a green bottle with a peeling label.

"Please."

Jamila set up two glasses and filled them almost to the rim.

"Thank goodness your country came to its senses about Prohibition." Jamila drank deeply from the glass.

Josephine didn't bother explaining that Prohibition was going to take a long time to be rolled back throughout the country, especially in the Deep South.

They walked out onto the porch. Josephine was enjoying the wine and it mixed well with the warm salt air. "You never really said why you chose to visit Cedar Island," she said.

"Neither did you," Jamila countered.

"I had an uncle who came here years ago. He wrote to me about the island. I wanted to see it for myself." *And that's all true*, Josephine thought, *as far as it goes*.

"I read about the island too, in an old journal. The author made it sound like a place that would be worth my time to visit, with many native animals to sketch." Jamila looked out across the docks at the calm Gulf waters.

"And has it been worth the trip?"

"I'm not sure yet, but it's becoming more interesting,"

she said, finishing her wine. "I think I will turn in now."

As the woman walked back inside, Josephine was left to wonder what exactly she'd meant.

CHAPTER SEVEN

Josephine was surprised to find Blasko pacing the floor in her bedroom.

"You have your own room," she reminded him.

"I want to compare notes with you," he said eagerly.

"Have you seen Grace?"

"No, but Anton said they had a fine dinner in the kitchen. There were several other staff who ate with them, including the cook, a maid and that waif of a girl who helped Mrs. Lachlan serve us."

"I can hear everything y'all are sayin'." Grace's voice came through the wall.

Josephine went over to the door of the bathroom that served both their rooms and knocked lightly. "Grace?"

"I'm in the finest tub I've ever been in," she said in a dreamy voice. "I might never get out. The water sure is fine."

"I want to talk to you about the other folks who ate dinner with you."

"Nothin' to tell. Those are the most closed-mouthed people I've ever met. Didn't get a dozen words from any of 'em. You ain't goin' to want in here for a while, are you?"

"Enjoy yourself," Josephine said with a smile.

"Sure 'nough," Grace responded with a satisfied tone.

Josephine walked over to where Blasko was staring out the window, pretending not hear Grace's voice from the bathroom. "Are we in agreement that the group downstairs is not some random assembly of tourists?" she asked.

Blasko nodded, glad to hear that she had sensed the same things he had. "I think they are hiding something, both individually and as a cabal of some sort."

"The question is: does it have anything to do with us or Uncle Petey's death?"

"Normally, I would think that highly unlikely. But after everything else we've experienced in the past year…" Blasko shook his head. "Maybe the letter your uncle left at the post office will tell us something."

"If there is a letter. Even if Uncle Petey really did leave one, it might not be there now."

"I know we'll have a hard time learning anything else from that crowd. I judge that they are all well practiced at keeping secrets."

"Captain Hume strikes me as sympathetic."

"Perhaps, but he is an old soldier. I wouldn't mistake sympathy for weakness. Tell me about the card game and what you learned."

Josephine shared the little she knew about the group.

"Interesting," Blasko said, looking down at the floor and stroking his chin in a thoughtful manner.

"What?"

"A connection. At least between three of them."

"I don't see it."

"You said that Hume was sent to Cairo to recover from his wounds. Neith is Egyptian and Jamila is Gitano."

"Jamila is from Spain."

"Yes, but the Gitano are said to have come to Spain after generations in Egypt."

"There doesn't seem to be any love lost between Jamila and Neith," Josephine said archly.

"Maybe it is a coincidence. I'm not sure how Zhao,

Brock and Donavan would fit anyway."

"Donavan invited me out on his boat. Actually, he invited both of us." She added the last part to see what sort of reaction she would get out of Blasko.

"Bah! I hate boats."

"And sunlight."

"Exactly. But I wouldn't go even at night."

"You need to have gold and your native earth under you to cross a river." Josephine brought the subject up carefully. The baron never liked to talk about his weaknesses.

"I told you that when you brought me here. I even had my car seats lined with a few gold coins and a light dusting of soil from Romania." His voice was stiff and he kept his chin elevated and eyes averted from her.

"Is the ocean the same as a river?"

"I don't know!" he snapped, irritation creeping into his tone. "I took precautions with the crate when I traveled across the Atlantic. Whether it was necessary or not, I do not really know. All I know is that running water makes me very... uncomfortable."

"I'm just trying to understand," Josephine said quietly, by way of an apology for mentioning his vulnerabilities.

"It's fine. Go with Donavan and find out what you can."

"I think I'll ask someone else to go with me. He looks like the type of guy who could be... difficult."

"Difficult?"

"Like an octopus."

"Ahh," Blasko said. "Be careful." He reached out and took her hand.

"Are you going out on the prowl tonight?"

"If you mean, am I going out to look around the town?—then yes, I am." He dropped her hand. He hated it when she suggested that he skulked around at night like some madman.

"Why don't you check out that bar they were talking about?"

"One of my first destinations."

"I picked this up from the front desk." She handed him a small matchbook. Written in red letters on a black background were simply the words: *The Dragon, Cedar Island.*

"It sits near the docks just north of us. I could smell the stale beer from the balcony," Blasko said.

"First thing tomorrow, I'm going to the post office to see if Uncle Petey's letter is there."

"And if it's not?"

"Let's cross our bridges one at a time."

"I'm done if you want to get yourself a bath!" Grace yelled from the bathroom.

"I'm off to go… prowling," Blasko said with a slight smirk and a bow.

"Wish me luck tomorrow."

Blasko could hear an underlying insecurity in her words, an emotion he seldom saw in Josephine. The memory of her uncle and this odd quest to find what he'd left behind were clearly affecting her self-confidence.

He reached out and touched her cheek lightly, brushing a strand of honey-brown hair away from her face. "Everything will be fine. I will see you tomorrow night." He leaned forward and gave her a gentle kiss. "And whatever you discover, we'll deal with it together."

Josephine grabbed for his hand and squeezed it before letting him go. She waited until he had closed the door before dabbing at the tears that had formed in her eyes. Josephine was forced to admit that this little adventure was bringing up feelings of loss that she thought she'd left behind a year ago when she'd said goodbye to her father. There was fear too. Fear that she would learn things about her uncle that she didn't want to know. Whatever he'd done on the island all those years ago had ended with him dead.

Blasko walked softly around the balcony outside his room until he was at the back of the hotel. Looking around to make sure he wasn't being watched, he slipped over the railing and dropped softly to the ground beside a palm tree.

After hundreds of years, Blasko still marveled when he encountered new sensations. The feel of the sand giving way beneath his feet was one of those, mixed with the exotic smells of the Gulf and the night-blooming jasmine growing along the wooden fence marking the hotel's property.

As he walked toward the docks, he could smell another odor, something lurking underneath the stale smell of beer and tobacco. At first he thought it was just the scent of fish brought in by the trawlers, but it was more than that. There was an organic smell like that of a wet animal, and it was coming from more than one location. Mixed with the odor was a hint of decay.

Over the centuries, Blasko had perfected the art of walking in the shadows. Tonight he was particularly careful to stay hidden from the casual observer as he made his way toward the bar. When he was a block away, he saw the red neon sign that clung to the clapboard wall. *The Dragon* was spelled out in garish red, but the letter "R" was burned out.

Blasko crouched beside an overturned rowboat whose splintered hull assured him that its days on the water were long over. From there he could see into a cloudy window on the side of the bar, plus he had a clear view of the front door opening out onto the sidewalk. Several men were leaning against the wall, talking and smoking.

Though they spoke in near whispers, Blasko was able to hear parts of their conversation. They were talking about going out in their boats, which seemed perfectly normal as they were obviously fishermen, but they never seemed to discuss a purpose or destination. Their voices all held an odd undertone, as if they were gasping for air, and sometimes their words seemed to be in a language unlike anything he'd ever heard. *"Fu'logg huq tov,"* he thought he heard one of the men say. As he puzzled this out, Blasko also wondered why they were all bundled up in jackets and knitted caps on a night that was warm and sticky, with only the breeze from the water to make it bearable.

A dozen men came and went from the bar. They would nod to the others standing outside and occasionally join them for a brief conversation. As an hour passed, the foot traffic toward the docks seemed to increase, then Blasko realized that he could hear the throbbing sound of diesel engines moving *away* from shore. While he wasn't familiar with the ways of fishermen, Blasko didn't think it was normal for them to be heading out after midnight. *Perhaps it has to do with the tides or the running of the fish*, he thought. *I'll have to make inquiries when I can.*

Blasko considered entering the bar, but the only thing that stopped him was the thought of Josephine. Solving the mystery of her uncle's death meant too much to her. If he barged into the bar and burned bridges with the locals, spoiling her chances of discovering what had happened to Peter Nicolson, he'd have a hard time making amends. It was better to save the direct approach for later. Instead, he slid away from his vantage point and walked toward the docks. He wanted to watch the boats going out to sea.

As he walked, Blasko noticed that there was mold growing on some of the houses and buildings. The fences around some of the yards were falling down and old cars and trucks parked on the streets looked like they hadn't moved for months. Many of the houses were lit by only the dim glow of gas lighting. *Obviously there is electricity on the island*, he thought. *Can this many people not afford it?* He guessed that even this remote fishing village had been unable to escape the effects of a national economy in tatters.

Blasko had intended on heading directly to the docks to watch the departing trawlers, but instead he turned down one of the residential streets near the waterfront. What he saw was unnerving. He remembered entering a mountain village centuries before, where everyone had been slaughtered by a warlord from the north. The village had been deathly quiet, yet still he had felt the sense of morbid life. He'd soon come to understand that his enhanced hearing was bringing him the sounds of insects as they devoured the corpses of the slain villagers. Walking down the sandy avenues of Cedar Island and looking at the rotted, moss-covered boards holding the houses together, he got the same feeling. Several times he saw someone come out of one of the homes and scuttle-hop eerily across the road to another house or down to the docks.

Disturbed, Blasko headed back toward the docks. He stuck to the shadows, as there were several men milling about and hauling equipment down to the dozen boats that were still secured to cleats. Quietly, Blasko eased into the sagging doorway of a derelict structure on the edge of the dock where he could watch the men through a dusty window.

The fishermen seemed as capable of moving about in the dark as he was. No one was using a lantern or flashlight, and yet they never stumbled or bumped into each other. The moon was almost full, which probably accounted for some of it. However, with all the various tools and equipment lying about, to say nothing of the rotted boards and railings, Blasko was impressed that the men were able to move around without hurting themselves.

One by one, the strange fishermen made their boats ready, then cast off and motored out into the Gulf. Though he couldn't be sure, Blasko's gut was telling him that there was something very odd about their behavior.

With only a few hours until sunrise, he left the docks. As he walked back to the hotel, he was surprised to see Eric Donavan leaning against a tree in a vacant lot, staring down at the docks. At first Blasko thought it best to avoid him, but feeling frustrated about how little he'd learned so far, he decided to talk to Donavan. He knew that Josephine had already floated the allergy-to-sunlight excuse, so he would be able to use that to explain why he was wandering around in the middle of the night. Blasko thought it would be interesting to hear Donavan's reason for being out at this hour.

"Good morning," he said, startling Donavan as he'd

planned.

"Baron Blasko, what are you doing out here?"

"I'm afraid that my aversion to sunlight forces me to live a nocturnal life. I saw you standing here and was wondering if you are another… What do they call it over here? Oh yes, a night owl." Blasko smiled.

Donavan nodded. "Sort of. I'm a professor of biological anthropology back in Vancouver, but I also have an interest in marine biology. I've been waiting for the boats to come back so I can collect anything… odd that they've caught."

"When do the boats come back?"

"Usually just before dawn."

"I don't know anything about fishing, but that seems unusual."

Donavan's feet shifted back and forth. "I've found most fishermen to be a clannish lot. These are no different." He paused for a moment, as though he were considering whether to go on. "You are right that the men on this island have some peculiar habits." He looked at Blasko keenly. "Can you keep a secret?"

"Of course."

"When I first got to the island, I went to them and asked if they would save anything unusual that they caught for me. I offered to pay them. I've done this in a dozen different fishing villages and have always been met with a grin and a handshake. But here, they told me to leave them alone. I did find one willing to rent me a trawler, but that's as far as it went."

"So?"

"So, some nights I hide here and wait for the boats to come back. I usually have about an hour between when the men leave the docks and the sun comes up to go down there and crawl around under the docks, collecting anything they've discarded."

Blasko was impressed with the man's determination. "Have you found any notable specimens?"

Donavan looked away. "I've found… bits and pieces that

seem… unique."

"Do they catch many fish?"

"An impressive amount of red snapper. They sell what they catch to Mrs. Lachlan's brother, who runs the local store. He gives them credit and takes the fish to the mainland, where I assume he sells it."

"Do they sell any locally?"

"The islanders won't eat fish."

They watched the docks in silence for a few more minutes. The moon was setting, so Blasko assumed that Donavan would be able to make his way down to the docks without being seen. He wanted to go down with him, but the risk of being caught in the sunrise was too great.

He was just about to depart when Donavan said, "You're from Romania, right?"

"Yes."

"Like Dracula."

Blasko tensed, but managed to give a little chuckle. "Ah, my famous countryman. We owe Bram Stoker a nod for putting our homeland on the map."

"Funny that *you* have an allergy to sunlight," Donavan said lightly.

"I do not find my condition humorous," Blasko said, mustering all the indignation he could, which was considerable.

"I'm sorry. I just thought it was curious. The moon has gone down. I should head for the docks." Donavan walked away with his hands in his pockets, looking only a little embarrassed.

Blasko turned toward the hotel. He was beginning to feel a gnawing craving for fresh blood. For the journey, they had packed on ice several bottles of the blood that Josephine ordered from a medical supply company. It was stale and never gave him the restorative energy of fresh blood, but Josephine was so squeamish about him hunting his own that he tried to stick to the legally acquired blood she provided. He had tried repeatedly to convince her that he did no harm when he hunted. After all, he was able to take enough for himself and leave the donor unconscious, but alive. *Besides, I only pick people who deserve to have the lives sucked out of them*, he thought to himself, knowing that wasn't the sort of argument that Josephine would appreciate.

Mrs. Lachlan had made a point of telling them that she locked the hotel at midnight, so he made his way around to the spot where he'd jumped down and deftly climbed up the palm tree. Once on the balcony, he brushed off his clothes and started to walk around to his room. However, he heard voices as he passed a window and moved closer to the wall, being careful not to make any noise.

"Why are they here? That's what we need to find out," said a voice that Blasko recognized as Neith's.

"You had to come to my room at five in the morning to tell me something I'd already figured out?" Captain Hume retorted.

"I have been thinking about it all night. Be grateful that I waited until morning."

"This is only morning if you were raised on a farm. For the rest of us, it's still the middle of the night."

"I don't like them showing up like this."

"I don't like it either. I played cards with the woman and she was definitely fishing for information."

"Who's going to look into this?"

"Zhao maybe. He's the great researcher."

"I'm going to keep an eye on them."

"We all need to do that. There's too much at stake. Now, get out of my room and let me go back to sleep."

"I don't think you're taking this seriously enough. We already have the man in the cabin by the cemetery to worry about."

"Rehashing it isn't going to solve anything now. Go on, get out."

Blasko walked quickly back to his room. Once inside, he heard Anton's loud snoring. The man had made himself invaluable, but his personal habits and refusal to leave

Blasko's side often grated on the baron's nerves.

"Anton, get up. I must prepare for the morning." Blasko tapped Anton's shoe.

"Yes, Baron."

Anton was on his feet almost before he was awake. He fussed around the baron, taking his coat and helping him settle in to sleep with his broadsword on his right side and a 1911 Colt .45 tucked into a holster built into the left side of the coffin. Blasko had recently been caught unawares while he slept and he wasn't going to allow that to happen again. In addition to his weapons, the coffin also had interior locks that he slipped into place after Anton closed the lid. Before drifting off, he thought about the strange conversation he'd overheard and wondered again about the odd group of tourists.

CHAPTER EIGHT

"See if you can talk to some folks today, find out what you can about the town," Josephine suggested to Grace the next morning.

"That's not goin' to be so easy. I'm the only black person on this island," Grace said doubtfully.

"Is this a sunset town?" There were still many communities throughout the South where black people weren't welcome after sunset.

"No, ma'am. I don't get that at all. Seems there were some livin' here years ago, but they all just moved."

"Was it a lack of jobs?"

"I'll ask around." Josephine knew that Grace actually enjoyed having a reason to snoop and gossip.

"I'm going to get a little breakfast, then head to the post office to see if Uncle Petey's letter is still there."

"You want me or Anton to come with you?"

"I'll be fine. The postmaster might speak more freely if I'm alone. Besides, Anton should stay with Dragomir during the day."

"What can I fetch for you while I'm out?"

"I don't need anything, thank you."

"Miss Josephine, you have to need somethin'. If you want

me to walk around town askin' questions, I got to have a reason for bein' out and about."

"Good point." Josephine took a minute to think. "We're on the water so I'll need a scarf, maybe two." She reached into her purse and took out a ten-dollar bill.

"That's goin' to be a nice scarf," Grace said, looking at the money.

"Get yourself whatever you want with what's left."

With her clothes and hair in order, Josephine made her way downstairs to the dining room. Neith was seated at the main table, drinking tea and writing in a small journal. She looked up as Josephine walked in.

"Mrs. Lachlan will be back momentarily," she said.

"Some tea and toast will be a good start," Josephine said, going to the sideboard.

With a plate and cup in hand, Josephine sat at the table close enough to see what Neith was writing, but one glance told her it was a wasted effort. The script was in Arabic.

"Are you excavating the mound today?"

Neith gave her a look of annoyance. "We have made several preliminary excavations. I am currently drawing up plans for a large dig next month when I will have several undergraduates to assist me." She turned back to her writing without making further eye contact with Josephine.

"I'd love to see the mound." Josephine was determined to ignore Neith's attempts to ignore *her*.

"Perhaps."

"We don't have much of an agenda for the next couple of weeks."

Neith sighed. "I will be very busy."

Josephine gave up and let Neith concentrate on her work while Mrs. Lachlan served a breakfast of eggs, bacon and grits.

Once Josephine was finished, she headed out to the post office. It was located in a small brick building a block away from the hotel. It was separated from the dry goods store next door by a short alley that was barely as wide as a man's shoulders. Josephine looked down the alley as she walked past and saw an orange tabby saunter into a doorway.

A bell above the door rang loudly as Josephine entered the tiny lobby of the post office. An older woman in a faded print dress with a drooping bow in her hair came out of the back.

"May I help you?"

"I hope so. My name is Josephine Nicolson. This is going to sound—"

"Who did you say you were?" The woman looked like she had seen a ghost.

"Josephine Nicolson."

"Where… um… are you from?" the woman stuttered.

"Sumter, Alabama."

"After all these years!" The woman glanced at the side window. "Oh my, come on back here." The woman lifted a section of the counter and motioned Josephine into the back room.

"You know who I am?" Josephine asked. Of all the reactions she had expected, this was not one of them.

"You're Pete's niece."

"You knew my uncle?"

"We were… friends," the woman said, blushing, then shook her head. "I'm sorry. I've forgotten my manners. I'm Mitzi Alexander. This is just so overwhelming."

"I found a letter my uncle wrote before leaving home. It said he would leave another letter here."

"He did. I've guarded it all these years." As Mitzi spoke, she kept looking around as though she thought someone might be listening. The room had several windows that were open to catch what little breeze there was. Mitzi quickly shut all of them. "I hid it," she said, coming back to Josephine.

"Were you worried someone would steal it?"

"If they knew I had a letter from Pete, they would have tortured me to find it."

Suspecting that the woman was being a little melodramatic, Josephine asked, "Do you know what's in the letter?"

"I don't want to know. I begged him to stop. I didn't care about the gold or treasure or whatever it was he was after."

"Treasure?"

"He was digging into the secrets that have destroyed this island."

"I don't understand."

"I've lived as long as I have by being ignorant of most of it. I'm going to give you the letter, then you have to go. You need to leave Cedar Island."

"You realize how crazy you sound?" Josephine didn't want to insult this woman she'd just met, but nothing she was saying made any sense.

"Worse than crazy. It's evil."

Mitzi went over to a safe in the corner. Josephine assumed that the letter was locked up inside, so she was surprised when Mitzi got down on her belly and reached as far as she could underneath the safe. The legs were just high enough to allow her to push her arm under it. "Can you help me?"

Josephine knelt down on the floor next to her.

"I'm not as nimble as I used to be. Can you see the board I'm trying to pull up?"

Josephine looked under the safe and saw that Mitzi was trying to lift a small section of the pine flooring.

"Let me try."

Mitzi moved over and Josephine reached under the safe. A cloud of dust made her sneeze.

"Bless you," Mitzi said.

"Thank you. Yes, I've got it up. I can feel a letter and a ring." Josephine brought them both out. "This is his school ring." She remembered seeing her uncle wear it, and how large the simple blue stone at its center had seemed to her child's eyes.

Mitzi took the ring. "He gave it to me and told me I was his girl. Pete was such a funny man."

"He must have loved you." Secretly, Josephine wondered

how serious her uncle had been about Mitzi. He'd once promised to marry a girl in Sumter, but had jilted her before making it to the altar. Peter Nicolson had not liked to be tied down.

"And I loved him. When he died…" Mitzi started to cry.

"It must have been horrible for you."

"The worst of it was, I couldn't tell anyone. If they'd known, they would have killed me."

"Who?"

"I told you, Pete was dredging up old secrets, and some that weren't all that old. Take the letter and go. Quickly."

The woman's urgency was infectious. For a moment, Josephine thought she saw movement outside one of the windows. *Maybe her paranoia is contagious too*, she wondered. Aloud, she said, "I have more questions."

"I don't know anything and I don't want to. And I don't know what brought you here after all of these years, but it's a good thing you came when you did. I'm going to leave the island as soon as I can. I have someone to go with now." She was physically pushing Josephine toward the door.

Puzzled at the woman's intense reaction, Josephine looked down at the letter. It was the old-fashioned kind where the letter folded up so that it also served as the envelope. Both her father's name and her own were written neatly on the front.

"But—"

"Go!" Mitzi insisted, crying harder now.

Josephine reluctantly left the post office. She was still looking at the letter as she walked back past the alley. In a flash, a small body hopped out from between the buildings and tried to grab the letter from her hands.

Josephine didn't let go and was pulled into the narrow alley. She tried to see the thief's face, but he was wearing a peacoat with the collar turned up and a knit cap pulled low over his head. He seemed hardly larger than a boy, but he pulled and yanked on the letter with considerable strength.

Josephine fought to keep her hold on the letter. Both she

and the thief were gripping the letter with both hands, throwing each other repeatedly against the brick walls in the confined space. Battered and bruised, Josephine refused to let go… until she heard a ripping sound and then fell hard to the ground on her knees. The thief scuttled away to the other end of the alley, disappearing around the corner with a large piece of the letter in his hand.

Josephine looked down to see that she held only a ragged third of the letter. Furious, she jumped to her feet. She was debating the wisdom of running after the thief when she saw him suddenly reappear in the alley, running back toward her. Before she could react, the thief fell face-down in front of her. She was shocked to see a knife sticking out of his back.

Still shaken by the fight and aching all over from the struggle, Josephine stared at the body, unsure what to do. If she had been home, then she wouldn't have hesitated to call the sheriff. But here on Cedar Island, with no phone lines and no local law enforcement that she knew of, she was at a loss.

She finally decided that the most sensible thing to do would be to go back to the post office and tell Mitzi what had happened. She'd know who they should inform about the murder.

Josephine walked a bit unsteadily out of the alley, looking around nervously to make sure there wasn't anyone else lurking nearby.

"Damn it!" she hissed when she found the door of the post office locked. She knocked loudly, but there was no answer. Looking around, she didn't see anyone else on the street, though it was nearly nine-thirty. Surely the stores should be opening soon.

Still in shock, she almost forgot the reason she was there. Remembering the torn letter in her hand, Josephine realized that there was something she needed to do. Reluctantly, she turned back toward the alley, hoping that the killer wasn't still hiding nearby.

She took a deep breath as she approached the body.

Bending over, she looked at his hands. The skin was crusty with an odd, pale green tint that made her stomach turn. Both hands were empty. With a feeling of revulsion, she reached into the dirty and threadbare coat to search his pockets, but found nothing. She looked at the knitted cap pulled down almost to his nose and saw scaly patches on his chin and around his mouth. She briefly considered pulling the cap off of his head, but she couldn't bring herself to do it.

Nothing else to do but go back to the hotel, she told herself. She slipped the torn letter into a pocket of her skirt, then started walking as fast as she could, constantly looking over her shoulder.

Eric Donavan and Jamila were sitting on the porch having coffee when she returned.

"Morning," Donavan said with a nod.

"Do you know where I can find Mrs. Lachlan?" she asked them.

"Why? What's going on?" Donavan asked, noticing that Josephine was flushed and sweating.

"There's been an… accident. I need to get some help."

"I'll do what I can." Donavan stood up.

"I'm afraid we need the sheriff."

"There's no phone—"

"Someone around here must have some authority!" Josephine said, exasperated. "I just need to find Mrs. Lachlan."

"Okay, I'll look in the back. She might be in the kitchen. You might check upstairs. She sometimes starts cleaning early in the morning."

"I believe I did see her going upstairs," Jamila said, looking only mildly interested in Josephine's anxiety.

"I'll check there. If you see her, ask her to meet me upstairs," Josephine said, hurrying through the door to the staircase.

Grace was just coming out of her room.

"Have you seen Mrs. Lachlan?"

"She's in your room right now, makin' the bed," Grace said. "What on earth is goin' on?"

"Stay here. I may need your help."

Josephine rushed into her room and found Mrs. Lachlan finishing the bed with the help of the strange young woman they'd seen last night.

"We're just about done in—" Mrs. Lachlan started to say.

"There's been a terrible accident down by the post office."

"What type of accident?"

"The kind where someone dies." Josephine didn't think that now was the time to sugarcoat the truth.

"Oh my! We'll have to send over to the mainland for the sheriff. That's going to take time. Are you sure the person is dead?"

"He has a foot-long knife rammed into his back."

The young woman looked frightened, making Josephine briefly regret her choice of words.

"We need to get help," she emphasized, trying to sound calmer.

"Yes, of course. I'll send my son for the sheriff." Mrs. Lachlan turned to the girl. "Go get Edward." The girl didn't seem to hear. "Go, girl, now!" Mrs. Lachlan clapped her hands and the girl jumped, hustling out of the room.

"I'm going to get my maid and go back to the post office," Josephine said.

"You should take one of the other men too. Mr. Donavan or Mr. Brock," Mrs. Lachlan said, looking concerned as they left Josephine's room.

Josephine decided she was probably right. Two more hands might be a good idea.

"Come with me to the post office," Josephine told Grace, who was still standing by her bedroom door.

"Did I hear you say that a man is dead?"

"Yes. He was stabbed in the back." Reluctantly, she also admitted, "He tried to steal my uncle's letter from me."

Grace's eyes widened. "I guess the shoppin' trip ain't

happenin'. Do you think it's a good idea goin' back there now?"

"I need to."

"I feel crazy for sayin' it, but I sure do wish the baron could go with us," Grace muttered as she followed Josephine and Mrs. Lachlan down the stairs.

Mrs. Lachlan's son was waiting in the lobby. Josephine left her to explain about the sheriff and headed out the door. Donavan was standing on the porch, looking interested in all of the activity.

"Will you come with me to the post office?" Josephine asked.

"Certainly. I can see from here that there are some people gathering around outside it," he said, falling in step with Josephine and Grace.

Sure enough, Josephine could see four people standing by the post office. She assumed that they had found the body and were waiting for help… or maybe they were just gawking. Like her attacker, two of the people were wearing coats and hats, even though the temperature was already above eighty and the air was humid. They all drifted away silently as Josephine and her companions approached.

"What kind of accident was it?" Donavan asked.

"It wasn't an accident. A man was murdered," Josephine told him.

"Murdered? Are you serious?"

They stopped at the entrance to the alley and Josephine looked into the narrow passage. The corpse was gone.

CHAPTER NINE

"I don't believe it!"

Josephine stalked into the alley with Donavan following in her wake. She stopped at the spot where she had last seen the body. "It was right here."

"Maybe he wasn't dead."

"He most certainly *was* dead." Josephine was on the brink of telling him that she had rifled through the man's coat, but she didn't want to have to explain what she was looking for.

"I doubt that someone moved a dead body," Donavan said with an irritating, know-it-all tone.

"Well, he didn't get up and walk away." She squatted and examined the ground. "There's blood here," she said, pointing to a spot on the ground. The blood showed clearly against the crushed white shells that comprised most streets on the island.

Donavan bent over and peered closely at the spot. "It's blood, I'll give you that, but it's not very much. I'm sure you were very upset. I don't blame you for jumping to conclusions. Most likely the guy got up and wandered off," he said, his voice annoyingly superior.

"This isn't the first dead body I've seen, but it's the first one that's ever disappeared."

"You see a lot of dead bodies in Alabama?" Donavan asked with a lopsided grin.

"You'd be surprised."

Josephine walked to the other end of the alley. She saw several empty lots and a couple of houses with fishnets drying in the yard next to crab traps and floats, but there was no sign of the dead man.

Frustrated, Josephine returned to the post office and knocked loudly on the door. There was still no answer. *Where can Mitzi have gone?* she asked herself, pounding on the door until her knuckles hurt.

"That's probably why those people were standing out front," Donavan said. "The postmistress must have closed up."

"Why would she do that in the middle of the morning?" Josephine gave up and stopped knocking. *She was so upset after talking to me, maybe she just needed a break*, she rationalized. But another voice in her head suggested darker reasons why Mitzi wasn't answering the door. She went around the building and peered inside all of the windows, now securely closed and locked. She saw no signs of anything sinister having happened.

"I really think you're blowing this out of proportion," Donavan said as he followed her from window to window.

Josephine sighed. "Perhaps you're right. You can go back to the hotel." She looked around and noticed for the first time that the maid wasn't with them. "Where's Grace?"

"I'm right here," Grace called from the street a few feet from the post office. "If you think I'm walkin' down that narrow alley where you saw a dead body, you got another thing comin'."

"Stay close," Josephine encouraged her, then turned back to Donavan. "I do appreciate you coming down here with me."

"I'm sorry if I offended you, but you have to admit that the idea someone carted off a dead body in broad daylight is a bit crazy."

"Crazy is suggesting that I don't know a dead body when I see one. The man had a knife stuck in his back." Josephine thought how much the whole situation sounded like a plot from one of the Gothic novels she'd devoured as a young woman. She reached into her pocket and felt what was left of the letter the dead man had attempted to snatch from her. She wanted to examine it, but couldn't with Donavan hovering over her.

"The sheriff isn't going to be too happy when he gets here," he said.

"Honestly, you don't have to stay."

"I'll wait. If there really is a murderer running about, I wouldn't want to leave you out here by yourself. Tell me exactly what happened."

Josephine debated how much she wanted to tell him. "I came out of the post office and the man in the coat was waiting in the alley. He jumped me and tried to take my… purse. I resisted and he ran off down the passageway between the two buildings, only to reappear and fall to the ground with a knife sticking out of his back." She thought this summed it up nicely without giving away anything about the letter or her talk with Mitzi.

"Maybe it was a gag."

"Don't be an idiot." Josephine walked over to Grace, all the while scanning the ground for any clues as to what might have happened to the body or Mitzi. "How long do you think it will take for the sheriff to get here?"

"I don't know," Donavan answered. "An hour, maybe longer. It's fifteen miles before you get to anything you could call a town. And if he's on the other side of the county, you're talking a couple of hours."

"Great."

"There's no sense waiting here."

"Do you know where Mitzi Alexander lives?"

"I'm as much a tourist as you are." Donavan shrugged his shoulders.

Grace was watching him closely. He had two strikes

against him in her eyes; he was a man, and he was a stranger.

"I don't believe we've met," Donavan said to Grace. "I'm Eric Donavan. You work for Miss Nicolson?"

"I do. You can call me Grace," she snapped. Another strike in her book was a man who would presume to talk to a woman without her speaking to him first.

"I say we should all go back to the hotel and wait for the sheriff. Then you can tell him your story when he gets here," Donavan said to Josephine.

"It's not a story," she grumbled, though she realized there wasn't much point in standing around if there wasn't a body to guard. The body could have been anywhere by now. "Okay, let's go back," she said grudgingly.

"Who was it?" Mrs. Lachlan asked when they entered the hotel.

"Poof, gone." Donavan moved his hands apart, palms up like a magician. Josephine wanted to clobber him.

"What do you mean 'gone?'" Mrs. Lachlan said with a stern expression.

"Someone moved the body," Josephine said before Donavan had a chance to make any more snide remarks.

"I don't understand." Mrs. Lachlan looked like she was about to faint.

"Apparently someone didn't want anyone else to get a good look at it," Josephine said, thinking about the body's scaly skin and odd color. Could there have been another reason to move the body other than to cover up the murder?

"The sheriff isn't going to be happy about this. No, sir, not happy at all." Mrs. Lachlan was sweating profusely.

"I think you should sit down." Josephine didn't want her passing out or having a heart attack.

"That's a good idea." Mrs. Lachlan dropped into one of the chairs in the lobby and began to fan herself with her apron.

Josephine turned on the metal fan sitting on the corner of the reception desk while Grace went to fetch a glass of lemonade for Mrs. Lachlan.

"Another odd thing," Josephine said to Mrs. Lachlan as they waited for Grace to come back from the kitchen. "The postmistress closed up the post office."

"She's probably just out. Mitzi is the only employee and, if she has to run an errand, she just locks it up. Usually puts a note on the door."

"There wasn't a note."

"She *is* getting pretty old. Forgetful, you know. If they keep her on the job too much longer, who knows who will get whose mail. Thank you, dear," she said as Grace handed her a cool glass of lemonade.

Suddenly Anton came trotting down the stairs, looking more focused than usual. He stopped a foot from Josephine and, as if making a pronouncement at a formal affair, he said, "The baron wants to see you."

Josephine was shocked. Blasko had never summoned her to his room during the day. Hiding her surprise, she said, "Please excuse me," then headed quickly up the stairs with Anton at her heels.

"It's me," she said, knocking on Blasko's door. Anton squeezed around her and opened it before she could turn the knob.

"He said for *me* to bring you," the little man said as they entered the darkened room where the curtains had been pinned tightly shut. Anton opened the lid of the portable coffin.

"We need a bier for this," Blasko muttered as he climbed weakly out of the coffin. "Excellent design, but I do not like being down on the floor." Gripping the back of a chair to steady himself, he looked closely at Josephine. "You are safe?" he asked, his voice full of concern.

Josephine realized that, even through his deep sleep, Blasko had known about the attack. Ever since the first day they'd met when she'd accidentally drank some of his blood in self-defense, they had been bound together by an inextricable force. This bond gave Blasko a sixth sense about Josephine and he'd never failed to know when she was in danger.

"Yes… Well, there was some difficulty."

"Tell me."

She explained the whole series of events from her first meeting with the postmistress to the body's mysterious disappearance.

"Excellent!"

"Which part? When I get attacked or when I lose half of my uncle's letter?" Josephine asked, frowning. She pulled the letter out of her pocket.

"Let me see that," Blasko said, reaching for it.

"Not so fast. I haven't had time to look at it myself. Now I wish I'd read it when Mitzi gave it to me." She looked at the tattered paper. "This is less than half of it."

She stepped over to the bedside lamp and turned it on. Blasko moved next to her and read over her shoulder. The letter had been two pages, both printed front and back. It had torn almost across the middle.

"What do you think?" Josephine asked once they'd both been able to read what little they could.

"It is hard to decipher from what we have, but this seems to imply that your uncle found out about some sort of… treasure. He mentions a sailor he met who claimed to have seen it buried on another island near here. The last part of the letter looks like the start of directions, nautical coordinates and such."

"But we only have part of them, which won't do us much good."

"On the other hand, the person who killed for the letter also only has part of it."

"Which means they're not likely to find the treasure either."

"Probably not. And they have killed once. I doubt they will hesitate to kill again to get this half of the letter," Blasko said solemnly. "There's a morbid air about this town. The fishermen in particular seem to be suffering from some odd metamorphosis."

"There was something wrong with the man who was murdered. The skin on his face was scaly. And now that I think about it, his ears were odd too."

"You say he wore a coat and hat? That sounds like the fishermen I observed last night." Blasko touched his temples and winced. "I can't tell you about it now. I must rest. But promise me that you won't do anything more until I wake at dusk."

"The sheriff is on his way. I'll have to talk to him and show him where the attack and the murder took place."

"You'll be safe with him. But I'm serious. Don't go about town on your own."

As a rule, Josephine hated to give in to his demands. However, she could tell that this request came from his heart. She wondered what he'd seen during his nighttime walk through the town.

"I promise," she told him, touching his arm softly.

He nodded and returned to his coffin. Josephine left the room as Anton shut the lid.

As she came back down the stairs, she heard a commotion in the lobby.

"What do you mean, the body is gone?" a gruff male voice asked.

"I'm just telling you what that woman said," Mrs. Lachlan responded.

"I'm here, Mrs. Lachlan."

She could see Mrs. Lachlan standing next to a tall, thin man wearing a button-down shirt and dark pants. He held his hat in one hand and was slapping it absentmindedly against his thigh as he watched Josephine come down. There was a star pinned to his shirt and a revolver strapped to his waist.

"You must be the sheriff. I'm Josephine Nicolson." She extended her hand and tried hard to seem like a level-headed person who didn't imagine murders.

He shook her hand like it was a water moccasin. "Yes, I'm Sheriff Gentry. Miss Nicolson, you say you saw a murder?" His face was skeptical, but Josephine thought that underneath his tough veneer was a man who wanted very much to run out the door and drive away as fast as he could.

"First, I was assaulted. Then the person who attacked me was killed," she said calmly.

"Where did this happen?"

"At the post office," Mrs. Lachlan said. Both Josephine and the sheriff gave her a look making it clear she should butt out.

"The attacker came out of the alley next to the post office," Josephine explained.

"Why don't we go down there and see where it happened?" Gentry said and turned to Mrs. Lachlan. "Thank you for your help." It was clear he didn't want her following them to the scene.

"Well, if you don't need me," Mrs. Lachlan said, a touch of annoyance in her voice. She didn't budge, but watched them as they left the hotel.

Sheriff Gentry didn't speak as they walked down the street. Josephine had decided not to volunteer any information. She thought it would sound desperate if she threw facts at him. As they walked, she thought she saw a few of the locals peering out at them from the storefronts.

"So tell me what happened," Gentry said when they were standing next to the post office.

"I came out of the post office and walked along the sidewalk. I should have been more careful, but it was morning and…" She shrugged.

"What had you been doing at the post office?"

"I was talking to the postmistress." Josephine didn't want to mention the letter.

"Did you buy anything?"

"No."

"So what were you talking to her about? You're from out of town, aren't you?" He gave her a hard look that made it clear he knew she was being evasive.

"It's personal…" Josephine paused before coming up with an answer. "She knew my uncle before the war. I wanted to meet the woman he'd spoken of so fondly," she lied.

"Okay, so you came out of the post office and this man was hiding in the alley and attacked you. Did he take anything?"

"No." Another lie. "He grabbed at my purse and I fought with him."

"Were you injured?"

Josephine showed him her elbows, where the bruises she'd sustained in the scuffle were already turning a yellowish purple. "And I assume you will believe me when I tell you that my knees are also scraped." She thought it would give a better impression if she didn't raise her skirt and show him her damaged knees.

"Of course," he said, looking sympathetic for the first time. "What happened after he tried to grab your purse?"

"We struggled until he gave up and ran down the alley. It took me a minute to recover and, when I did, I looked where he'd gone. I was in shock and didn't know what to do, but then he stumbled back into the alley. When he fell to the ground, I could see a knife sticking out of his back."

"So you're telling me that, after he jumped you, someone else stabbed him in the back?" Gentry's voice made it clear that he thought she was either crazy or lying through her teeth.

"That is exactly what happened."

"Do you think someone killed him *because* he attacked you?" Gentry asked, his eyes narrowed.

"Maybe." Josephine hadn't considered that possibility. Of course, the sheriff didn't know that the victim had stolen part of a letter that was still missing. It had seemed clear to Josephine from the start that the second attack was motivated by the same thing as the first—the letter. But she wasn't going to mention it to the sheriff. The last thing she wanted was for him to take the letter as evidence.

"Show me exactly where the man fell," Gentry said, entering the alley. Josephine followed. "Did you approach the body?"

"I did. I… don't know what I was thinking." This at least was the whole truth. Looking back on it, Josephine realized she could have gotten herself into even deeper trouble.

"Then you and this other guest, Mr. Donavan, came back and the body was gone?"

"That's right," she said, trying to get ahead of the narrative. "The body was right there. Just inside this end of the alley. See, there was blood here." She pointed to the fading spot on the crushed shells.

The sheriff was thorough. He got down on his hands and knees, examining the ground and the walls on both sides of the alley. "Humph," he grunted, looking closely at the spot Josephine had indicated. "This *could* be blood," he said, just barely touching the spot. With the sun and heat, the stain had mostly faded into the dry shells.

Gentry stood up and walked out of the alley. After a few minutes, he came back and faced Josephine. "Sheriff Avery told me about you and your friends."

"He took us for gangsters," Josephine said with more than a hint of derision.

"Now be fair. The hotel called it in. The point is, he told me that y'all were coming down here and that, in his estimate, trouble was going to follow. And now here we are." He glowered at her.

"Why don't you like coming to Cedar Island?" Josephine asked. She didn't like his attitude and figured she didn't have much to lose by turning the tables on him.

Gentry's face turned a deep scarlet as his jaw muscles tightened. Josephine realized she might have miscalculated. He took a couple of deep breaths, then stepped in closer so that they were only a foot apart.

"There is a smell to this place. Has been as long as I've been with the sheriff's office. You're darn right I don't like coming out here. And I think you should count your lucky stars that the body disappeared and not you." He paused, still looking her in the eye. It was obvious to Josephine that he had more to say, but was trying to decide how much he wanted to tell her. Finally he said, "I'm assuming that if you're a part of whatever strange and… I'll just say it, wicked, business is going on here, then you wouldn't have called me. So I'll tell you, don't go near the water or the fishermen. Better yet, pack up and leave. There is nothing but trouble out here."

"What about the body?"

"It's gone. Even if I found it, I wouldn't find anyone interested in solving the murder. That's how it is out here. Any law there is comes from those that live here."

"Have there been other murders on the island?"

He shrugged. "People come out here and never come back. What I *can* tell you is that, in my lifetime, no one has ever been arrested for any crime that happened on Cedar Island."

"Why don't you do something about it?"

"Like what? There's me and five deputies. You don't get it. These people aren't interested in my help." Gentry looked down at the ground. "I don't know what the hell is going on out here. As far as I'm concerned, my job is to see that whatever corruption has sunk its roots on the island doesn't cross the bridge." He started to walk away from her. "Don't send for me again." Then he stopped and turned back. "And if someone calls me up in a month and says they haven't heard from you, I won't come looking either."

With that, he spun on his heel and headed back toward the hotel. Josephine trailed after him, baffled by his attitude and even more aware of the eyes watching them from the windows of the town.

CHAPTER TEN

"I could have told you that he wouldn't do much," Mrs. Lachlan said as she and Josephine watched the sheriff drive away. "He didn't do anything when my hus—" She stopped talking and looked embarrassed.

"What's happening on this island?" Josephine asked her bluntly.

"Don't know what you mean. I'm not saying there aren't some odd ones living here, but bad things happen everywhere." Josephine heard a sad weariness in Mrs. Lachlan's voice.

"Bodies don't disappear in most towns."

"You want a suspect? I'd suggest looking at that nut staying in the old Sharp place."

"What?"

"A real strange one. Came in a while back asking all sorts of questions. Stayed overnight with me before renting the Sharp house. Then, about two weeks ago, he closed and locked the shutters. No one's seen him since."

"You mean he disappeared?" Josephine's interest was piqued.

"No. Not like that. He's in that house, just no one has seen him. He's got the Martin boy delivering food to him.

Pays him by pushing the money under the door. When the boy leaves, he opens the door and grabs the food."

"Who is he?"

"Said his name was Howard Phillips. Not that I believed that bit of malarkey."

"Why not?"

"'Cause I watched him write his name in the register. He had to *think* about writing that name down. I've been in this business a bunch of years. People don't think about writing their own names. Not unless they're… you know, not real bright."

"You said he asked questions?"

"All kinds. Started out asking about the fishing. Nothing odd there, but then he started in on the fishermen. Wanted to know when they fished, the names of the best fishermen. He also asked a bunch of questions about shipwrecks. I finally told him he'd have to go down to the docks and ask the men themselves. Didn't seem too keen on that."

"What did he look like?"

"Tall, gangly fella. Dark hair. Guess he was thirty years old, maybe a bit older. Had one of them Yankee accents." Mrs. Lachlan was frowning as she recalled the man.

"You say he made arrangements to rent a house for a few weeks?"

"That's right. The owner, Mrs. Sharp, said he's still paying the rent so she don't care what he does as long as the house is still standing when he leaves."

"Where does Mrs. Sharp live?"

"Up by the church. It was her father-in-law's house until he went out on his boat a few years ago and never came back."

Josephine was already trying to decide whether she should go knock on the man's door or his landlord's. Something about Mrs. Lachlan's description of the man was niggling at a part of her mind.

"Would she talk to me?"

"Ha! Maddie will talk to anyone who doesn't run away."

"Do you think she'd be home now?"

"Don't see why she wouldn't be."

"I'm going over there," Josephine said, making up her mind as she said it.

"She won't like it if you're trying to get her tenant in trouble. That's the first cash money she's seen for a while," Mrs. Lachlan warned.

"I just want to find out what's going on."

"Around here? Good luck! Folks around here know how to keep secrets."

Josephine headed upstairs to find Grace. After everything that had happened, she didn't want to go across town by herself. The maid was on the balcony sitting in a rocking chair, looking out on the Gulf waters in the distance.

"I'm going back outside. Will you come with me?"

"After you were attacked and that man killed? You should just wait until the baron wakes up." Grace's tone held a hint of finality.

Josephine thought back to the days not so long ago when Grace hadn't trusted the baron. Now, after he'd saved her brother from accusations of murder and had proved capable of tackling the malignant forces that had been plaguing Sumter, she'd seen him more often than not as the solution to their problems rather than the cause of them.

"I'm not going to wait until it's dark. I want to talk to a woman about a house she's renting," Josephine told her.

"I've been watchin' the town from up here. This place is mighty strange. Folks skulkin' around. That sundry store across the street… she's done locked the door a dozen times when she's seen somebody comin'. Other times she swings the door wide and near 'bouts drags some people in."

Josephine looked across the street at the five-and-dime store. "Who does she let in and who does she lock the door on?"

"The ones she keeps out are those that are practically hiding under their hats. There! Like that fella down the street." Grace pointed to a man who was walking slowly down the road with his hat pulled low over his eyes and the collar of his coat turned up. Like Josephine's attacker, he was over-dressed for the heat and his movements looked awkward and unnatural.

"Please come with me," Josephine said. She was afraid that if she thought about it anymore, she'd chicken out of leaving the hotel. As it was, she was feeling guilty for breaking her promise to Blasko.

"Is Anton coming?" Grace asked.

"He needs to watch over the baron," Josephine said. As much as she would have liked having a man with them, she thought it was best to leave Anton with Blasko. "But we'll tell him where we're going."

Anton took the news with his usual stoic attitude. Josephine told him to let the baron know immediately if they didn't return by sundown, though her heart was sure that Blasko would already know.

"There's an odd man renting a house in town," she explained to Grace as they walked up a small sandy hill toward a church steeple at the center of town.

"I thought we'd agreed that half this town is made up of creepy people. What's so special about this one?" Grace asked.

"He's a stranger. Came into town a few weeks ago."

As they climbed the short hill, Josephine could see that the church was in need of repair. There were shingles missing from the roof and most of the paint was peeling off of the boards. Next door was a small house with a porch running across the front. According to the directions she'd wrangled from Mrs. Lachlan, this was the home of Mrs. Sharp. Like the church, her house was also in need of fresh boards and a new coat of paint.

Once they were on the porch, Josephine could hear someone washing dishes through the open windows. She knocked on the door while Grace stood back, looking down at her hands.

"Who is it?" asked a suspicious voice from the other side

of the grey cypress door.

"I'm Josephine Nicolson. I'm new in town and I'd like to ask you a few questions." Josephine hadn't been able to come up with any other excuse, so she'd decided to go with the truth.

"I don't want to answer no questions," the woman said with stern determination.

"I understand your hesitation, Mrs. Sharp. Mrs. Lachlan up at the hotel said that you're renting your house to a rather strange young man." Josephine threw this out in an effort to tease Mrs. Sharp into talking to her. Based on what Mrs. Lachlan had said, the woman badly needed the money the man was paying her, so anyone asking questions about her golden goose was going to be met with suspicion.

"You mean Mr. Phillips?" Mrs. Sharp sounded less sure of herself.

"That's right. I just have a few questions."

"He pays his rent on time. That's all you need to know." Mrs. Sharp still didn't open the door, but Josephine could tell that she was standing just on the other side.

"I hope he's able to *keep* paying your rent." Josephine made it sound as though she knew something about the man that could cause the money to stop flowing.

"What is it you want to know?" There was a hint of fear in the woman's voice.

"I'd rather talk face to face," Josephine answered, pushing her advantage.

She heard the sound of a bolt being slid aside, then the door creaked open a few inches. A worn woman's face appeared in the opening and she looked Josephine and Grace up and down. When the door opened wide, Josephine assumed that they had passed inspection.

"Come on in," Mrs. Sharp told them. The flower print dress she wore was old, but well mended. "I can offer you some tea."

"Thank you, that would be lovely."

Josephine and Grace followed her into the front parlor,

where the three women filled up the little room. Most of the space was occupied by heavy wooden, empire-style furniture that would have fit much better in a grander house.

"Have a seat and I'll put the pot on."

The woman didn't wait for them to sit before she shuffled off to the kitchen in the back of house. They could hear the sound of water running and a pot being set on the stove. Josephine looked around at the tattered drapes and old pictures covering one wall. The house felt oddly deserted, as though Mrs. Sharp were nothing more than a shadow of a past occupant.

"This ain't no house for the livin'," Grace whispered, echoing Josephine's own thoughts. The black woman shivered a little as she sat back against the sofa.

Mrs. Sharp soon returned with a wooden tray holding three mismatched china cups.

"These are very nice," Josephine said, admiring the delicate cups.

"My father-in-law was a merchant seaman for many years. My husband told me that his father always brought his wife back a china cup from his travels. I still have a cabinet full."

"Is your husband a fisherman?"

"Was. He and my father-in-law went out four years ago and never returned." There was deep pain in her voice.

"I'm sorry," Josephine said, and saw Grace mouth a quick prayer up to God for the woman's family.

"I have nights when I think, maybe, just maybe, they'll come back." Mrs. Sharp looked quickly toward the door, biting her lip.

"It must be awful not knowing what happened to them," Josephine sympathized.

"I know what happened to them." She was silent so long that Josephine was getting ready to prompt her for more when she finally said, "What do you want to know about my tenant? Why'd you make it sound like he might not keep paying his rent?"

"I've just heard some odd things about him." Josephine paused. She'd considered making up an elaborate lie, but again settled on an answer close to the truth. "I was attacked this morning near the post office."

Mrs. Sharp didn't react as much as Josephine would have expected to the news that she had been attacked on the street in broad daylight.

"I'm trying to find the man who did it," Josephine finished, leaving out the fact that the person who'd attacked her was already dead.

"I doubt Mr. Phillips had anything to do with you being attacked. He never leaves the house that I know of. Lord knows, I've tried to get him to come out or to let me in. I worry that he's tearing up the place. Of course, with the rent he's paying…" It was clear that the situation had been bothering Mrs. Sharp and she appeared relieved to voice her concerns.

"Can you tell me what he looks like?"

"Tall man, weedy lookin'. Not young, but he has a boyish face."

"How's he dress?"

"Not like he's from around here. 'Course I knew that as soon as he opened his mouth. High-pitched Yankee speech. His clothes are like a preacher's, dark and cheap. Now that I think about it, he has the same know-it-all manner of a preacher."

"You didn't like him?" Josephine asked, noticing how Mrs. Sharp's eyes narrowed and her lip curled as she talked about her tenant.

"No, I didn't. Like I said, he had that looking-down-your-nose Yankee attitude about him. But like most Yankees, his money was green. I'm not ashamed to say that I've been suffering since the loss of my family. For a while I had to live off the…" She stopped as though she was afraid to admit something, then said, "…the fish that the men left on my porch."

Josephine felt that it had been a kindness for the

fishermen to help out a widow, but something about Mrs. Sharp's voice suggested she didn't feel the same.

"Did Mr. Phillips say why he wanted to rent the house?"

"Just said he was interested in the fishing hereabouts. I'm sure that was a lie."

"Why?"

Mrs. Sharp snorted derisively. "I don't think he'd know which end of the line to throw in the water. I got no idea why he rented the place. At the time, I didn't care."

"But you care now?"

"I don't want the money to stop, but there's something wrong about it."

"I want to go see him," Josephine said and felt Grace stiffen beside her. "If he won't let me in, maybe I can talk to him through the door."

"That's all I've been able to do for weeks. If you find out anything, I'd appreciate you tellin' me."

"I will. And I promise that I won't try to get him into trouble. I understand about the money."

Mrs. Sharp looked at Josephine's clothes disbelievingly. "I don't see how you'd know about money problems."

"I run a bank. Every day, more so since the stock market crashed, I see people who are struggling to make it on the little bit of money they make."

"You run a bank?" Mrs. Sharp's eyes were wide. "I never heard tell of a woman owning a bank."

"You come up to Sumter, Alabama and I'll show you what it looks like," Josephine said with a smile. She took a card out of her purse and handed it to Mrs. Sharp, who took it as gently as she would one of her china cups.

Josephine stood up. "We'll go right over there and knock on his door."

Mrs. Sharp gave them directions to the rented cottage. All the while, Grace looked at Josephine like she'd lost her mind.

When they were back outside in the road, she reached out and grabbed Josephine's arm. "Surely you ain't that crazy," she scolded.

Josephine pulled her arm away. "You can come with me or not, but there's something strange about the man who's renting her house. I want to see him."

"This whole island is full of loony people."

"You know I came here to try to find out what happened to my uncle. Someone stole that letter from me and I want to know who."

"Nobody cares more 'bout family than I do. No, ma'am. But you almost got yourself killed this mornin', so why you got to try again this afternoon?" Grace pleaded.

"And I'll still be in danger until we find out what's going on."

"How you goin' to catch that killer if the sheriff doesn't even believe there is one?"

"He knows I was telling the truth. The sheriff is just scared." Josephine started walking in the direction of Mrs. Sharp's rental house.

"That right there!" Grace said, loud enough to stop Josephine again. She turned to look back at her. "If the sheriff is afraid, that should tell you somethin'." Grace stomped her foot for emphasis.

Reluctantly, Josephine walked back to her. "You're right. This could be dangerous. It already has been and that's why I need your help. I promise you that, if the situation gets any worse, we'll leave the island. I don't want any of us hurt over something that occurred twenty years ago."

Grace pursed her lips and looked down at the ground. Josephine waited. "You give your word? More crazy comes our way, we all leave?"

"Yes."

"Lord, give us strength! Okay, let's get this done." Grace started walking and Josephine fell into step with her determined strides.

They found the house two blocks down the street. It stood on a little rise near the cemetery with a clear view down to the docks. Like most of the houses on the island, it was built of cypress clapboards. Never painted, it loomed grey and brooding under a pair of live oak trees. The wooden shutters were closed and a light breeze blew leaves across the porch.

"Looks like it's home to a whole share of haunts," Grace said under her breath, but she followed Josephine through the gate and across the dirt yard.

"It *could* use some attention," Josephine agreed, not wanting to admit that there was an air of melancholy surrounding the place. Ignoring her own inner voice of caution, she walked up the creaky wooden steps to the porch and gave the door a few solid knocks.

"Leave the food," came a distant voice from inside. Muffled by the distance and the wooden door between them, Josephine still thought she heard an oddly familiar quality to the voice.

She knocked again and said loudly, "We'd like to talk with you."

They heard the sound of feet crossing a wooden floor, then a sliver of skin showed through the shutters at the window to her right. But by the time she turned to look, it was gone and the feet were walking quickly away from the door.

Josephine waited, thinking perhaps that the man wanted to dress or make some other preparation before opening the door. However, the minutes dragged on until she felt that she had to knock again.

This time there was no sound from inside the house. More knocking and calling yielded nothing. Finally, Josephine turned to Grace. "What do you think?"

"I think we're in luck. Nothin' in this house is goin' to bring us any good."

"Maybe," Josephine said, disappointed by her lack of success at breaching this domestic fortress. She wanted to go around the house and try to peek through the shutters, but the house stood on limestone blocks that lifted it several feet off the ground. Even if there *were* cracks in the shutters, she wouldn't be able to look in without something to stand on. Even she didn't think that was a good idea.

They made their way back toward the hotel. Josephine took the time to look around at the houses and shops. Like the people on the island, there seemed to be two types—those that looked normal, if a little rundown, and those with an aura of decay and rot to them. The stale smell of fish was not confined to the breezes coming from the docks. Josephine thought that several of the buildings were emitting their own odd fetid odor.

"This place smells like a fisherman's underthings," Grace said, scrunching up her nose.

"Maybe they use some of these buildings to clean fish or shuck oysters."

"Far as I can see, they don't clean nothin' around here."

"Not enjoying your seaside vacation?" Josephine joked. Grace frowned at her, but Josephine could see a small twinkle of amusement in her eyes.

"Hummmph! Would have been more relaxin' to go to Hamilton's slaughterhouse back home. And it would have smelled better."

Josephine dragged Grace down the main street to the post office, which was still closed.

"Where can she be?" Josephine muttered to herself.

"I thought we were just goin' to check on that man in the house and be done." Grace used a handkerchief to wipe the sweat from her face and bosom.

"I know, but this is another… problem that's bothering me."

"Honey, you know you need to work harder on worryin' about your own business." Grace stopped when she saw the look on Josephine's face. "Fine, then. Ask someone where this woman lives and let's get that over with too so we can go back the hotel. This heat is just awful."

Josephine backtracked to the five-and-dime store where the woman behind the counter seemed to decide on an individual basis who gained admittance and who didn't.

Apparently they made the cut, for Josephine had no more than stopped at the door when it sprung open for them.

"Hot day for keeping the door closed," Josephine said lightly, trying to tease information from the frowzy woman who'd opened the door.

"The owner's out. I don't like lettin' just anyone in when I'm alone." The shop clerk wiped nervously at a glass display case with a cloth in her hand. "How can I help you?"

"We're looking for some postcards to send home," Josephine said, coming up with an excuse on the fly.

"The rack is right over there."

"I'll need some stamps too, but the post office seems to be closed."

"I know." The woman's voice sounded fearful.

"Do you know when Mitzi will be back?" Josephine decided that name-dropping couldn't hurt.

"Oh, do you know Mitzi?" the woman asked, sounding both more friendly and interested.

"I had the chance to talk with her this morning, but unfortunately I didn't think to get stamps while I was there."

"I heard that something happened this morning down by the post office."

"Mitzi wasn't involved, was she?" Josephine said, playing dumb.

"No, no, but she closed up right after."

"Do you think she'll be back soon?"

There was a long pause as the clerk considered this. "I've never known her to lock up the post office in the middle of the day without putting a note on the door." There was worry in her voice.

"Do you think it would be okay if I go around to her house to ask if she plans to reopen?"

"She's very nice."

"I thought so too."

"Maybe someone should check on her." The clerk was biting her nails now.

"Where does she live?"

"Just a few blocks over, away from the water," she said pointedly, as if suggesting that Mitzi lived in a better part of town.

"Just give me directions and I'll check on her," Josephine assured her.

"Will you come back and let me know she's all right?"

"Of course."

The woman took out a pencil and sketched a map to the postmistress's house on a piece of brown wrapping paper

"This is the last house we're goin' to visit today, right?" Grace asked as they trudged through the heat on their way to Mitzi Alexander's house.

"Cross my heart." The hot, sticky air was hard to breathe as Josephine looked at the map.

At last they came to a neat little cottage painted white with green shutters. Josephine took a moment to enjoy the shade of the front porch before opening the screen door and knocking. In what was becoming a familiar pattern, there was no answer.

"She ain't home!" yelled a woman's voice from the house next door. "You're the third person to come looking for her today. Tell everyone she's not there."

"Has she been here at all?" Josephine shouted back.

"No. Now go away. It's too hot to be yelling back and forth," the grumpy voice said.

"I think we've reached the end of the trail," Josephine said, not looking forward to the hot trek back to the hotel.

When they finally returned, they saw Wallace Brock on the porch steps, leaning against the bannister. He glared at them as they walked up.

"Good day," Josephine said with a nod.

"I want to talk to you," he said, his voice gruff.

Josephine stopped. "About?"

"What happened this morning and… all this asking questions."

"So talk."

"Not here. Come around to the side." Brock turned and

headed for the small ornamental garden beside the hotel. It was mostly wild flowers and seashells, with a couple of benches and a small fountain.

"Can't we talk in the shade of the porch?" Josephine asked, but Brock kept walking.

"I'll wait right here," Grace assured her.

Josephine didn't like his attitude, but she didn't feel like she could ignore any information he might have for her. "I don't intend to stroll through the garden with you," she said when she caught up with him.

Once they were around the corner of the building, Brock turned and gave her an aggressive and condescending stare. "You need to stop asking questions and get off this island."

Josephine laughed lightly. "Why in the world would I do that?"

"You've already been attacked. Do you want to be the next victim?"

"Is that a threat?"

Brock looked taken aback by the suggestion. "No, it's a warning. Blast it! Don't you know when you're in danger?"

"Why are you so worried about me?"

Brock pursed his lips in anger. Though he looked like he had something in particular on his mind, he stayed silent.

"I think there is something strange going on around here and that you know something about it," Josephine accused him.

"I don't have any idea what's going on. But I will tell you that, unlike some people, I believe your story that a man was killed this morning."

"What do you know about it?" Josephine couldn't decide whether Brock was warning her about a threat or if he *was* the threat.

"I just know that, whether it's smuggling or something else, there are folks who will kill to keep it a secret." Josephine heard the ring of truth in what he said. "Ignore my advice at your peril." Brock gave a dramatic wave of his hand and walked back toward the porch.

Pompous ass, Josephine thought. His dark suit, shining black shoes and grey fedora seemed out of place on the coast. She thought he looked more like a gangster than a tourist, and his arrogant attitude was infuriating.

Back inside the hotel, the heat was oppressive, with no breeze from the Gulf to cool the air. Brock was the only person in sight, having come straight in and headed for the liquor cabinet to pour himself a large whiskey. Tired from their excursion, both Josephine and Grace decided to head to their rooms to lie down and wait for the world to cool off.

CHAPTER ELEVEN

Josephine was surprised at the long shadows in the room when she woke up. Looking at the clock, she saw that she had only a couple of hours to wait before she would be able to talk with Blasko.

She bathed and dressed for the evening, then headed downstairs for a cocktail while she waited for sunset. After pouring herself a glass of cool water with a little bit of gin and lime, she went out on the porch, managing to avoid the other guests. Sitting in a soft chair and watching as the sun slowly slipped below the tree line, she soon drifted off again.

"Are you asleep?"

Josephine awoke with a start to see Blasko's face inches from hers.

"No," she lied.

"Come on. Let's go up to my room where we can talk," he whispered. The other guests were starting to wander into the dining room.

"We should talk about what happened this morning. Jolly bad luck," Captain Hume said as Josephine and Blasko walked past him.

"We'll be back down for dinner," Josephine said, feeling light-headed as she climbed back up the stairs.

"Afraid it's a cold dinner this evening. The cook didn't show up or something or other," Hume called over his shoulder.

Once upstairs, Josephine told Blasko about the trip to the rental house and her search for the missing postmistress.

"You were almost killed this morning, yet you went back out knocking on strangers' doors?" Blasko growled, his green eyes flashing with anger.

"What was I supposed to do? I couldn't just sit around here all day. Grace was with me."

"People are being murdered. Was it worth the risk? Did you learn anything?" he challenged.

"Only one person has been murdered since we got here," Josephine muttered, then went on to explain everything they *hadn't* learned.

"One person dead and one person missing. As I said earlier, whoever killed for that letter will most likely come back for the rest of it." Blasko went to the door and looked suspiciously at the second-floor hallway, then he came back and rapped once on the door connecting his room to Anton's before opening it. "Take a chair and sit in the hall. Let me know if anyone approaches Josephine's or Grace's rooms."

"Do you think that's necessary?" Josephine asked after Anton had dutifully carried a chair into the hallway.

"I think that you and Grace should return home."

"No. At least I'm not. I'll give Grace the choice."

"There is something very dangerous lurking below the surface of this island. And I mean that both in the figurative and literal sense."

"I'm not disagreeing with you. Don't forget that I *saw* the dead body."

"If you're going to stay then we need to push our investigations forward as fast as possible," Blasko said, doing his Sherlock Holmes impression. "Both the one into the death of your Uncle Petey and the one into the murder of the thief."

"I feel sure that there's a link between the thief stealing my letter and his own murder. And since the stolen letter was the one from my uncle then, if only in a circumstantial way, his death is linked to the murder this morning."

"But is the dark miasma hovering over this town related to it?" Blasko wondered.

"Without knowing the source of the underlying malevolence, it's hard to make a judgment," Josephine said, teasing him. She found him both amusing and, though she hated to admit it, a bit exciting when he became enthused with his own deductive reasoning.

"Exactly! I will try to learn more tonight." His excitement had eroded his earlier anger.

"You can start with the stranger in town who wouldn't answer his door."

Blasko nodded enthusiastically. "Yes, I'll…" He stopped and a puzzled look crossed his face. As if talking to himself, he said softly, "That smell… I could smell blood on you this morning and when I was downstairs…"

"What?"

Instead of answering her, Blasko strode out into the corridor with Josephine at his heels. He marched past Anton, sitting stoically in his chair, and opened the door to Josephine's room. In three strides, he was across the room and picking up a white cloth bag.

"Wait a minute, that's my dirty… things," Josephine protested.

Without a word in response, he opened the bag and started digging through her clothes.

"I smelled the blood when you woke me, but I was too groggy to give it much thought."

"What the hell are you talking about? And put that down!" she yelled in an attempt to get him to drop her camisole.

"Here!" he said, holding up the blouse she'd worn that morning.

Josephine moved to grab it away from him until he

pointed out several spots of blood on the dark blue sleeve.

"That must have happened when I checked the dead man's pockets for the letter," Josephine said. Neither spot was larger than the end of a pencil eraser.

Blasko put the cloth up to his nose and inhaled like a wine connoisseur with a cork. "Yes. Follow me." He tossed the blouse onto the bed before hurrying back out of the room and down the stairs. Josephine jogged to catch up with him.

"Whatever you're doing, please do it discreetly," she hissed in his ear.

"Bah! I am the soul of discretion."

"You have got to be kidding me." Josephine rolled her eyes.

At the bottom of the stairs, they could hear conversation coming from the dining room. Like a weathervane following the wind, Blasko turned toward the voices.

"Here they come!" Eric Donavan hailed them.

The other guests were seated round the room in two groups. Wallace Brock was playing cards with Donavan and the Egyptian woman, while Captain Hume, Jamila and Elliot Zhao were sipping cocktails. The latter three looked flushed, as though they had been in a heated argument.

"Please come in and tell us all about your adventures." Hume waved them toward his table. "Not that I'm making light of the assault on your person."

"Go on. Sit and tell them about your… adventure," Blasko urged, receiving a dirty look for his efforts.

"I'm sure you've heard everything that I can tell you." Josephine didn't want to get trapped in a conversation at the moment.

"Rumors are all that anyone deals in around here. We heard you saw someone get killed." Jamila looked like she was trying very hard to appear sad, but without much success.

Hume stood up and pulled a chair out for Josephine. "Have a seat, my lady," he said with a toothy smile.

"I don't know…" She looked at Blasko.

"Sit. Would you like me to make you a drink?" he asked with just enough inflection to suggest that he wanted her to say yes.

"A whiskey sour."

"Tell us *all* that happened to you," Jamila encouraged.

Josephine went into some detail, giving them the same story she'd told the sheriff. Out of the corner of her eye, she saw Blasko take a drink stirrer out of a glass and bend forward to place the glass on the table in front of her. As he leaned over, he dropped the stirrer and it fell at Josephine's feet.

"Clumsy of me." He knelt down to fetch it and Josephine was sure that he lingered for a moment before standing up. Then he drifted over to the table where Brock, Donavan and Neith were playing a laconic game of cards.

"We can deal you in if you want. All penny ante," Donavan said, nodding toward the cards.

"They've been teaching me how to play poker." Neith pushed a quarter toward the pot. "I call."

"You've been teaching us lately," Brock guffawed, dropping a quarter next to hers.

"I'm out. Care to join us?" Donavan looked at Blasko.

"Maybe a couple of… What do you call it… rounds?"

"Hands." Brock turned over his cards to reveal a pair of sixes. Neith smiled and showed three fours.

Blasko sat down to join them.

Now Josephine was sure that he was up to something, but she had no idea what. She couldn't watch him without drawing attention to herself, so she sipped her drink and parried questions from the three people at her table.

"Could you see the face of the man who attacked you?" Zhao asked.

"And he was stabbed?" Jamila said.

"What kind of knife?" Hume asked.

This went on until the whiskey sour was only a fond memory.

"Enough!" Josephine finally heard Blasko exclaim. "I'll need to make a little study of the game before playing again." His tone was light and good-natured as he stood up, looking across the room at Josephine and nodding his head toward the stairs. She excused herself from the group and followed him up to her room.

"What was that performance all about?" Josephine whispered once they were alone.

"The drops of blood on your sleeve. I smelled that same blood twice today. Once on your sleeve this morning and later this evening when I came down looking for you."

"The dead man's blood?" Josephine was still surprised at the power of Blasko's senses.

"Yes."

"So who had the blood on them?"

"I didn't pay that much attention earlier. You would be surprised how often I smell blood when I'm around... people. And remember, I didn't have any reason at the time to associate it with the murder."

"That's why you dragged me back down to the dining room."

"Precisely."

"Ahhhh! It was on their shoes! That's why you had to get close to the floor."

He smiled. "I smelled it as soon as we entered the room, but I couldn't tell where it was coming from. I narrowed it down to the three playing poker. Joining them, I managed to drop a card. When I bent down, I was able to discern that the blood was on Donavan's shoes."

"Not Brock's?"

"Why him?"

"I get an odd feeling from him. His arrogance is part of it." Josephine was having a hard time quantifying her suspicions.

"I am sure that it was on Donavan's shoes."

"Which doesn't mean he's the killer. He could have stepped in it when he followed me back to the body."

"True. Did you see him get near it?"

"Not close enough to stand on it. But I don't see how this gets us anywhere."

"It places Donavan at the scene of the crime and on the top of the list of suspects."

"Only because the suspect list is short."

"Currently composed of one, yes," Blasko admitted. "Unless you want to include everyone who is acting suspicious, which would include the entire population of this island."

"Especially the man who's locked himself in that house."

"Tonight I will confront the mysterious boarder."

"Which might tell us if we can cross him off of our list of suspects. What's bothering me is that this isn't getting us any closer to finding out what happened to Uncle Petey."

"If we can find out who killed your attacker, then we should be able to find the other half of the letter."

"I'm angry with myself for losing it."

"You did not lose it. Someone tried to take it from you. A lesser person would have lost all of it." Blasko reached out and took her hand. "Remember, the killer only has as much of the letter as the thief was able to get from you."

"Which means that if they want the information in the letter, they'll come back for the rest of it." For the first time, Josephine realized the danger she might be in, but being cautious didn't come naturally to her.

"I don't want to leave you alone tonight," Blasko told her, squeezing her hand.

"You need to find out what you can about Mr. Phillips. Grace will be with me. And I brought a .45 revolver."

"Anton will sit in the hall."

"He can't stay out there all night." Josephine thought she was stating the obvious, but from the look Blasko gave her, it hadn't occurred to him.

"Anton is able."

"Even if he is, I think he's going to draw attention from Mrs. Lachlan and the other guests."

"You might have a point," Blasko said thoughtfully. "Don't worry. I'll take care of it."

"I'll be fine," Josephine reassured him. The truth was that she *was* worried, but she really wanted Blasko to find out what he could about the stranger. The man had gotten under her skin when he'd refused to open the door for her.

"If I run into Donavan again tonight, I'll press him for some answers," Blasko said.

"Tomorrow I'm going to the mainland to call Bobby," Josephine said suddenly, making a quick decision. "I'll give him the names of all the other guests and see if he can find out if any of them have a criminal background."

"Assuming they've told us their real names," Blasko pointed out.

"We can only do so much."

"It's convenient that your old beau is a deputy." There was no sarcasm in the words, but Josephine couldn't help but wonder if she heard the smallest bit of jealously.

"Hopefully we'll learn something useful."

"Be careful." Blasko gave her a stern look.

"I didn't think there was any risk in simply going to the post office," she responded. "What do you think is really going on here?"

"Something ominous. The docks and the homes near the water have a putrid odor that reminds me of the pit that opened beneath Mrs. Rosehill's place."

Josephine shuddered. "I hope you're wrong."

Blasko pulled her into his arms and kissed her lightly, his lips lingering on hers for a moment. "I have to go. Please be vigilant. Let Anton watch over you and Grace."

Before she could say a word, he turned and left the room.

CHAPTER TWELVE

Once he was gone, Josephine knocked on the door connecting her room with Grace's. Quickly she warned the maid to be on her guard in case someone came looking for Josephine's half of the letter.

"Where is it now?" Grace asked.

"Let's just say that it's close to my skin."

Grace squinted. "Just give the letter to whoever wants it and let's go home."

"I can send *you* home," Josephine offered.

"If you stay, I stay."

"Right then. I'm going for a stroll around the hotel. I'll check in when I get back. If you haven't heard from me by midnight, go tell Anton."

"Is that man still sitting in the hall?"

"I told Blasko that isn't going to work. He's going to cause a scene sitting out there and watching everyone."

Josephine left Grace doing needlework and shaking her head, still convinced that they should all pack up and leave.

Out in the hallway, Josephine was glad to see that Anton and the chair he'd been sitting on were gone. Satisfied, she started for the stairs, then stopped short as she passed Blasko's door. There was a hole in the door, about chest-height and just large enough to push a pencil through. Josephine leaned over to look at it, trying to remember if it had been there before, and saw a flash of movement on the other side of the door.

Frowning, she knocked on the door. She was feeling like she'd spent the whole day on the wrong side of various doors.

"Open up, Anton," she commanded, softly but firmly. "Now."

The door slowly opened to reveal the little man. Not far behind him was the chair he'd been using in the hallway.

"Who drilled this hole in the door?" Josephine asked, knowing damn well who had done it.

"The baron said watch the hallway. You tell him I have to be out of the hallway. He was very anxious that no one creep up on you. I was worried. A little hole, no one will even notice," Anton explained, gesturing to the very obvious hole in the door.

"You can tell the baron that I'm not paying for the door."

"He doesn't know I drilled hole. My idea. I regret if I cost you for door." Anton was obviously ashamed and his English suffered for it.

Josephine rolled her eyes and sighed. "Don't worry about it."

"May I sit here and watch now?"

"I suppose the damage is done."

"Good! I want to see when they come out." Anton smiled.

"Who?"

"Them. Other guests."

"Where are they?"

"All go into that room across the hall. Very sneaky."

"Are you telling me that *all* of the other guests are in Mr. Donavan's room?" Josephine's curiosity was roused.

"They each come upstairs and, one by one, they go inside."

"Close the door and keep an eye out," Josephine told him as she left the room. Anton nodded enthusiastically and shut the door behind her.

Josephine walked slowly and carefully over to Eric Donavan's room. Trying to be as quiet as possible, she leaned in and placed her ear against the door while also trying to keep a lookout for anyone coming up the stairs.

She could hear low voices talking earnestly. She leaned in closer to the door, accidentally bumping it with the side of her head. Before she could move back, the door flew open and Donavan frowned down at her.

"Hear anything?" he asked brusquely. The other guests were standing in the room behind him and staring at her.

"I was just…" She started to make an excuse, but realized that nothing would make any sense. "Actually, I was going to knock on your door and see if anyone wanted to play a game of cards." It was a poor bluff.

"Tell her to get in here," Neith said.

"Come in, Miss Nicolson." Donavan stepped back and swung the door open wide.

Josephine followed him, suddenly very glad to know that Anton was watching from across the hall.

"We've been discussing you," Elliot Zhao said once Donavan had shut the door.

"I guess that's fair enough since the baron and I have talked some about all of you too," Josephine said with as much moxie as she could muster when the odds were six to one.

"I bet you have," Jamila sneered. "Do you think you've fooled us?"

"Why are you here? And try telling us the truth this time," Wallace Brock said with his usual arrogant manner.

"We told you, we're here on vacation." As soon as the words were out of her mouth, everyone in the room shook their heads in disbelief. "Okay, then, tell me why all of *you* are really here," Josephine shot back.

"We suspect for the same reason you are," Captain

Hume answered, his demeanor no longer open and friendly.

"Come on, let's compare secrets," Donavan urged her.

"Never mind. I'll tell you who *you* are," Brock said. "You're related to Peter Nicolson and you're here looking for the same gold and artifacts that we are."

Josephine was stunned into silence, both by the fact that they knew who she was and that they knew why her uncle had come to the island.

"She refuses to talk," Jamila said in a tone that implied she was willing to *make* Josephine talk if necessary.

"I'm not sure what we have to talk about," Josephine stammered.

"Even though you're looking for the treasure, same as us?" Donavan asked.

"*Treasure?* Is that all you think this is about? It is my country's heritage," Neith said, casting a look of scorn at Donavan.

"Neith is right. I don't know why you were even allowed to join the group." Jamila's dark eyes stared daggers at Donavan.

Josephine was more than willing to let them fight amongst themselves while she gathered her wits and took mental notes of the divisions within their ranks. Had one of them killed the man who'd stolen her uncle's letter? Or had one of them *hired* the man to steal the letter. Or… She could think of a dozen possibilities.

"Stop bickering!" Hume commanded, silencing the others. He turned to Josephine. "Why keep up the pretense? We're giving you a chance to come clean and maybe to… join forces with us."

"I didn't agree to that," Donavan groused.

"Don't worry, Donavan, you'll get your gold," Neith told him. "But first we must find it."

"Exactly why the lady here should be a part of the group. She undoubtedly has some knowledge that we lack," Hume stated.

"I don't…" Josephine wanted to deny any knowledge of

what they were talking about, but she didn't see the point. "Fine. Yes, Peter Nicolson was my uncle. But I didn't know anything about treasure."

"Why are you here now?" Jamila asked.

"He left my father a letter."

"Is that why you were at the post office this morning?" Donavan asked.

"Yes. I mean, not exactly. He left one at our house. I only discovered it a few months ago."

"Was there another letter left here?" Donavan pushed.

"I'd rather not say at this point. I think it's y'all's turn to share."

"We all got letters. We thought maybe you'd sent them." Zhao held up an envelope that had clearly passed through many hands and gave it to Josephine.

She quickly scanned the two pages. The first paragraph simply stated that certain items had been identified by Peter Nicolson, now deceased, and that they could be found near Cedar Island. The rest of Zhao's letter described various Chinese artifacts.

"Each letter described different national artifacts particular to our interests," Jamila said, grinding her teeth.

"I had nothing to do with the letters. Why do you think you all received them?"

"Obviously, whoever it was wanted us all to come here." Neith shrugged.

"But why?"

"We've been trying to figure that out," Hume admitted.

"I've already told you why!" Donavan fumed. "Whoever wrote those letters wants us to do all of the footwork, then they'll swoop in and take whatever we find."

"Possibly," Hume said.

"And you all just want to retrieve the items for your various countries?" Josephine watched as they exchanged glances.

"For the most part," Brock answered.

"There are some of us who are more patriotic than

others," Jamila said, smirking.

"I wouldn't go casting stones." Donavan frowned at her.

"Now that you know I had nothing to do with the letters, I'll be going." Josephine turned and started toward the door.

"Not so fast," Brock said, blocking her exit. "You still haven't explained why you're here."

"Obviously, she is just a thief looking for the gold," Jamila said.

"Little harsh," Hume said. "I think we've established that each of us plans on wanting a little bit of gold for our troubles."

"There are artifacts and coins. You all are welcome to the artifacts." Donavan sounded annoyed.

"I told you," Josephine said. "I recently found a letter that my uncle left for us. It mentioned Cedar Island and, since I knew he'd died here, I wanted to see if I could learn more about what happened to him."

"After more than twenty years?" Brock sounded unconvinced.

"I only just found it."

"What did the letter say?" Donavan moved a step closer, his eyes searching Josephine's face.

"Not much. He wrote something about a legacy for my father and me, but nothing specific."

"He was murdered," Brock stated.

"Why do you say that?" Josephine asked.

"Why would he mention a legacy and not tell you how to find it?" Donavan acted as if Brock had not spoken.

Ignoring Donavan, Brock said, "I say he was murdered because he was. I did some research on the mainland and found a copy of the sheriff's report."

Josephine was stunned. "The sheriff *knew* he was murdered? No one ever told us."

"He knew. Covered it up. Even the half-ass autopsy was enough to show that he'd been killed. There was no water in his lungs. Skull was cracked. Sheriff's report said he'd fallen off the dock and hit his head, or was hit by a boat."

"He left you a clue to the treasure, didn't he?" Donavan said, trying to bring the conversation back to the present.

"I…"

"What did you pick up from the post office?" Brock asked pointedly.

"Something worth killing for?" Neith said, her eyebrows raised.

"Yes, there was a second letter." Josephine couldn't see the point in denying it anymore. Besides, she might have been able to use their help.

"And someone attacked you for it," Hume said thoughtfully.

Josephine noticed that the members of this rather odd group of treasure hunters were all looking at each other suspiciously.

"Yes. The person who attacked me grabbed the letter. I fought with him and he ran off. Next thing I knew, he was dead."

"Very succinct, Miss Nicolson," Zhao said, looking at her closely.

They spent the next few minutes questioning her about the incident. Josephine felt as if she repeated the same story twelve times, but she didn't really mind. She was using the time to try to decide who in the group was most likely to be a killer. She hoped that the person might slip up while pretending to be interested in events that they already knew better than she did.

"Who cares about the damn murder? I want to know what was in the letter," Donavan said dismissively.

"Don't be a fool. Whoever killed that man today undoubtedly knew about the letter and, therefore, also about the treasure and Peter Nicolson," Hume said.

"And who is more interested in finding the trea… artifacts than the six of us?" Neith asked.

"I see where you're going. I guess that makes sense," Donavan reflected.

"It's not just the murder. The postmistress is missing,"

Josephine told them.

"One question comes to mind," said Brock, looking contemplative. "Is there someone else on the island who knows about the treasure? If not, then the murderer is probably in this room."

"But we know the thief wasn't part of our group," Hume reasoned.

"Maybe one of us hired the thief." Jamila was staring at Donavan as she spoke. "And then killed him."

"You have a rather nasty opinion of the rest of us," Hume chuckled.

"I say it was one of our rather strange island brethren… the fishermen. Other folks around here must have heard about the treasure. Remember that, according to Brock here, someone killed Peter Nicolson," Donavan pointed out.

"Those things may be brethren to you, but not me," Jamila spat.

"Let's not get sidetracked." Brock glared at both Jamila and Donavan. Josephine could tell that the subject of the fishermen was a sore one. "I think we have to agree that there is at least a *possibility* that one of us is a murderer." He looked around as if he might find a red letter "M" burned onto one of their foreheads.

"This is all well and good, but how does it help us find the treasure? Far as I can see, you all are just stirring the pot to no good purpose." Donavan's voice held a mix of anxiety, excitement and irritation. He turned to Josephine. "So make with the letter."

"Shut up!" Hume ordered, moving toward Donavan. "You are making an ass of yourself."

"I don't want to stay on this island one day longer than I have to."

"Go home, then. No one will miss you," Jamila sneered.

"Don't act so high and mighty. I know you need the money just as much as I do."

"There's the difference. I need the money. You just *want* the money."

"Children, let's settle down. Remember, we have a guest." Brock gestured toward Josephine.

"Don't mind me." Josephine smiled, watching the dynamics of the group closely.

"Make her give us the letter." Donavan pointed his finger at Brock.

"Yes, I agree. She should turn the letter over to us." Zhao's voice was calm and icy. "We need the letter. Like the impetuous and greedy Mr. Donavan, I also want to get off this island."

"You can't make me give you the letter," Josephine bluffed. "But you can trade for it."

CHAPTER THIRTEEN

"A trade?" Captain Hume sounded intrigued.

"What do you want for it?" Donavan asked suspiciously.

"Cooperation." She wasn't the least bit ashamed that she was only offering up *part* of a letter.

"What exactly are you talking about?" Brock asked.

"I want to know who murdered that man this morning, and I think one of you knows more than you're admitting. I'll turn over the letter to all of you if you'll allow the baron and me to interview each one of you. Since the sheriff won't investigate the murder, we will."

"Do you fancy yourselves some sort of half-ass detectives?" Brock said with a scornful laugh.

"Take my offer and you'll find out," Josephine said, looking him square in the eyes.

"I do not understand. If she has the letter and it tells where the treasure is located, then why is she bargaining with us?" Neith reasoned.

"Our Egyptian goddess has a point," Donavan said. "Maybe she doesn't really have anything to trade."

"You're the one who's been demanding the letter," Josephine challenged him.

"Yeah, but still… Why didn't you spend the afternoon

digging up the treasure?"

"Because I only have part of the letter," Josephine admitted. Several people groaned.

"Cripes!" Brock exclaimed. "Why didn't you say that from the beginning?"

"I would have if I had thought it was any of your business."

"So you're going to trade us damaged goods?" Donavan shouted.

"The letter isn't the only damaged goods," Jamila said, tapping her head and looking at Donavan.

"What exactly do you mean by *part* of the letter?" Hume asked.

"The person who attacked me tried to steal the letter. I fought him off, but he managed to get away with about half of it."

"You searched the body for it?" Brock asked.

"Of course."

"So the murderer must have the rest of it," Hume mused.

"That's what I assume," Josephine said.

There was silence in the room as everyone traded glances.

"I agree to her conditions," Jamila finally said.

"Sure, if it gets us a look at her part of the letter," Donavan agreed. "At this point, anything is better than nothing."

"I don't see the point in them doing any sort of investigation," Brock said. When he saw the looks he got from the others, he added. "But I guess it isn't going to hurt anything."

"Count me in," Hume said with a smile.

"If it finds us the artifacts so I can get off this island, I will cooperate," Neith allowed.

Everyone looked at Zhao. He smiled broadly. "I will not go against the wishes of the group."

"Of course, if one of us is the killer, then they will have both parts of the puzzle," Donavan pointed out.

"That's obvious," Brock groused.

"Which brings up the next question," Neith said. "How do we keep the murderer from using their part of the letter to beat us to the treasure?"

"Not much we can do about that," Donavan said.

There was a moment of silence before Hume spoke up. "I've got an idea. We will elect one person to look at Miss Nicolson's part of the letter. He—" Receiving murderous looks from Jamila and Neith, he amended: "—or *she* will keep the information close to their vest, so to speak, using it only when it might assist our group search."

"Kinda like letting one person hold the map," Brock said.

"Exactly, and if that person does anything suspicious, we'll know who the killer is."

"That way we only have one person to watch instead of five." Jamila nodded.

"Sounds fine, but how will the vote be taken?" Zhao did not look interested in the idea.

"No majority crap," Donavan said.

"I agree. There might be someone in league with the killer," Hume said.

"Or maybe three." Neith was looking very unhappy.

"It's got to be a unanimous vote." Jamila stared at everyone.

"Is there anyone we all trust?" Donavan asked.

More looks were exchanged. The group seemed at an impasse.

"Why don't we draw cards for it?" Hume said. This suggestion received frosty looks from everyone.

The silence grew as each member of the group tried to come up with a solution to their dilemma.

"We just need to pick someone," Jamila said in frustration.

"Yes. What's the problem?" Donavan agreed.

"*Quis custodiet ipsos germen radicum eius?*" Zhao said.

"He is not wrong," Neith said.

"What's that gibberish?" Brock asked.

"'Who watches the watchers' is a rough translation."

Hume smiled. "Indeed."

"I think that's pretty obvious. We've all been watching each other since the day we showed up at this cursed hotel," Donavan grumbled.

"And for very good reason." Again, Jamila looked at Donavan.

Josephine had been a little worried about making a deal with this group. What would happen if they all just used the information to find the treasure, then ran out on her and Blasko? But watching this childish display, she realized that her instincts had been right. It would take a more tightly knit group than this to pull off an organized swindle.

"I was simply honest and you've been holding it against me ever since. All I said was that I was personally interested in the gold. The artifacts that my university is interested in are Inuit, but not gold."

"I cannot believe that you teach at a university," Jamila scoffed.

"Go to hell," Donavan flung back at her.

"The trouble is, I *am* here to recover gold artifacts," Neith pointed out.

"And I told *you* that I don't care about them, just any gold bullion that might be found along with the rest. I said we'd share." Donavan sounded exasperated.

"Enough! We'll do what Captain Hume originally suggested." Zhao stood up. "I'll get the cards and we will draw to see who has the privilege of reading Miss Nicolson's letter."

Everyone stopped talking and there was a begrudging acceptance of the plan. The members of the group shifted nervously in place while Zhao left the room to find a deck of cards.

"While we wait, why don't you tell us about your cousin the baron?" Neith smiled at Josephine.

"How is that relevant?"

"I assume he knows all about the letter, so we are essentially making a pact with him as well as you. You did say that he would be involved in your little game of detective, did you not?"

Josephine noted that all of the eyes in the room were judging her and she didn't see any way to wriggle out of answering. "There's nothing to tell, really. When he heard that I was coming here to look into my uncle's death, he insisted on coming with me."

"It is nice to have a protector. Even if his strange sun allergy keeps him indoors during the day." Neith's smile grew a bit larger.

Josephine didn't like her tone at all. There was an underlying mockery suggesting that Neith knew that something other than allergies afflicted Blasko.

Zhao finally returned, holding up a deck of cards.

"Don't mind if I have a look at those cards, do you?" Donavan held out his hand.

"Really?" Jamila asked.

Josephine wondered about the animosity between Jamila and Donavan. While the rest of the group wasn't overly friendly with Donavan, they treated him equally. But Jamila seemed incensed by everything he did.

Zhao handed the cards to Donavan. He flipped through them, with Brock watching closely.

"They look okay." Donavan set the cards down on a small table between the windows.

"High card?" Brock asked.

There were nods and mutters of agreement as the six people gathered around the cards.

Hume quickly shuffled the cards and spread them around the table. Then he drew his own card, flipping it over to reveal the nine of clubs.

Hands reached out and took cards. Neith showed the seven of diamonds and Brock the ten of diamonds. Jamila, to her disgust, revealed the three of hearts. Zhao pulled up the queen of clubs while Donavan tossed his ten of hearts on the table in irritation.

"Zhao's the man for the job," Brock said, looking more

relaxed about the situation than Josephine expected. She was sure there was something off about Brock, but she couldn't put her finger on it.

The group turned to her.

"How would you like to proceed?" Hume asked.

"With the interrogation or with the letter reveal?" Josephine asked sweetly.

"Both, I guess."

"I'm going to trust you to hold up your end of the bargain." Josephine looked around at all of them. When she was as satisfied as she was going to get, she said, "If Mr. Zhao will meet me downstairs in the dining room, I will give him time to study the letter. But I don't want him to make a copy."

"I have an excellent memory," Zhao assured the group.

"I can't stop you from making notes after you see the letter."

"I fear *that* would be dangerous," Zhao said.

"Which brings up a question. How do we know the letter is safe in *your* hands?" Hume asked Josephine.

"You'll have to trust me." She paused, then clarified, "It is in a safe place, but I'll destroy it if I ever feel as though I or my friends are in any danger. That includes if I find that someone has attempted to search our rooms."

"I would never…" Hume started, then looked around at the others as if deciding that he couldn't vouch for everyone else. "…Of course. Understood."

"How do we know Zhao's going to tell us the truth?" Donavan seemed to be having second thoughts.

"I will tell you what I think the group needs to know and no more. If I reveal too much information from Miss Nicolson's letter, then the person who might have the other part of the letter would be in an excellent position to outmaneuver us."

"We trust you," Brock told him. "But we're going to keep a very close eye on you too… For your safety, of course."

"I won't mind having extra pairs of eyes on my back. I

assume that if the murderer is among us that he, also, will be watching me."

"Meet me downstairs," Josephine said, tired of the group paranoia.

She quickly went to her room and pulled the letter from underneath her skirt. She'd been able to secure it with a small safety pin at her waist, just behind her hip, where it was reasonably comfortable and secure.

Heading downstairs, she wondered how Blasko would react to her deal with the group. *What choice did I have?* she thought.

Josephine wasn't surprised to see that Zhao was already waiting for her near one of the tables. He pulled out a chair for her and she offered him the torn letter as soon as they were both seated.

With an academic thoroughness, he scrutinized the letter for half an hour. At one point, Jamila came down and got a dirty look from him before fixing herself a drink and sitting as far from them as she could.

Zhao handed the letter back to Josephine, having not said a word from the time they sat down.

"Bad luck that there are important clues missing," he said. "However, I believe that we can narrow down the possible location from this information."

"Who do you think might have killed the thief?"

"I believe that any one of the other members of the group could kill with the right motivation. The question is, who had both the motivation and the opportunity?"

"The killer used a knife."

"So you said. That would not eliminate any of us. Including myself."

"What's the issue between Jamila and Donavan?"

Zhao smiled broadly. "I am sure that you can guess. We all arrived within days of each other. Hume was the first, followed by Jamila and Donavan. By the time I checked into the hotel, they were already having a rather torrid affair. But after only a few days, their relationship was as you see it now."

"I thought that might be it. Is Donavan as mercenary as he acts?"

"I believe it would be safe to assume that he is no more or less a mercenary than the rest of us."

"You're saying that none of you should be trusted?" Josephine was surprised at his candor. "Despite the reasons y'all originally gave for being here, I gather that you're all really academics of one sort or another."

He gave a heartfelt laugh. "Yes, and that makes us the worst kind of thieves because we can justify it. And we are not the… cream of the crop of academics. Most serious scholars scoff at the thought that the artifacts we're after are real."

"Yet you believe the letter you received is genuine."

"Yes. The descriptions of the artifacts are very good. Based on what I was able to read in your part of the letter, the descriptions came from your uncle. He had an excellent eye for detail."

"But those letters couldn't have come from my uncle. He's been dead for twenty years."

"I believe someone simply copied your uncle's descriptions and sent them to us. I've examined the letters that were sent to the other members of our group and they each read the same. A short introduction, followed by descriptions of the artifacts that would be of most interest to the person who received the letter."

"And you think you can figure out where the treasure is located?"

"I think we can get in the general area. Notice the description of the island is as detailed as his descriptions of the various artifacts were in our letters. Donavan, for all of his pomposity, is an excellent cartographer."

"How will you proceed from here?"

"I'll talk with the others." He glanced over at Jamila, who was sipping her whiskey and pretending to be interested in whatever was going on outside the window. "Come see us in the morning and we'll tell you what our plans are."

"And I may want to question some of you as we agreed."

"Of course."

"Before you go, tell me what you know about Brock."

"American from Chicago. He teaches anthropology at the University of Chicago, but was refused a tenured position based on a flirtation he had with a visiting professor's wife. I believe the trip down here came at an opportune time for him to… I believe he said, get out of Dodge."

"I see."

"If you will excuse me, I want to begin my analysis of the information in the letter."

Josephine stood and Zhao started to leave. "Be careful," she told him and he gave her a small smile in return. Jamila dropped all pretense and left the room right behind Zhao.

Josephine went back upstairs and was about to knock on Blasko's door when Anton swung it open wide.

"Please ask the baron to come onto the balcony and knock on my window when he returns, whatever the hour. I need to speak with him," Josephine said.

"The balcony, knock on your window, yes," Anton agreed.

"You did well letting me know about the gathering across the hall."

"I watch like the baron told me."

"I may even pay for the door," Josephine said, looking at the hole again as she turned away.

Back in her room, she found Grace still working on her needlepoint.

"We leaving?" Grace asked without looking up from her work.

"You may be." Josephine wasn't surprised when Grace snapped her head around to look at her.

"What do you mean?"

"I may need you to leave the island tomorrow and phone Bobby Tucker."

"You don't want me doing that," Grace said

emphatically. "I'll tell him to come get you."

"You will *not*. I'll write out a list of questions for you to ask him."

"How am I going to get there? And where am I going call him from?"

"Don't worry about the details. I'll work them out."

"I don't feel comfortable alone in these backwoods. It ain't like I'm at home where people know me," Grace said, all petulance gone and real concern in her voice.

Josephine was aware of the dangers that a black woman could face in a strange part of the country. "I'll make sure you have a safe escort."

An hour later, after a long soak in the tub, Josephine lay in bed on top of the covers, letting the warm Gulf breezes do their best to cool her off. She couldn't help but wonder where Blasko was and if he'd been able to discover any of the island's secrets.

CHAPTER FOURTEEN

After revising his orders to Anton, Blasko headed for Mrs. Sharp's house in search of its mysterious occupant. As he walked through the dark streets, he felt the hunger growing within him. In order to honor his promise to Josephine not to hunt for his own blood, he usually worked hard to keep his mind occupied with other distractions. Most of the time he was successful, but tonight's focus on the trail of the dead man's blood from Josephine's clothes to the dining room had taxed him. He'd felt the old sensations and desires rising in him every time he'd inhaled the sweet, coppery aroma of the blood, and now he was having to fight the urge to hunt.

Before long, he found himself in front of the small rental house, where he could see the faint yellow glow of lamplight through the cracks in the shutters. Blasko blended in with the shadows as he sidled up to the clapboard house. His keen hearing was able to pick up the breathing of a single person, rapid and shallow. Like an experienced predator, Blasko could tell that the person inside was in distress. He could also detect the whiff of the same putrid odor that permeated the docks, and underneath that something floral, but very faint.

Blasko circled the house, trying the shutters. They were

all high off the ground and secured from the inside, so he gave up hope of a stealthy entry. It would have to be through the front door. If he could get the man to open the door even the slightest crack, then he'd be able to force his way inside whether he was invited in or not. Of course, Josephine had told him that the man had refused to even acknowledge her presence when she'd knocked. Knocking would alert the occupant, but simply barging his way in could lead to a confrontation that might cause the person inside to be rendered unconscious, uncooperative or worse.

Blasko went over the options and their probable outcomes in an effort to approach the situation with cold logic. A deliberative process would give him cover if everything went south and he had to explain his actions to Josephine. With this last thought in mind, he decided to knock on the door and force his way in only if necessary. At least then he would be able to tell Josephine that he had tried reasoning with the lodger first.

He climbed the steps to the front porch and stood awkwardly in front of the door. Knocking was a social nicety he'd never had to practice in the old country. If he'd ridden up to a house on horseback, he'd simply called to the people inside who would come out in deference to his peerage. If he'd ever had to knock, it meant that the door came down and he followed up by killing everyone inside who failed to surrender. If he hadn't been plagued by his condition, then he might have acquired more friends and acquaintances of his own social standing. *But if it weren't for my condition, I'd have been dust in the grave hundreds of years ago*, Blasko thought with an ironic grin.

Finally, he gave the door five thunderous raps with his fist. He heard the person inside stand up and move stealthily toward the door. He knocked again several times, loud enough that he could sense the person on the other side startle in fear. But there was still no answer.

He was about to kick the door down when he decided to try one more tactic—asking politely.

"I don't know who you are, but I'd like to speak with you. I—"

Blasko was going to assure the person that he meant no harm., but before he could get the words out he heard the bolt being thrown back and the door flew open in his face.

"Blasko, damn you, get in here!" a harsh voice barked from the shadows behind the door.

A voice that was all too familiar.

"Carter!" Blasko bellowed, stunned that Josephine's cousin was on the island and even more surprised that he'd opened the door.

"Get in here! Consider that the best invitation you're going to get," Franklin Carter hissed from the darkness.

Blasko stepped into the house, fully prepared for a cage covered in garlic to crash down over him. Carter had never trusted him and the feeling was mutual. The last time they'd met, Carter had tried to kill the vampire before leaving Sumter in possession of a valuable and very dangerous book.

"What are you doing here?" Blasko asked, staring at the man. Anyone else would have had a difficult time making out his features in the dim light, but not Blasko. He was perfectly able to tell that the once-pompous man was now a shadow of himself, gaunt and pale. He also noticed that Carter had a burlap sack tied firmly over his left hand.

"Have you gone mad?" Blasko said. "Or should I say madder! Where the devil is the *Necronomicon* you stole?"

"I've been punished enough for that, thank you. Let me shut the door." He slammed the door with his right hand and stumbled back toward the bedroom where an oil lamp glowed.

Blasko followed him, wanting to toss Carter against the wall and demand that he return the dark grimoire. The only thing stopping him was the pitiable state of the man. He also couldn't help but take note of the rancid, fishy smell coming off of Carter, which had almost completely masked his usual tell-tale scent of orange-blossom perfume. Curious, Blasko decided to hear him out.

Carter sat down on the side of a rickety, metal-framed bed that took up one wall of the cramped room. "I'm actually glad you're here. I'm desperate for assistance." He gestured to a straight-backed wooden chair across from the bed. "Sit."

Despite his curiosity, Blasko still couldn't let go of his anger toward the man… for so many things. "How dare you send Josephine that abominable book?" Months earlier, he had discovered Josephine reading a book that was filled with myths and lies about vampirism. She'd admitted that Carter had sent it to her.

"You have to admit that vampires can… present some… dangers," Carter said, treading lightly. "But maybe I was wrong about you." He waved dismissively with the hand that wasn't in the bag. "Sit… please."

Blasko didn't want to sit, but Carter's obvious desperation blunted his anger. *Best to humor the man*, he thought.

A silence drew out as Carter sat staring down at the floor. Blasko saw the man's shoulders moving and realized that he was crying. At last, Carter wiped his eyes and began to speak.

"You were right about the *Necronomicon*. I never should have kept it."

"You murdered a man for that book," Blasko couldn't help reminding him.

"Yes, yes, you're right. But Mayor Thornton couldn't have been allowed to keep it, not after he'd opened that portal to hell. Look, I'd been on the trail of the book for almost a decade. I couldn't let you destroy it before I had a chance to do some research." He looked up for the first time. "Damn it, I meant well!"

"Most of the world's grief can be laid at the feet of men who uttered those words."

"No worries for the world. I'm the only one who is suffering now because of my hubris," Carter said through clenched teeth. He untied the string from around his forearm and pulled the burlap bag off of his hand, revealing the most fascinating and revolting melding of man and monster that Blasko had ever seen.

The lower part of Carter's arm was no longer human. From just below his elbow, it looked like someone had grafted an octopus where his hand should have been. Five pink tentacles seemed to move with their own undulating purpose as he held the monstrosity up in front of Blasko.

Mesmerized, Blasko studied the flexing tentacles. He noticed that they didn't look damp; rather they appeared to be dry and scaly like a lizard's skin. The suckers opened and closed reflexively.

"Are you able to control the tentacles and the individual suckers?" Blasko asked, entranced.

"After a fashion. That's not the point! This… thing is not something I wish to become accustomed to."

"Yes, I can understand that," Blasko said with genuine sympathy. "How did…" Blasko gestured at the tentacles, wiggling away where Carter's hand should be. "Start at the beginning. Why are you here on Cedar Island?"

Carter sighed loudly. "After our last encounter with the… thing under the gentlemen's club and that strange cult, I decided to do some research into Semmes County… to see if there is a reason so many odd things seem to be happening there. I also looked into Josephine's family history. I knew some of it, but very little, as it turned out. When I realized she had an uncle named Peter Nicolson, I remembered that I'd seen the name in some papers archived at Miskatonic University. I soon discovered that there were ties to Innsmouth."

"What were these papers about Nicolson? Was it a letter?" Blasko interrupted, and Carter gave him the squint-eye.

"If you'll give me a chance, I'll tell you." His tentacles became more agitated as his temper flared. Carter pinned them down and put the bag back over them. "This settles them. Anyway, yes, I saw a letter from Josephine's uncle. In fact, there were several correspondences between Nicolson and a Professor Weller. Weller was an archeologist at the university. The letters described various objects that Nicolson claimed to have seen, or possibly found. He was vague on that point."

"Why did he write to the professor?"

"Because the objects were so out of place. Nicolson was also aware of Innsmouth and the strange reputation it already had, and he thought some of the objects might have a connection. Weller had done surveys of the population around Innsmouth at the turn of the century, when he was studying anthropology. It turned out that Weller's attempts to get a master's in anthropology based on his hypothesis of the genetic and cultural origins of the Innsmouth-type were consistently turned down, which is why he wound up in archeology."

"What were these objects?"

"That was the odd part. They were a mix of gold items from various ancient cultures. Nicolson wanted the professor's opinion on whether they could be real. Weller told him that they might be. In fact, one of the items had been reported stolen form the first Egyptian antiquity museum in 1837."

"You mentioned Innsmouth. What is the connection?"

"There were also some very strange items described in the letter. Several were similar to esoteric pieces that the professor had seen during his research."

"How did Nicolson know that?"

"He referenced an article in the *Miskatonic Archeology Journal*. The professor had written a short monograph on several items he'd found in Innsmouth. Nicolson saw the journal article and contacted the professor. Look, can I tell you about my hand now?" Carter was clearly irritated.

"No. You still haven't told me why you are here. Do you have the *Necronomicon* with you?"

"Yes," Carter admitted. "Specifically, I came here looking for the Innsmouth connection. I arrived on the island before the end of May. I did some scouting around and thought I was on to something. I found some strange carvings on several of the trawlers. In the process of getting a closer look at them, I brushed some barnacles off one of the boats and cut my hand. I didn't think much of it and hurried back here to consult the *Necronomicon*. I was sure the symbols I'd found on the boat were identical to symbols in the book.

"I was searching through the book when blood from my hand dripped onto the page. Then I started to feel a tingling and smelled an awful odor, like fish rotting on the beach. When I looked down, there was a tendril of putrefying flesh stretching from the book to my hand. I managed to cut it away, but not before my hand started to change into this." He removed the bag again. The tentacles writhed and twisted in the air.

"The worse part is that I think, whatever this horrid corruption is, it's creeping farther up my arm." Carter's eyes were wide and panicked-looking. It was clear that he could only maintain his composure for short stretches. "You've got to help me!"

Blasko could barely resist repeating his original warnings about the use of the *Necronomicon*. But the almost suicidal expression on Carter's face made him bite back his retort. "What have you tried?" he asked in his best clinical manner.

"I went back through the *Necronomicon*. Carefully." Carter emphasized this last part. "But I couldn't find anything about how to reverse this. Hell, I couldn't find anything that would have done this in the first place!" He waved his hand in the air while the tentacles wiggled obscenely.

"Of course not. This wasn't something you called up. Instead, it was the result of you unwittingly bringing various unsavory elements together." Blasko stared at Carter's hand, fascinated in spite of himself. "Do you have a knife?"

"I thought of that," Carter said flatly. "I... don't know if I can do it."

"Do you have any feeling in the tentacles?"

"I do and, as I said, I have some control over them."

Gingerly, Blasko reached out and felt the moving digits.

The half dozen suckers on each tentacle slurped at Blasko's hand as he flexed the appendages tentatively. He tried not to shudder.

"Look away," Blasko said. When Carter turned his head, Blasko took a small folding knife from his pocket. He opened it and stuck it into the smallest tentacle. Carter screamed.

"What the devil are you doing?"

"Confirming that your nerves are connected to the ones in the tentacles."

"I already told you they were."

"So… How much liquor do you have on hand and how badly do you want to get rid of this abomination?"

"I can't… You can't… My hand." Carter's words were barely audible.

"Would you rather keep it as it is?" Blasko asked bluntly.

Carter shook his head. "I can feel it creeping up my arm. I've measured its progress. I lose a quarter of an inch every day."

"Then you want it gone?"

"Please. Think of something."

Blasko took a small pouch out of his jacket pocket and pulled out a gold coin, holding it up in front of Carter's face.

"Look at the design on this coin," Blasko said softly. The gold reflected the lamplight as Blasko moved it back and forth in front of Carter's eyes. "Breathe deeply. Fall into the darkness. Watch the coin move back and forth…"

Blasko figured Carter knew that he was being brought under the vampire's control, but his desperation and exhaustion made it easy for him to let go, like a man freezing to death in a snowstorm.

Once Blasko could hear the man's steady, rhythmic breathing and he was sure that he controlled all of Carter's thoughts and emotions, he told him to lie down on the floor. As Carter followed his instructions, Blasko felt the slightest tug on his desires. As he'd taken over Carter's mind, Blasko had sensed the blood pulsing in his veins. For a moment the craving was intense. *It wouldn't be right to take advantage of the poor man*, Blasko thought. *Besides, his blood is tainted by whatever caused that monstrosity to grow in place of his hand.*

Blasko went to the kitchen and found a large butcher knife lying on the counter. He figured it was even odds that Carter had already contemplated using it for what Blasko intended. Stepping over to the gas stove, Blasko lit the burner and set the blade of the knife on the flames. Then he searched until he found a ten-inch cast-iron skillet.

Five minutes later, Blasko was back with his patient, checking on his breathing.

"Lay your left arm out straight," he told Carter in a low, firm voice. Dutifully, Carter placed his arm out. The tentacles were writhing frantically, as though they knew what was coming.

The change had spread up Carter's arm to about four inches below his elbow. Blasko wondered how much of the apparently normal part of Carter's arm he should remove, along with the hellish appendage, in order to get rid of all of the affected tissue. *Best not to be too conservative*, he decided before placing the blade of the knife at the joint of the elbow.

"Makes more sense anyway, because I doubt that I'd be able to cut through the bone with this knife. At the elbow, I'll be able to cut through the joint," he said to Carter, though the man was not likely to hear him. "Gruesome work. Best if I finish it quickly."

Blasko began to saw through the flesh. The gristle around the elbow proved too much of a task for the butcher knife. When the handle snapped off, Blasko hurled the broken instrument across the room. "Bah! I should have brought my sword."

Before he got up to look for more tools, he instructed Carter to slow his heart rate down. His gentle suggestions brought the man's pulse low enough that the wound bled only a little. The smell of it almost overwhelmed Blasko. He kept his hunger pinned down through sheer force of will, knowing that if he gave in to it, he might not be able to control himself.

He found a metal toolbox under the kitchen sink. He clutched the small-toothed saw he found inside and rushed back to his patient. After just a few minutes of steady sawing, the foul thing was finally separated from Carter's body.

Blasko retrieved the skillet that he'd left warming on the stove burner. He came back to Carter and placed the searing hot pan against the nub of Carter's arm, cauterizing the wound. Taking a clean undershirt from Carter's bag, he wrapped the stub of the arm tightly. The shirt slowly turned red as Carter's arm continued to bleed. Blasko kept his hand pressed firmly against the shirt, fighting the urge to rip it off and drink from Carter's wound.

The presence of the blood was engulfing and intoxicating. Blasko tried to focus on the withering tentacles, still squirming around on the floor, to remind himself that while the blood smelled enticing, it was most likely infused with whatever evil filth had grown out of the *Necronomicon*. After a while, Blasko could feel through the makeshift bandage that he'd managed to stem the flow of blood. The searing of the flesh had done most of the work.

Once again, he searched the small house until he found several bottles of liquor. He set these down beside Carter and slowly began to bring him out of the trance. Blasko had learned by experience that it was dangerous to leave someone in one of his induced trances for too long. There was danger of drifting into a coma from which they would never return.

Blasko could order Carter not to feel the pain of his wound, but that would have a very limited effect. The body could be fooled for only so long. He did what he could and hoped that the alcohol would serve to deaden the pain that remained.

CHAPTER FIFTEEN

"Heaven help me!" Carter begged as he awoke. His eyes were rolling madly as he looked around the room.

"I've removed the… infection from your arm," Blasko told him, watching him placidly.

"What kind of bastard are you?" Carter clutched the stump of his left arm. "You butcher!"

"You know that removing the corruption was the only chance you had."

"I don't know any such thing. You're a half-ass surgeon. Did you lap up my blood while you were mangling me?"

"I'm offended that you would even suggest such a thing." Blasko stood up and looked down his nose at Carter, who was rocking back and forth with tears of pain streaming down his face. He would never admit to the man that he *had* been drawn to his blood. "I am sure your angry words are just an outgrowth of your pain."

"They bloody well aren't."

"Drink some whiskey. That will help the pain." Blasko scooted a half-full bottle of amber liquid closer to Carter, who grabbed it, pulled the cork and downed everything in the bottle in three swigs, followed by a coughing fit.

"Okay, okay." Carter coughed again. "Is it dead?" he

asked, looking at the remains of arm on the floor.

Blasko poked it with the broken blade of the butcher knife. The tentacles clenched reflexively, then remained still.

"Yes. The thing is dead."

"That's good." Carter looked at his stump. "There really wasn't a choice."

"Exactly."

"But don't expect me to thank you any time soon."

"Of course not. Now, do you know anything about the strange guests at the hotel?" Blasko asked, ready to get back to his investigation.

A guilty look crossed Carter's face, but he shook his head. "I'm in pain! I'm not up to answering questions right now." Carter's eyes closed as he fought off another wave of agony.

"I could have extracted information from you while you were in a trance." Blasko's tone made it clear that he wasn't going to be sidetracked.

"All right, all right, yes, I sent them letters before I left Arkham. When I saw the list of the different artifacts that Peter Nicolson claimed to have found, I developed a list of institutions that might be interested in acquiring them."

"Why?"

"I didn't want to be the only stranger in town. One stranger among half a dozen or more would receive less attention. And if there was an… infection like the one that overtook Innsmouth, I wanted some cover in order to come to the island and get to the bottom of things. Besides, I'm not interested in the museum trinkets."

"But they don't know that you're here?"

"I sent them the information anonymously. Like I said, I just wanted them here to create… a little chaos."

"Did you know that a local man was murdered this morning?" Blasko was gratified by the shocked expression on Carter's face. "He attempted to steal a letter from Josephine. She resisted. The man got away with half the letter, but was stabbed by a third party." Blasko recited this as if narrating a newsreel.

"What… The man who tried to steal a letter from Josephine was then killed by someone else?" Carter reached out and uncorked another bottle of whiskey.

"That's what I said."

"What letter? I'm assuming it was from her uncle. He mentioned in several of the letters to Professor Weller that he was prepared to bring in outside resources, and I was reasonably sure that he meant hitting up his brother the banker. When did he send the letter?"

"The letter she was carrying had been left at the post office for Josephine's father to pick up."

"What did it say?"

"Why do you care if you're not interested in the gold?"

The look on Carter's face told Blasko what he already knew. "Damn! More accursed literature."

"Nicolson described journals and several volumes that would be… rare." Carter saw the look on Blasko's face. "You have a right to be scornful." Carter held up his stump. "The pain is less now." His words were slightly slurred as the alcohol took effect.

"You deserve some pain," Blasko said, then relented. "Though I'm not sure you deserve to be turned into a mutant octopus."

The tentacles were now a rotting mess on the floor. Blasko decided to get rid of the hideous thing. With some effort and not a little nausea, he managed to carry it outside on a piece of wood and bury it in the backyard. Back inside the house, he found Carter half asleep on the floor.

"Come on. Let me help you into bed."

"Yeah, all right…" Carter muttered as Blasko all but lifted him off of the floor.

"Do you have any idea where Peter Nicolson found all those items, or where they came from?" Blasko didn't feel the least bit guilty for taking advantage of Carter's present state to wheedle more information out of him.

"No. Maybe."

Blasko nudged him. When the man didn't say anything, he nudged him harder. "Maybe what?"

"A manifest," Carter said groggily, rubbing at his stump.

Blasko slapped his hand. "Don't pick at it. What manifest?"

"Ship. Found in papers from Innsmouth."

"A ship's manifest?" When he received no answer, Blasko gave Carter a poke. "You found a ship's manifest that had some of the same items on it?"

"Library in Arkham. Private collection. Recovered from Innsmouth during…. all that stuff." Carter was making less sense as he fell into unconsciousness.

Blasko stood and considered pulling a sheet over the man, but the room was stifling. Instead he picked up the empty bottles and took them into the kitchen. He tried to remember what it had felt like to be drunk. After hundreds of years he had the vaguest recollection of intoxication, but not of the aftereffects—though Blasko figured that the pain of Carter's stump would override any headache he might have. As a last gesture, Blasko filled a glass with water and set it on the nightstand beside Carter's bed.

He found a key by the door and locked up the house as he was leaving. With a sigh, he decided that he would need to check on Carter's condition before returning to the hotel to sleep.

Outside, the air was warm and humid. The moon was directly overhead and Blasko could hear the sound of boat engines idling down at the docks. He was determined to get a closer look at some of the odd men who went out fishing late at night.

As he walked to the docks, he tried to decide how he would use the information he'd received from Carter. He knew he'd have to tell Josephine, though Blasko was sure that the man wouldn't want her to know about his hand. Not that he was going to be able to hide the fact from anyone now that all he had left was a stump.

Once he was in sight of the boats, Blasko shook the

other thoughts out of his head and tried to concentrate on the challenge before him. He made his way to the same spot where he and Donavan had watched the boats the night before, but tonight he was alone. He watched as the fishermen shambled around the dock, their heads downcast as they went about their various tasks.

Six trawlers were lined up at the docks and, offshore, Blasko could see the lights of half a dozen more. He watched the boats at the dock move off one by one, until there were only two left. One boat's engine was idling and its crew moved about anxiously, while the men on the other boat seemed concerned. One man was pounding on something at the stern of the boat, and Blasko assumed there must be a problem with the engine. There was some excited chatter that even Blasko's ears couldn't make out, and the volume wasn't the only problem. It sounded like more of the strange tongue he'd heard the previous night. There was a little more conversation, then almost all of the men joined the crew of the functioning trawler. Soon they cast off, leaving the one man alone on the dark and silent boat.

Once Blasko was sure that the man was focused on his work, he began to move toward the dock. There were lights in a few houses nearby, but there was no one else outside. Blasko walked at a steady pace, seeming to blend in with the shadows and making no sound. Willing himself to drift across the wooden planks as though he weighed nothing, he approached the back of the trawler. Suddenly the man seemed to sense that he wasn't alone, but before he could turn his head, Blasko leaped onto the boat and grabbed the man by the wet, firm skin of his neck.

"Don't make a sound. I just want—"

The man opened his mouth, issuing a fetid odor that so surprised Blasko that he lost his grip. The creature, for Blasko was no longer sure that it was a man, took advantage of his lapse and slipped out of his grasp.

"Arggg! Youal die fosure for thissss, whoyou may be," the creature said, before opening a hideous mouth that was impossibly large and full of sharp teeth. He lunged toward Blasko, who was taken completely off guard by the thing's appearance and aggressive attack.

At first all Blasko could do was retreat from the onslaught. He didn't know what would happen if the creature bit him, but he doubted it would be anything good. His backed away along the gunwale toward the bow of the boat, with the monster snapping at him every step of the way, its teeth mere inches from Blasko's arms and face.

Blasko's shoes were not designed for walking on a slippery deck. Twice he almost lost his balance. The second time they were passing the entrance to the wheelhouse. When he reached up and grabbed the roof to steady himself, he saw that the creature had grabbed something from his belt.

Before Blasko could react, the creature reached out and plunged a long marlin spike into Blasko's chest. The pain almost brought him to his knees, but Blasko kept his grip on the roof, and then it was the creature's turn to be surprised. It had clearly expected Blasko to succumb to an attack that would have been fatal to any normal human. Instead, fighting through the pain, Blasko withdrew the spike and rammed it into the creature's chest. Its gaping mouth opened and closed a few times in shock before it stumbled back and fell into the water.

Breathing hard and clutching his chest, Blasko glanced around to make sure no one had seen the fight. Then he took a minute to assess his wound. While it was bad, he'd survived much worse.

Thinking hard, he decided to risk taking a quick look around the boat. He certainly didn't want to linger, but he also wasn't going to pass up the chance to look for evidence of who these mutant fishermen were and what they were doing.

He looked around the wheelhouse, where nothing seemed unusual except for four dark robes hanging on pegs by the door where foul-weather gear normally would have been. The robes resembled what medieval monks had worn during their devotionals.

Cautiously, Blasko approached the door that led down into the hold. At the bottom of the steps, he found himself in what appeared to be a small, cramped temple. The walls were covered with disturbing representations of animal sacrifices, while at the far end of the cabin was a stone tablet, six feet by three. It rested on two more stones that raised it three feet off of the deck. While he couldn't make out the meaning of the words carved into the stone, it seemed to be a shrine to a god called Dagon. The stone was worn smooth, with dry blood crusted along its sides. Blasko inhaled reluctantly and was only a little relieved to detect mostly animal blood.

Realizing that he'd been there much longer than he'd planned, Blasko quickly retreated up the steps and back into the humid Florida night. The dock was still deserted. He slipped off of the boat and back into the shadows.

With his wound burning in his chest, Blasko decided that he'd had enough of the eldritch creatures who worked the fishing boats. He wasn't sure if he'd killed the thing and he wasn't sure if he cared. And he was weak from the fight. *Where can I get fresh blood on this cursed island?* he grumbled to himself. The last thing he wanted was to drink any of the blood that flowed in local veins. He had a brief moment when he imagined tentacles growing out of his arms and, for the first time in nearly a century, he felt a twinge of real fear.

He made his way back to Carter's cabin and unlocked the door, not bothering to knock as he figured the man would still be sleeping off his alcoholic fog. He walked quietly to the bedroom, where he found Carter covered in sweat and moaning softly. The lamp by the bed had long since burned out, but Blasko didn't need it. He felt the man's forehead and sensed a slight temperature. He shook Carter by the shoulder.

"Wake up. I need to see how you're doing," he told his groggy patient.

"I'm… Yes… It hurts… Damn it…" Carter was rubbing at the shirt tied around his stump.

"I told you to leave it alone. You will cause it to start bleeding again."

"The wrappings are too tight," Carter complained, more awake now.

"Let me see."

"It would help if you lit a lamp."

"Bah! I don't need a lamp." Blasko took Carter's arm and examined the stump. "We need to unwrap this."

"Light a lamp so I can see." Carter's voice was full of anxiety.

Blasko lit the lamp and heard Carter gasp.

"What happened to you?" Carter asked, looking at the bloody hole in Blasko's chest.

"An encounter with a reluctant fishman."

"You mean fisherman?"

"Definitely *fish*man," Blasko told him.

Carter grunted. "Then this *is* like Innsmouth."

"Enough. Let me look at your arm."

Carefully, Blasko removed the shirt that he'd used as a bandage. When the stump was completely uncovered, he stared dumbfounded at what he saw.

"What the hell…" Carter muttered. "Oh no, no, no!" he chanted rhythmically as he looked at the stump.

"I'm sorry, Franklin. I… didn't expect this."

Both men looked at his arm with varying degrees of dread, revulsion and hopelessness. Where Blasko had cauterized the wound, a small nub had appeared like a seedling pushing through the soil. The tentacles were growing back.

"This can't be happening," Carter said, his voice cracking.

"Whatever you are infected with has the power to regenerate. We are going to have to find a more… supernatural solution to your problem. We shouldn't be surprised since we know the source of the mutation," Blasko observed.

"Don't just stand there! Figure something out."

"There is nothing to be done tonight."

"Take the *Necronomicon*. Find a cure for this abomination," Carter pleaded.

"That *book* is an abomination." Blasko hesitated. He didn't want to have the book in his possession, but he also didn't want to leave it where Carter could get himself into more trouble. "Where is it?"

"In the fireplace. I dug out some of the bricks and hid the book behind them."

Blasko went to the fireplace, which was large enough that it could have once been used for cooking. It didn't take Blasko long to find the fresh scratches where Carter had dug out the stones. Using a fire poker, he pried them away and removed the large, dusty tome from its resting place.

Carter was crying softly in the bedroom. Blasko handed him the last bottle of liquor. "Drink and sleep. I'll be back tomorrow night."

Blasko locked the door behind him and hurried through the night with the book tucked tightly under his arm. He felt a heavy responsibility settle on his shoulders. His first impulse was to burn the book. Watching the damned thing go up in flames would have been very satisfying. If only there wasn't the matter of Carter's tentacles to deal with. There was a slight chance that they still might find something in the book that could be used to remove whatever corruption had taken hold of him.

Blasko slunk quietly along the side of the hotel. His ears picked up no sound as he climbed back up onto the balcony. But when he opened the door to his room, there was a scrambling that caused him to prepare to defend himself.

"It is only me, Baron." Anton picked up the chair he'd knocked over in his surprise. "I was watching the hall like you wanted."

"And you didn't hear me open the door?"

"I might have fallen asleep." Anton's voice was full of shame. "You are hurt?"

Blasko touched the large blood stain on his chest. The wound was throbbing as his body and spirit tried to garner the energy to repair itself, a feat made doubly hard without fresh blood.

"Never mind. I have another job for you." Blasko held out the large book to the diminutive Anton. "You must protect this book with your life."

"Yes, Baron." Anton reached out and took the book gingerly.

"If, for any reason, you fear that you cannot protect it, the book must be destroyed. Do you understand?"

"I must protect the book or destroy it." Anton's confusion was evident.

"This book is too dangerous to allow anyone to gain possession of it." Blasko remembered that Carter had hinted to Josephine that the *Necronomicon* might contain a way to reverse the blood bond that bound them together. "No one includes Miss Josephine."

"Yes, Baron."

Blasko knew that while Anton had the simple nature of an old country peasant, he also had the loyalty and strength of a man of the fields.

"Oh, Baron, I almost forgot. She wishes to see you. She said for you to come to her by the balcony."

Blasko nodded and turned back to the balcony. But before he opened the door, he said to Anton. "Do not open that book. Under *any* circumstances."

Anton looked down at the book and nodded. Blasko knew that Anton couldn't read the archaic script, but he wasn't sure that the book would care.

Josephine had slept fitfully. There was a fine sheen of sweat across her body from the humid air when she was startled awake by a soft knock on the balcony door. Shaking off strange, unremembered dreams, she got up and pulled on a light robe.

After checking to make sure it was Blasko, she unlocked the door and opened it, then walked away to light the oil lamp next to the bed. When she turned back, her eyes were drawn to the blood on Blasko's chest. Her hand flew to her mouth.

"Is that your blood?"

"As much as any blood that comes out of my body can be considered mine," he said with a tired smile.

"What happened?" she asked, rushing over to him to determine the extent of his injuries.

"I met one of the local fishermen. More fish than man, I would say." He told her about the encounter on the boat. "These… things are some sort of hybrid."

"Here, take off your coat and shirt. We can't let anyone else see this."

Blasko struggled to get out of his bloody clothes, fighting against pain and fatigue.

"We can soak them in the tub. Grace and I will work on them," she said, taking each piece of clothing as he handed it to her. Her breath caught when she saw the wound. It was no longer bleeding, but the puncture was still open, red and angry.

"What do you need?" Josephine asked when she returned from the bathroom. She was remembering another night when Blasko had been shot. It had taken fresh blood and more than a little time for him to heal.

"I think you know. But even if I wanted to draw blood from one of the locals, I fear that what runs through their veins is contaminated. It carries whatever has transformed the fishermen into living nightmares."

Josephine looked into Blasko's eyes, her heart racing. When she'd first let him into her room, she'd realized that her body, caressed by the warm salt air, had wanted him. Now she knew that she was going to give herself to him, but not in the way she desired.

"You must drink from me," she said softly.

"I don't know if I trust myself." Blasko's eyes were

locked on hers.

She smiled. "It's all right. *I* trust you, Dragomir."

He returned her smile, then pulled her into his arms and lowered his fangs to her neck. Guided by her faith in him, he drank just to the point of satiation, then pulled away. He lifted the semi-conscious Josephine into his arms and carried her to the bed, lying down beside her.

After a while, he stroked her hand and asked, "How do you feel?"

"I'm a little light-headed, but I promise to eat a good breakfast." She rolled over to face him, propping her head on her hand. "I need to tell you about my evening. I may have made a deal with the devil." She went on to tell him about her meeting with the other guests and their agreement to share the letter.

"You did the right thing. The faster we can get off this island, the better." Josephine was surprised to detect fear in Blasko's voice. "You're not the only one with a story to tell," he said, and explained about Carter.

"Franklin is here? And he's turning into a giant squid? I don't believe it!"

"The malformation is as much supernatural as it is biological. It reminded me of the creature that rose out of the fissure below Mrs. Rosehill's house."

"Can anything be done for him?"

"I'll try to come up with something. He has some time. Maybe a couple of weeks, or even a month, before the contamination moves up his arm and consumes who he is."

"My cousin is a bit of an ass, but that…"

"No one deserves what's happening to him," Blasko agreed.

"Well, at least we know who invited the treasure hunters. Speaking of which, I'm supposed to meet with them again in the morning."

Blasko looked at the darkness beyond the windows, where he perceived the faintest hint of dawn. He turned back to Josephine. "I must go. The sun will be up soon."

As he rose from the bed, Josephine thought his color looked better and the wound on his bare chest was almost closed. "Will you be okay now?"

"I won't be fully recovered after I sleep, but I'll be much better. Thanks to you."

He leaned down and kissed her. The kiss turned passionate and, with his arms tightly around her, Josephine allowed herself to hope that it would lead to more. *But how can it, with so little time?* she thought regretfully as he pulled away. In another moment he was gone.

CHAPTER SIXTEEN

Josephine still felt a little woozy when she got out of bed two hours later.

"What the sweet Jesus happened in the tub?" Grace yelled from the bathroom.

Josephine smiled to herself, then went to explain things to Grace. She told her all about Blasko's fight with the fisherman, leaving out only the details of the assailant's hybrid nature.

"There's a hole that's got to be mended," Grace said, looking at a ragged tear in Blasko's shirt.

"You'll be glad to hear that the baron is as anxious to get off this island as you are."

"After this, I'd expect so."

Josephine dressed and headed down to breakfast, keeping her word to Blasko as she tucked into Mrs. Lachlan's hearty fare. The only other guests in the dining room were Jamila and Neith, who kept giving her sideways glances. They had all exchanged greetings, but seemed to be of one mind about skipping any small talk.

"We are meeting in Captain Hume's room," Jamila told Josephine as she headed for the stairs, followed closely by Neith.

Feeling much more herself, Josephine joined them just before nine.

"We should wait until everyone has assembled," Hume said as the group started to talk. "Mr. Brock has not yet joined us."

Fifteen minutes later, they were still waiting for him.

"That man has never shown very good manners," Elliot Zhao observed.

"Someone should go knock on his door," Jamila said, sounding more like she wanted to go knock on his head. "You go," she said to Zhao.

He gave her a *Why me?* look.

"That would be a good chap," Hume agreed, apparently reluctant to leave everyone alone in his room.

Zhao stood without another word and went out into the hall. He was back in less than five minutes. "He didn't answer and the door is locked."

"That's odd. The man was quite keen to get to the hunt this morning," Hume said.

"Could he have the other part of the letter?" Jamila asked.

"And got a jump on us!" Donavan finished the thought.

"Hold on. Let's make sure we're chasing the right fox." Hume stood up and went to the French doors leading to the balcony. "We can go around to his balcony door. It'll be easy enough to get in there."

"You sound like you've broken into people's rooms before," Jamila said with a hint of approval in her voice.

"I've done a lot of things. Come on."

Josephine followed Zhao, Donavan and Hume onto the balcony. When they reached Brock's door, they were surprised to find that it was unlocked.

"I say, Brock, we're coming in!" Hume announced before stepping over the threshold.

The tall four-poster bed had obviously been slept in. Half the covers had been dragged off and lay stretched out on the floor, pointing toward the bathroom.

As a group, they moved toward the closed bathroom door. As Hume turned the knob, Josephine was sure that they all had a bad feeling about what they would find. Sure enough, as soon as the door was open, they could see Brock in his underwear and wife-beater undershirt, lying in the clawfoot tub. His bluish face was underwater, while his feet stuck up in the air at the other end. A rusty trail of blood ran down the back of the tub above his head.

"We found him," Donavan said unnecessarily.

"We should leave and call the sheriff," Josephine said, trying to take note of everything in the bathroom. She didn't have Blasko's powerful sense of smell, but she was good at observing items that were out of place. She noticed that there was water around the tub, and a few drops clinging to the wall behind it.

The others still seemed unsure what to do.

"She's right. There's no sense standing here and gawking," Donavan finally said.

"How much good did calling the sheriff do yesterday?" Zhao asked Josephine.

"Not much. But we have a body this time. Just to make sure that we *still* have a body when the sheriff gets here, one of us should stay and keep an eye on it."

"Two of us," Hume interjected. "Otherwise, there could be some question about what the watcher got up to alone."

"Who watches the watcher," Zhao said, remembering their conversation from the night before.

"I'll stay," Josephine volunteered.

"I'll keep her company." Donavan looked around at the others as though he expected objections.

"I'll ask Mrs. Lachlan to send someone for the sheriff," Hume said.

"So who do you think iced him?" Donavan asked Josephine after the others had left.

"I was going to ask you the same thing. I had him pegged as the one who'd killed my thief."

Donavan shook his head. "Nah, I think you read him

wrong. He reminded me of an insurance investigator or the like."

As soon as he said it, Josephine saw that her line of thinking had been all wrong. She realized that what Brock's attitude had really reminded her of was Bobby Tucker at his most serious.

"I guess if we're careful, we can look around the room a little," Josephine suggested, knowing that it was wrong but unable to help herself.

"I'm right behind you. We'll need to keep this on the hush-hush."

"I won't be snitching," Josephine assured him. "But let's do it together so we can vouch for the fact that we didn't steal or disturb anything."

"Deal."

"I'll do the snooping if you'll do the supervising."

"Lead on."

Josephine went to the two suitcases beside the wardrobe and carefully placed the larger of the two onto the bed. She opened the leather bag and ran her hands all along the inside. She found a tin of aspirin, a ticket for a Chicago White Sox game at Comiskey Park, a half-used pack of matches that advertised some cheap elixir and, finally, a pencil. Josephine put everything back and replaced the first suitcase before repeating the exercise with the second one, finding only a second pencil and a damaged collar.

In the wardrobe, she methodically searched the pockets of his coats and pants, finding mostly lint and old gum wrappers. It was only when she got to the last suitcoat that she found anything interesting—a bullet from a .38 special.

"A lot of bulls use those," Donavan said. "You know, Colt Police Specials."

"You sound more like you're from Chicago than Canada." Josephine stopped searching and looked at him hard.

"I was born in Chicago. But my folks are from Canada and my father moved us back for business reasons," he said, looking up at the ceiling.

"During Prohibition?"

"I think you get the picture. Lots of trips across the border and gangster talk before Mom made sure I got off to university."

"Now you're all grown up," Josephine joked.

"Yes, but now I'm fighting to keep my assistant professor position at the University of British Columbia. There was going to be a round of layoffs, so I grabbed the letter when it came into the Anthropology Department. I figured they couldn't fire me if I was off on a project. Of course, they made me agree to pay my own travel expenses."

Josephine went back to searching the drawers in the wardrobe. Brock had placed everything neatly.

"Military man. Rolling up his socks like that," Donavan said.

Josephine was very careful to put everything back where she'd found it as she searched. In the bottom drawer, she found a paperback hidden under several T-shirts.

"Got something," she said, holding up the book. *Diamond Jim's Bad Girls Rodeo* read the title, and the cover was graced with a couple of buxom ladies in their underwear, drawn in lurid detail.

"I take that back," Josephine blushed. She started to return the book to where she'd found it when she realized that a tawdry novel would be a great place to hide something. "Maybe I'd better flip through it."

"Don't let me stop you," Donavan said with a smirk on his face. "I'll just read over your shoulder."

"Any part of your body touches mine and I promise you'll regret it," Josephine said, emphasizing her words with a menacing look. Donavan held up his hands.

Josephine flipped through the pages until she found a piece of paper, about an inch wide and four inches long, that had been used as a bookmark. Obviously torn from a larger document, they could make out only a few typed words on it.

"You might be right about him. There's the word 'district,' part of a word 'sum,' which could be summons, a few names. I'd say it's a court document."

"I told you he had cop written all over him."

Josephine put the makeshift bookmark back into the book and returned it to the drawer.

Next she went over to the bed and looked at the depressions in the mattress and pillows. There was no blood or dirt; nothing that would suggest anything other than a man who got up in the middle of the night on his own. Then a thought occurred to her. She ran her hand under the mattress near the headboard, until she felt a bulky metal object. Carefully, she withdrew a .38 special and held it up for Donavan to see.

"Again, what did I tell you?"

Josephine sniffed the gun, smelling only gun oil. "It hasn't been fired since it was cleaned."

"Nobody's been shot," he said as though she were stupid.

"Not yet."

The fact that the gun was still under the mattress told Josephine that Brock hadn't been concerned when he'd gotten out of bed. If someone had knocked on his door and he let them in, then he must have trusted them. She looked around the room again. There were no signs of a fight. Sure, the room could have been cleaned up, but the hotel's walls were thin and a wrestling match in one of the rooms would have been heard by other guests. She put the gun back under the mattress just as she'd found it.

Lastly, Josephine checked the door into the hall. It was locked and didn't look like it had been tampered with. She returned to the French door that led out onto the balcony, which they had found unlocked. Would a man who kept a gun under his bed leave a door unlocked when he went to bed? *Unlikely*, Josephine decided. But the lock on the door didn't look like anyone had tried to pry it open, leading her to believe that Brock had let his killer into the room.

"I hear someone," Donavan said in a hoarse whisper.

Josephine also heard the footsteps coming along the balcony. She tried to look like they hadn't been snooping as Neith entered the room.

"They have sent for the sheriff." Neith looked from Josephine to Donavan suspiciously.

"What?" Donavan asked.

"You look… Never mind. I'll stay and wait."

"If you're going to be here, I need to go back to my room for a moment." Josephine wanted to talk with Grace and see if she could arrange for her to get onto the mainland to make a call to Bobby.

"I heard already: there's been another murder. I'm packin' my bags right now," Grace said when Josephine came to her room. "You aren't talkin' me into stayin' no longer."

A thought occurred to Josephine. "I wouldn't dream of trying."

Grace was shocked. "You wouldn't?"

"No. But I'm going to write down the names of six people and give them to you. Call Bobby as soon as you get to the mainland. I need him or the colonel to do some background checks for me."

Grace was standing in the middle of the room, holding her carpetbag and wearing a stunned expression. "You mean to say you aren't goin' back with me?" she asked, sounding less sure of herself.

"No. I'm going to send Anton home with you. When you get home, find out what Bobby and the colonel were able to learn and send their reply back with Anton."

"Anton? Can that man even drive a car?" Grace looked worried that her plan to return home was not going the way she'd envisioned.

"Blasko's been giving him lessons." In truth, Blasko had hopes of adding "chauffer" to Anton's list of duties. It hadn't been going well, but Josephine wasn't going to tell Grace.

"The baron can't hardly back out of the driveway

himself." Grace sounded dubious.

"Anton can drive well enough, though you might need to make sure he doesn't get lost." Grace was an excellent navigator. On the trip down, she'd been good with the map and shown an uncanny sense of direction.

"If he can keep the car on the pavement, I'll get us home," Grace said firmly. "Though I don't like you stayin' here one bit. What happened to me just makin' a phone call to Mr. Bobby?"

"This will be more certain. Anyway, you can't wait by the phone while they do the background checks. I'll be fine. The baron is here. And so, I just found out, is Franklin Carter."

"That bean pole? I never trusted him and his Yankee ways. And the baron… Don't he need Anton to look after things when he's…" Grace didn't like to talk about the baron's unusual habits. "…resting?"

"I can keep an eye on him. With luck, Anton can be back by sunset tomorrow."

"You think that man can get back here by hisself?"

"He managed to get to our house from Romania by himself."

"I guess you got a point there." Grace opened her leather suitcase. "I don't feel right leavin' you."

"This is important, Grace. Any information that Bobby or Colonel Etheridge can dig up will be useful."

Josephine was able to convince Grace, but Anton took a little more persuading.

"I do not have the baron's permission," he said, shaking his head.

"You don't have the baron's permission, but you have my orders. If the baron is angry, he can take it out on me."

"It is not a question of his being angry with me. I must protect him while he rests. He was gravely wounded last night," Anton argued.

Josephine rubbed absently at the small marks on her neck. "I know. And I appreciate your concern for him. But I can look after him."

Anton looked at her as though she'd just told him that she could lift a car over her head. "I don't…"

"You will drive Grace back to Sumter in my car and—"

"Drive? You want me to *drive*?" Anton interrupted, his eyes aglow at the thought of driving

"Yes, drive. Now listen, Grace needs to make a call once you reach the mainland. When you get to Sumter, Deputy Tucker should have a message for me. Once you have it, you must get back here as quickly… as *safely* and quickly as you can. Do you understand?"

"I will get to drive your car," Anton said with the same awe usually reserved for holy relics.

Josephine wasn't sure he'd heard anything she'd said other than the fact that he was going to get to drive. It didn't matter. She'd give Grace very explicit instructions that would include sending Anton back with any information Bobby was able to obtain.

"I have a… just one… question, Miss Josephine." Anton wiped his hands up and down his pants nervously.

"What is it?"

"The pedals… You know, the pedals on the floor of your car. Yes, are they the same… order as in the baron's car?" She stared at him. "I don't suppose it matters…"

"It matters a great deal, Anton. How often has the baron let you drive his car?"

"Oh, many… several many times." He waved the question away. "I was very good. Just like driving a wagon." He smiled broadly.

Josephine had ridden with Mr. Gassmann on his milkman's wagon when she was a child. He'd let her hold the reins and steer the horses around town for a couple of blocks. She couldn't think of a single way that driving horses and driving a car were similar.

"Yes, the pedals are on the same side. Clutch, brake, pedal."

"Good, good!" Anton said with a broad smile.

Josephine left Blasko's room wondering if it wouldn't be

better to let Grace drive, even though she had never driven a car in her life as far as Josephine knew.

Josephine spent the next half hour writing up the list of names and background questions that she wanted Bobby to research. At least as much as he could in twenty-four hours. At one point, she had to go down to the foyer and sneak a look at the hotel's register to make sure she had the correct spelling of all the guests' names.

Back upstairs, she folded the message into an envelope and gave it to Grace, then they both went to fetch Anton.

"What is that?" Josephine asked, when Anton met them at the door holding a package the size of dress box in his hands.

"Nothing," Anton told her, remembering what Blasko had said about not letting even Josephine see the book.

"It is clearly something," she said, exasperated.

"Sorry, Miss… It is… my undergarments. I wish to wash them when I get home," Anton said, showing his crooked teeth in a small smile.

Josephine didn't believe for a minute that he was taking his underwear with him, but there wasn't time to argue.

"Fine. Just go," she said, and they followed him down the stairs and out to the car.

"Show me how you start it and how you change gears," Josephine told Anton once he was seated behind the wheel with the seat adjusted as far forward as it would go.

He gave her a passable explanation of how to operate the car. Josephine decided it was the best she could hope for.

"Be safe. Go as fast as you can without speeding or running off the road. If anyone stops you, give them this note."

She'd written a short letter explaining that the two occupants of the car were on a mission to deliver a letter to the acting sheriff of Semmes County, Alabama. At the bottom, she'd added contact information for herself, Colonel Etheridge and Bobby Tucker.

Watching Anton hesitantly drive away from the curb with

Grace sitting nervously beside him, Josephine raised her eyes to heaven and said a little prayer.

CHAPTER SEVENTEEN

As she turned to go back into the hotel, two other vehicles pulled up. One was an old Model A Ford with a star on the side. Its engine sputtered to a halt as Sheriff Gentry climbed out, brushing past Josephine as he headed onto the porch and into the hotel. He was followed by the two local men who had gone to the mainland to find him. They all looked grim.

Josephine hurried inside and up the stairs as quickly as she could. She saw one of the men point to the door of Brock's room and the sheriff barged inside without knocking. The two men hung back, but Josephine slipped by them and followed the sheriff into the room.

"Where's the body?" Sheriff Gentry barked at Donavan.

"In the tub." Donavan pointed toward the bathroom.

The sheriff's boots clumped across the pine floor as he entered the bathroom. Josephine glanced at Neith and Donavan as she followed the sheriff.

He went to the body without even glancing around the room. Gentry stood looking down at the dead Wallace Brock for a couple of minutes, as though looking into a reflecting pool. When he finally turned, he was shocked to see Josephine standing behind him.

"What the hell are you doing in here?" He didn't wait for her to answer. "It was an accidental death."

He started to push past her, but Josephine held her ground. Gentry's only two options were to push her out of the way or to stop. He stopped.

"You didn't even check the body," Josephine accused him.

"Didn't have to. It's obvious he tripped getting into the tub, hit his head and drowned."

"He was getting into the tub in his underwear?"

"People do odd things. What are you doing in here anyway?"

"Apparently I'm keeping an eye on you," she snapped, and could almost see his hackles rise.

"Look, lady. And I say lady, though I don't know what kind of lady would be in a dead man's bathroom looking at him in his underwear. You need to back off."

"I'm not going to respect you as the sheriff until you start acting like one." Josephine crossed her arms and held her ground.

"How would you like to go to jail for obstructing justice?"

"I don't see any justice happening here." As soon as the words were out of her mouth, Josephine saw the sheriff turn a bright red.

"That's enough," he said through gritted teeth. His left hand reached back and pulled a pair of handcuffs from somewhere under his jacket.

Josephine realized that she'd pushed him too far. *What will happen to Dragomir if I'm arrested?* she wondered. With Anton and Grace on their way back to Sumter, she was the only one left who could protect Blasko during the day. The weight of that responsibility hadn't dawned on her until that moment.

"Sheriff, I'm sorry. Two murd… deaths in two days just has me really upset." She did her best little-ol'-me impression and, to her relief, saw the sheriff's muscles relax.

"I'm not sure there *were* two deaths," Gentry said, giving her the eye.

"Yesterday was confusing." She couldn't bring herself to pretend like there hadn't been a murder the day before, but for Blasko's sake she was willing to give the sheriff an out. *It doesn't matter. He's not going to conduct any sort of investigation anyway*, she told herself. Her only objective now was to get through the next ten minutes without being arrested.

"Yeah. I found it a bit confusing myself," the sheriff said with a smirk.

Don't say a word, just smile, Josephine told herself, biting hard on her tongue and moving aside to let Gentry out of the bathroom.

The sheriff stalked out to the hall and told the two men still waiting there that the guest had slipped in the tub and they could do whatever they liked with the body.

"That went well," Donavan said sarcastically once the sheriff was gone.

"Everyone knows that bad things happen on this island," Neith said grimly. "We need to conduct our business as quickly as possible." She headed out of the room before she was done speaking.

"I guess we can finish searching his room. We need to find out if he has any relatives," Josephine said.

"I'm going back to Captain Hume's room. Neith is right. We need to start the search for the treasure as soon as we can," Donavan told her and followed Neith down the hall.

"You can't... leave me with this mess," Josephine finished to herself once she realized she was alone. "Damn it," she muttered. "Okay, if I was an undercover cop, where would I put my wallet when I went to bed?"

She walked around the room again. A coat and a pair of pants were hanging on the back of a chair, but neither of them revealed a wallet.

"Oh, I'd keep it with my gun," she said aloud as the thought came to her. Going back to the bed, she lifted the mattress as best she could and saw a brown leather wallet just beyond the gun.

Inside the wallet, she found fifty-two dollars and a pay stub from the University of Chicago made out to Wallace Brock. Digging a little deeper, she found an ID hidden in a fold of the wallet. It was for a Manfred Brock with the Chicago Police Department. Josephine put everything back inside the wallet and slipped it into the pocket of her dress.

Out in the hallway, she could hear Mrs. Lachlan down in the lobby, talking with the two local men. "He can't lie up there all day," the woman said, sounding scandalized.

"I don't think Henry can get over here much before two or three. He's got a funeral in Perry."

"He's got men working for him, doesn't he?" Mrs. Lachlan's voice was growing shrill.

"Okay, I'll drive over and see if we can't get them to do something," one of the men said, trying to placate Mrs. Lachlan.

"Someone should let the water out of the tub. Otherwise he'll… get… Well, it won't help matters."

"You have a point there. I'll go up and take care of it. Guess I'll cover him up too."

"Someone will have to notify his family," the other man said.

"You'd think that good-for-nothing sheriff would have taken that on."

"I'll search the room and see if I can come up with a home address or something."

"Maybe one of the other guests would know. They've all been very chummy lately." Mrs. Lachlan sounded like she didn't approve of her guests being so friendly with each other.

Josephine patted the wallet in her pocket, realizing that she'd assumed some responsibility for contacting Brock's family. She wished she'd known about the other name he used before she'd sent Grace off, but without access to a phone there wasn't much she could do until Anton returned.

She went to Blasko's room to check on him. She found

everything neat and tidy. For all of Anton's scruffy appearance, she had to hand it to him that he took good care of Blasko's personal affairs. She double-checked to make sure that the coffin was securely closed and that all the curtains where pinned tightly shut.

She was hesitant to leave Blasko unattended, but she was too worked up to stay inside the room and wait for nightfall. Despite all that had happened, it was still only eleven o'clock. She wondered what the treasure hunters were up to, but she also knew that she should check on Franklin Carter. She wanted to talk with him.

"I'm going to be gone for a little while, but I promise I'll be as quick as I can," Josephine said, placing a hand on Blasko's coffin. She didn't know if he could hear her or not, but saying it made her feel better about leaving him.

Out in the hall, she hesitated, then decided to go to her room and retrieve the revolver she'd brought with her. However, she didn't want to carry it in town with her, so she decided to leave it in Blasko's room so that it would be there when she got back. When she returned, she planned to spend the rest of the afternoon guarding his coffin while she read a book.

Downstairs, she saw Donavan on his way out, carrying a satchel.

"Where are you off to?" she asked, following him into the street.

"Well… I'm… You should have been at the meeting," he said, evading her question.

"I was dealing with other matters. Like your partner's dead body."

"He wasn't my partner." Donavan sighed. "Okay, look, we think we've figured out what island your letter was talking about. We're headed out there now."

"You don't think you need the rest of the letter?"

"We're hoping something will stick out when we get there. Otherwise I doubt we stand much of a chance of finding the treasure without more of the directions." He looked anxiously toward one of the boats tied up at the docks. Josephine could just make out a couple of figures walking on deck.

"They'll leave without me if I don't get down there," Donavan said, already walking away.

"Didn't you offer to take me out on your boat?" she chided him.

"Maybe tomorrow," Donavan yelled over his shoulder.

"Yeah, thanks," Josephine said, irritated at the turn of events. She wanted to go down and get on the boat with the others, but she couldn't bring herself to leave Blasko or abandon Carter in whatever condition he was in. With a sigh, she turned in the direction of Mrs. Sharp's cabin.

"It's Josephine. Let me in," she said once she was on the porch.

"No," Carter said from the other side of the door.

"At least you're answering me today."

"I couldn't let you in yesterday. And not today either. I can't let you to see me… like this." From the sound of his voice, Carter was barely hanging on to his sanity.

"Franklin, please let me in. I want to talk with you. You can hide—"

"I don't know… I need more liquor. Can you get me more liquor?"

"Yes, I promise. Let me in now, then I'll see about getting you something more to drink."

Finally, she heard him throw back the latch on the door and he opened it slowly. His angular face was covered in sweat.

A horrible smell assaulted Josephine's nostrils as a small bit of air escaped the house. She pushed her way inside with a gentle nudge of the door. Carter kept his arm hidden behind him as he backed away into the room.

"Don't try to see it," he warned her.

"No, of course not." She moved toward the kitchen. "Let me open some of the shutters and let a little fresh air in. I promise no one will see you."

Josephine took it as consent when he didn't answer. With several of the shutters open and some fresh air moving through the cottage, he seemed to relax. And Josephine was able to breathe.

"I messed up," Carter said, dropping into a chair at the kitchen table.

"Dragomir told me what happened."

"He was right about that book."

"You misjudged him before. He is a good man."

"Man?" Carter appeared about to argue, then looked down at the bag covering his arm and gave an eerie laugh that caused a chill to run up Josephine's back. "I guess I shouldn't be too judgmental about who's a man and who isn't."

"Don't be too hard on yourself."

His face scrunched up into a look of self-loathing and he pulled the bag from his arm, holding it up in front of Josephine

She couldn't help but be repulsed. The tentacles were still in the process of growing back, now about half the size they'd been when Blasko had first seen them. With sick fascination, Josephine counted five of the four-inch-long wiggly appendages on the end of his arm. Scaly, leathery skin extended up from his elbow.

"What do you say now? Do I have a right to wallow in self-pity?"

Internally, Josephine screamed, *Yes! Yes, you do!* But aloud she said, "We'll help you through this," hoping that she wasn't being too optimistic.

"Did Blasko tell you that he chopped it off? It grew back. A freakish miracle if there ever was one." With that, he broke into peals of laughter so loud that Josephine thought she should close the shutters again so the neighbors wouldn't hear.

Reluctantly, Josephine moved closer to him and, with a great effort of will, put her arm around him and hugged him. His maniacal laughter turned into soft tears, which quickly gave way to sobs. At one point his tentacles touched her back, and every muscle in her body tensed as she tried desperately not to scream.

Carter's weeping finally ended and Josephine sat down across from him at the table. For her own sanity, she needed to put distance between herself and the wriggling set of tentacles growing out of the end of his arm.

He looked at her and said, his voice calm and flat, "Make me a promise."

"What?"

"If we can't find a… cure for this, promise that you'll kill me, or have Blasko do it. Just don't leave me like this."

A part of Josephine wanted to give him a bunch of platitudes to reassure him that it wouldn't come to that, but she knew that wouldn't be fair. "I promise."

Eventually, she closed the shutters and left him sitting at the kitchen table after assuring him that she'd run up to the hotel and return quickly with some hard liquor to help medicate the horrors filling his mind.

"I just want to buy a couple of pints," Josephine told Mrs. Lachlan.

"Hard to come by still, even though the national prohibition is over. Not like you can buy it free and clear anywhere around here."

Josephine held up a twenty-dollar bill and all of Mrs. Lachlan's objections vanished. With the two bottles in hand, Josephine made her way back to Carter's house.

"Leave it on the porch," he told her through the door.

"That's silly. I've already seen… everything." She tried to sound persuasive, though the truth was she didn't want to have to confront that horror again. "Fine. I'm leaving two bottles."

She hadn't even made it to the road when she heard the door open and close behind her.

Instead of turning back for the hotel, Josephine found

herself wandering down to the water and along the docks. She was curious to see if there would be any sign of Blasko's altercation with the fisherman. Sure enough, she could see a streak of red on the side of the wheelhouse of one of the more ragged-looking boats.

"I wouldn't stare too long at them boats," said a voice, startling Josephine.

Looking around and seeing no one, she guessed that the voice had come from a boat docked next the one still stained with Blasko's blood.

"I was just admiring them," she said in the direction of the voice.

"Trawlers. That's what they're called. You're part of that bunch up at the hotel, aren't ya?" The man still did not reveal himself and Josephine wondered why. What hideous deformities was *he* hiding?

"You a fisherman?" she asked.

"Aye. Not up to the level of some, but I'm a competent hand."

Suddenly the old man came out of the shadows of the wheelhouse. After all that had happened, it was a shock for Josephine to see that he appeared almost completely normal. *Almost* normal, because he wore a hat pulled down low over his head. No hair showed and Josephine figured he was bald, but what caught her eye was the leathery skin around his temples and along the back of his neck. To her eyes, it closely resembled the skin of Carter's mutated arm.

"Why don't the men go fishing during the day?" Josephine was having a hard time not staring at the man's strange skin.

"Catch more fish at night." He looked at her with unblinking eyes.

"I just thought… Other fishermen I've known go out during the day."

"Do they catch as many fish?"

"I… Maybe not."

"See." He picked up a piece of hemp rope that was lying

across a wooden box and began to absentmindedly tie it into different knots. "'Sides, our men *like* fishing at night."

Josephine could swear that the man hadn't blinked the entire time they'd been talking.

"I guess I should get back to the hotel," she said awkwardly.

"Stay a minute if you want. I'll show you how to tie knots." He held out the rope to her.

The offer seemed more than a little bit odd. Josephine couldn't decide if he was mentally slow or if he was finding the conversation as awkward as she was.

"I learned some woodsmen knots when I was in school. We had a club. Now they have the Girl Scouts." She knew she was rambling, but he didn't seem to mind. He was still holding the rope out to her. Impulsively, she took it and tied a square knot.

"Good knot. Basic, but good."

Though her hands were shaking, she tied a sheet bend, though she couldn't have said what it was called. Her mind was screaming for her to leave this odd old man, but still she stayed.

"You can come onto the boat if you want to. I'd be glad to show you around."

Remembering Blasko's encounter, there was no way that she was going to set one foot onto this man's boat, even in broad daylight.

"I need to get back to the hotel." She held the rope out to him, her paranoia warning her not to let him reach out for the rope and grab her arm.

"You got a little time, surely. Hey, my name is Enoch. What's yours?"

"Josephine."

"Josie. That's nice. Let me take you on a tour." He took the rope from her hand and dropped it into the boat, then reached back out for her hand.

She backed away. "I really need to go."

"I thought you had questions. Wanted to know more

about us. Isn't that what all you tourists want?"

Josephine realized that he was trying to keep her there, but why? Was he going to assault her as soon as he had the chance? As she tried to break away from whatever strange mental hold Enoch had on her, an image of Blasko's coffin alone in the hotel flashed into her mind. While it had usually seemed that their shared blood bond only ever alerted Blasko when *she* was in danger, this time she was sure the tables were reversed. Someone was trying to get to Blasko!

CHAPTER EIGHTEEN

Without a word, she turned and began to hurry toward the hotel. At first she tried to keep calm and not attract attention. But as her heart pounded faster, she gave up all pretense and started to run.

"Hey, you come back here!" shouted the fisherman.

Josephine could hear him running behind her, but he was no match for her. The next time he shouted, his voice was far behind her and the hotel was only a block away.

She was mad at herself for leaving Blasko alone so long and her anger drove her to run faster. In her haste, she tripped climbing the porch steps of the hotel, falling hard on her knees. She ignored the pain and clambered back to her feet, running inside.

"Hey!" Mrs. Lachlan said, startled by Josephine's sudden appearance.

Josephine ignored her and hit the stairs still running, but being more careful where she placed her feet. At the top of the stairs, she could see that Blasko's door was slightly ajar and she headed straight for it.

Two men were standing over Blasko's coffin, looking startled as she burst into the room. The man farthest from her held a boat hook in his hand. The other man had been jostling the coffin, but now stood looking at Josephine. She had envisioned throwing herself at anyone who was in the room, but the men's appearance and the fact that there were two of them caused her to stop.

They were hideous abominations of men, with bulbous black eyes. They had large lips and their mouths opened and closed like fish out of water. There were only a few tufts of hair sticking to their scaly scalps and their hands were covered in the same rough skin as Carter's arm. When the man closest to her reached out to grab her, she realized that his fingers were webbed.

Josephine jumped back and looked around for a weapon, finally remembering the revolver. She'd left it in a drawer of the nightstand. She dodged the creature reaching for her and made for the nightstand. The monster lunged after her, but seemed to trip over its own feet. However, his movement carried enough momentum to send him crashing into Josephine and they both went down. Josephine reached out with her hand, but she was still a foot short of being able to open the nightstand drawer. The creature was clawing its way on top of her, while the other one was standing next to Blasko's coffin, looking indecisively back and forth from the fight to the boat hook in its hand.

Josephine had two choices. She could roll onto her back and face the creature or she could try to crawl closer to the nightstand. She knew she'd never be able to fight him off on her own, so her only real option was to acquire a weapon.

Pulling herself along the hard pine floor was next to impossible with almost two-hundred pounds of manfish on her back. What saved her was being able to get one foot lodged against a leg of the bed. Pushing off the bed with all her strength, she was just able to reach the nightstand. Without any hesitation, she pulled the piece of furniture down on top of herself and the thing clinging to her back.

She ducked her head as she pulled the nightstand over, leaving the creature's head to take the brunt of the marble top. The thing howled and let go of Josephine long enough that she rolled over and was able to open the drawer. Triumphantly retrieving the revolver, she pushed it flat up against the head of the beast that had been on her back, but was now keening softly while holding onto its skull.

"Neither of you move, or so help me I'll kill him," she growled as best she could between deep, panting breaths.

The creature standing above Blasko's coffin turned and stared at Josephine with those black, unblinking eyes. Josephine was sure that it was trying to assess her resolve.

"This is a .45 caliber Colt revolver. The hole that it will make in your friend's head would kill any animal in this state." She watched as the hand holding the boat hook slowly drifted down to the creature's side. "Drop it!" she ordered, cocking the pistol for emphasis. The boat hook was released with a loud *thunk* on the floor.

"This one damn near killed my father," the creature said in a watery voice, pointing a finger a Blasko's coffin.

"How did you know he was in there?"

"I know," the creature grumbled.

"Your… father attacked the baron," Josephine said, trying to scoot into a better position. She didn't like touching the one that was still holding its head and whining.

"Snooping, prying. One of you killed my friend yesterday." The creature hesitated for a moment before pointing his finger at Josephine. "You were there!"

"Your friend stole a letter from me."

"All of you must go. You are a threat to us."

Before Josephine could say anything, the creature on the floor flopped around and snapped at her arm. She yelped out of reflex and shock, dropping the pistol, which went off with an ear-shattering explosion. The bullet slammed harmlessly in the floorboards, but smoke filled the room and the creatures fled out onto the balcony.

As Josephine was recovering her wits, she heard footsteps pounding up the stairs. Thinking quickly, she slipped into the hallway, holding the gun by two fingers.

"What in heaven's name!" Mrs. Lachlan said when she

saw Josephine. The odd-looking young woman was behind her.

"I'm so sorry. I was fooling around with the baron's pistol and the darn thing just went off. Silly of me. I don't know a thing about guns. I just thought that, with a murder in the hotel, I ought to have some sort of protection." Josephine worked hard at selling her helpless-woman impression.

"You should leave those things alone. Where is the baron?"

"He's in his room. His sun allergy, you know. He told me that I better come out here and tell you what happened."

"Is he all right?" Mrs. Lachlan sounded unsure.

Josephine looked past her at the strange young woman who had helped with the meals and cleaning. The woman looked much more distressed than Mrs. Lachlan.

Did she know that those creatures were in Dragomir's room? Did she tell them where to find him? Josephine wondered. If so, then the fear in her eyes was all for her accomplices' safety.

"The baron is fine. He'll be down for dinner after it gets dark," Josephine reassured Mrs. Lachlan while watching the girl's eyes. They kept flicking toward Blasko's door. "He's fine," Josephine said, putting the emphasis on the pronoun.

The young woman seemed to pick up on it and looked straight at Josephine with suspicion in her eyes.

Josephine turned away from both of them and went back into Blasko's room. To her relief, the coffin seemed undamaged. Looking the box over carefully, she felt sure that he was all right.

She cleaned up the room and locked the door leading to the balcony. Satisfied that she'd done everything she could, she settled down in the most comfortable chair in the room with the revolver on her lap.

About four in the afternoon, she heard men coming up the stairs. From the conversation she could hear, she figured out they were the men sent from the funeral parlor on the mainland to gather up Wallace Brock's body. Forty-five minutes later, she heard them grunt and grumble as they carried the body down the stairs.

The treasure hunters returned at almost six. Josephine felt assured enough of Blasko's safety that she stepped out to talk with them. A single look at Donavan told her that she hadn't missed anything but bugs, heat and humidity.

"Nothing," he told her. "The island's all sand. I could bury a car out there today and, if there was a decent wind tonight, you wouldn't be able to tell where it was tomorrow. It's like the snow back home, only it never melts. Though I damn near melted in all this heat."

"What's the next step?" Josephine asked him.

"We'll go back tomorrow. There are only three choices. Find the other half of the letter, give up, or search some more. We all agreed to continue the search."

"What if one of you has the other half of the letter?"

"Ha! We've agreed to sleep in one room. The ladies get the bed." Donavan sighed. "I can't wait for a bath."

Josephine watched him walk away, his head hung low and his attitude defeated.

For the next two hours, Josephine paced Blasko's room. Her nerves were on edge as she wondered if Grace and Anton had made it home safely. Waiting for Blasko to wake up only added to her anxiety. Had the two creatures she'd found in the room done something that she hadn't noticed? Had Blasko been able to recover from the wound to his chest? As she waited for sunset, the hands of the clock on the mantel moved at a maddeningly slow pace.

At last she heard the sound of the interior locks on the coffin being pulled open. With a creak, the lid rose and Blasko sat up, looking much better than the night before.

Before he could say a word, Josephine threw herself across the room and wrapped her arms around him.

Shocked at her presence, he could only ask, "Where is Anton?"

"I asked him to drive Grace home."

"To Sumter? Why?"

"I have several questions for Bobby and the colonel."

"I thought I heard… Something disturbed my sleep. But I was still healing and couldn't…"

"Things have happened."

Josephine helped him out of the coffin. Taken aback by her distress, Blasko sat with her on the bed and held her close as she went on to tell him about Brock's death and the two intruders who had tried to break into his coffin.

"Who do you think killed Brock?" Blasko asked when she was done.

"One of the group… maybe. I was sure of it until I found those two… creatures in your room. If they broke in here, then they might have done the same to Brock. Drowning would seem like a logical way for them to kill someone."

"But you found his gun under the mattress… He would've had to have been taken by surprise, or been met by overwhelming force. Otherwise, there would have been a loud struggle."

"Add to that the fact that I think he was a police officer. Just from the way he was acting around us and the others, it's clear that he was cautious. I don't think he would have let the two men I saw into his room without his gun on him."

"Could they have picked the lock? Or come in from the balcony?"

"The door onto the balcony was unlocked. But there weren't any pry marks and I can't imagine that Brock wouldn't have locked it before going to bed."

"So he let whoever killed him into his room."

"There is one other possibility," Josephine said reluctantly. "I think the young woman who works for Mrs. Lachlan may be… one of those things. I'm pretty sure she knew that those two men were in your room. I suspect that she let them in… or gave them a key."

"So they could have come in without his knowing it and hit him with something in the back of the head."

"Maybe. But I looked at his pillow and there wasn't any

blood or hair on it."

"Mmmm. But you say there was definitely blood on the tub?"

"Yes. And I don't believe the sheriff's version of events for a moment. He just doesn't want anything to do with this island."

"After what I've seen, I can't say that I blame him." Blasko was deep in thought. "The easiest explanation is that someone Brock knew knocked on his balcony door, or came there by prearrangement."

"Someone he trusted."

"Precisely. He let them in and, during the course of their meeting, he turned his back and they took the opportunity to hit him over the head."

"Then dragged him into the bathroom and drowned him in the tub."

"Could you have done it?" When Josephine looked puzzled, Blasko explained. "Do you think that you could have physically hit him over the head and put his unconscious body into the tub?"

"He wasn't a big man. A little taller than me, but yes, I think I could," Josephine answered. "You're wondering if Neith or Jamila could have done it. I'd say yes. It wouldn't be easy, but it's definitely possible."

"Would he have answered the door in his underwear if it was one of the ladies?"

"Depends on why they were coming to his room," Josephine said and felt herself blushing. "Of course, he was an arrogant man, so if a lady knocked on his door in the middle of the night, he might have assumed that her reasons were romantic."

"But one of those two?"

"They're both attractive."

"That's not the point. If he was suspicious of the group, would he really have dropped his guard, even if he thought he might... ah... spend the night with one of them?"

"My experience with men is that they are always ready to

drop their… guard for a pretty woman," Josephine said.

"Yes. And I would have said that about myself until the day I saw a Turkish woman seduce and slaughter one of my closest allies. Now that I recall the incident, the word 'slaughter' doesn't do justice to her work," Blasko said thoughtfully.

"I don't want to hear about it." Josephine shook her head. "I say it must have been one of the remaining five."

"Motive?"

"Money. More of the treasure and less to split."

Blasko nodded, but suggested another theory. "If Brock was a policeman, then maybe he had information that the killer didn't want anyone else to know. Such as who killed your attacker."

"I can see that."

"Or Brock was the one with the other half of your letter," Blasko said contrarily.

"Then that would mean there are two murderers in the group. Brock and whoever killed *him*."

Blasko nodded. "It's not impossible, though I agree that it seems improbable. Especially if no one has yet found the treasure. I could more easily imagine someone going over the edge if they already knew the location of the artifacts and the gold."

"Makes sense. So if there is only one murderer, then he or she has the other half of the letter. Brock might have been onto him and so the killer had to silence him."

"It makes sense as to motive," Blasko cautioned, "but it confuses the opportunity. If Brock was on to the killer, he wouldn't have let them into his room without retrieving his gun."

"Maybe there are two people involved. A woman to entice him to open the door, followed by the killer. Maybe she even knocked Brock out before letting the killer inside."

"Anytime you involve more than one person, I think the probability goes down. No one in this group seems to trust any of the others enough to involve them in their plan."

They were silent as they thought about all the possibilities. Finally, Josephine said, "You need to get ready for dinner. I want to prove to Mrs. Lachlan that I didn't kill you."

"We'll tackle the suspects after dinner?"

Josephine nodded. "They will object after spending the day on that island, but they *did* agree to be questioned."

"If they're tired, then their guard might be down," Blasko said, reaching for his coat and tie.

Josephine went to her own room to freshen up. Spending the afternoon cooped up in a sultry hotel room had left her feeling like she'd been out in a rainstorm, and not even a refreshing rainstorm.

Downstairs they found a dispirited group sitting around the dining room table, picking at the pork chops Mrs. Lachlan had served them. The young woman who helped her was busy serving drinks and avoided making eye contact with Josephine.

After Blasko and Josephine joined the group, there was little conversation. Almost everyone who had gone out to the island seemed to be suffering from various degrees of sunburn. Only Neith appeared not to have been burned due to her dark complexion.

"Maybe we should take tomorrow off," Captain Hume suggested, looking up from his plate. This suggestion received hard stares from everyone else.

Josephine said, "The baron and I want to talk with each of you this evening. Remember our agreement."

"Why?" Donavan asked.

"Because we had a deal."

"Well, then, talk to me first. I don't plan on being awake much longer than it takes me to get upstairs," Donavan told her.

"We will all uphold our end of the bargain." Hume seemed to have aged ten years in the last twelve hours.

"Thank you," Blasko said. "We need to solve these murders before another person is killed." His words caused everyone around the table to look at each other with something less than charity in their eyes.

"Sheriff Gentry said that Brock's death was an accident." Jamila never looked up from her plate.

"None of us believes that," Zhao said. "I, too, want to see the killer caught."

"Are you saying I don't?" Donavan seemed to take an unusual amount of umbrage at Zhao's statement. Josephine suspected that something must have happened between them on the island that day.

"We all want the person who killed Brock to be apprehended. Plain and simple," Hume said with a bit of his old starch back in his voice. "I'll talk to you anytime you want."

"Thank you, Captain. We'll let you all choose the order you want," Josephine said.

"We're all staying in the same room now." He tapped his nose. "Security, you know."

"Good. And we'd prefer that you all don't talk about what we ask you. No comparing notes," Josephine told him.

"Like real detectives. I served on the adjutant general's staff for six months during the Great War. Did a little investigating myself. I'll help out if you need it."

Josephine just smiled politely at the captain.

CHAPTER NINETEEN

After dinner, Josephine and Blasko set up a table and chairs for the interviews in Josephine's room. Eric Donavan was the first to knock on the door.

"I want to say right off that I think this is a waste of time," Donavan stated as he took his seat across from them.

"You didn't raise any objections when you wanted to get a look at my letter," Josephine said.

"I didn't get a look at the letter. Zhao did."

"That was the deal."

"And I don't like it. I think he's got the other half and spent the day misleading the rest of us. I believe his plan is to sit on it until we all get tired and go home."

"You think he was purposefully misleading you today?"

"That's what I said. Can't prove it without looking at the letter."

"We went through that when we made the deal. Forget it," Josephine said. She let him pout for a minute, then asked, "How well did you know Wallace Brock?"

"Met him here like the everyone else. All I know is what he told me."

"Which was?"

"He said he was a professor of cultural anthropology at

the University of Chicago. Said his specialty was Mesoamerican culture; you know, Mayans, Aztecs. That's why he was here. The letter to his department listed a number of Aztec and Mayan artifacts."

"Did he seem like a professor to you?"

"Are you talking about the stereotypical professor with pince-nez glasses and his face always in a book? No, not really. Seemed like a tough guy; I thought he could be a cop of some sort. I wasn't at all surprised when we found that gun under his bed. 'Course he might have just been another guy who served in the Army. But my vote is 'no' on the professor gig."

"What about you?" Josephine asked.

"What do you mean?"

"Are you who you say you are?"

"Hey, I thought you were investigating the murder."

"Murders, plural. Yes, we are. And knowing all the players at the table is a good first step," Blasko said with authority.

Josephine watched him, amazed at the power of her blood to heal him. He'd waved away any concerns she still had about his wound as though it had been nothing.

"I'm exactly who I say I am," Donavan mumbled. "Trust me, no one else would want to be me, and *I* have a hard enough time being me. Not sure I could pull off being anyone else."

Josephine believed him.

"You told me who you are, and why you're here. Did you know any of the others before you came to the island?" she asked.

"I'd heard of Captain Hume. He's made a couple of impressive discoveries in the Middle East. The rest…" He shrugged.

"Who do you think is the killer?"

"I told you, Zhao."

"What makes you think it's him?"

"He's cold. Also, I was with him all day today. I tell you,

he was leading us around by the nose. We'd start searching one place and then he'd get some new idea. What's really screwy about it is, it's not like him. When we play cards, he knows what he's going to do as soon as he looks at his hand. Hell, he knows what *I'm* going to do before I do it. Trust me. He's your man."

"Where were you yesterday morning around nine-thirty?"

"When you were attacked? I guess I was up in my room writing," he said cagily.

"Writing what?"

"A bloody paper for a magazine. What do you think? My department head is breathing down my neck. If this treasure doesn't pan out, I need a back-up plan, so I'm writing a couple of articles."

"On the fishermen?" Blasko asked, thinking about his conversation with Donavan that first night near the docks.

"Anything I wrote about them, I couldn't get published. Not by any normal magazine."

"What would you write?" Blasko pressed.

"Have you seen them? I mean up close? I think they're a breeding… I should say an inbreeding population. You've seen the way they walk. Their skin is worse. A mutation or disease that's genetic. I don't know. I tried to talk to them down at The Dragon. Big mistake. I didn't tell anyone, but after I asked a couple of questions and didn't get any answers, I left the bar and got rolled. Funny thing was, they didn't take my wallet or my watch. They just pounded me with wooden clubs. The kind you use to kill a big fish when you land it. They kept hitting my chest and stomach so the bruises wouldn't show, telling me to stay away if I knew what was good for me."

"But they didn't kill you," Blasko said.

"Obviously not. They weren't trying to. They were sending a message and I got it loud and clear."

"Can you tell us anything else about them?"

Donavan sighed. "When I was working on my doctorate, I went to New Guinea to observe some of the tribes there.

They were peaceful as long as you posed no threat. Even friendly sometimes, but it was like walking on a razor's edge. If the mood shifted and they thought you were a danger to them, there'd be no question what would happen to you. No negotiation. No trial. No hesitation. They'd kill you, and they just might eat you as well. That's what it feels like when you get close to these fisherman, that they're all of a kind. Their deformities make them closer than a normal human social group. Like isolation and inbreeding did with those tribes in New Guinea."

"One of them attacked me last night," Blasko said, watching Donavan closely. Josephine tried to hide her surprise that he'd mentioned the attack.

"You got too close." Donavan shook his head. "I'm exhausted. Can we wrap this up?"

Blasko thought about the blood on Donavan's shoe. "Did you follow Josephine when she went to the post office yesterday?"

"No…" The way his voice trailed off suggested that he might have more to say.

"But you know something about her attack?" Blasko pressed.

"Not much. I…"

"*What* do you know?" Josephine demanded.

"I saw the dead body," Donavan admitted. "I was coming up from the docks when I heard something. I saw Josephine come out of the alley, so I looked in and saw the body with the knife sticking out of its back. I ran to the man, confirmed that he was very dead and hurried back to the hotel."

"Why didn't you say anything?"

"I didn't want to get involved. If I'd backed up your story with the sheriff, he might have started to ask questions and our attempts to find the gold might have been exposed. I couldn't afford for that to happen. Once the body went missing and the sheriff dropped it, I figured there wasn't any point."

Josephine glared at him.

"That's enough for now," Blasko said quickly, not wanting to see a full-blown fight break out between Josephine and Donavan. "Captain Hume told us that you are all staying in his room tonight."

"Yep. Guess that will give Mrs. Lachlan something to talk about if she finds out." He stood up, not meeting Josephine's angry gaze. "I tell you, I don't trust any of them. Especially not Zhao. I'll be sleeping right next to him and, I promise you, I won't be sleeping soundly."

"Send in Jamila," Blasko told him as he left.

He raised his hand in acknowledgement and staggered a little as he went out the door.

"He's being mostly honest. Which either means that he's innocent or he knows how to lie," Blasko said, neatly summing up Josephine's own thoughts on Donavan.

"He's an ass," she snarled, then relaxed a bit. "But I agree that he was being honest."

"Which blows up our one piece of solid evidence, the blood on his shoe," Blasko sighed.

"We'd already agreed that it wasn't much of a clue," Josephine reminded him.

The door opened and Jamila walked in, giving Blasko and Josephine a wary look. "I don't know what you two think you're playing at. You are not the police."

"Humor us," Blasko said, gesturing for her to have a seat.

"Ha! I don't even know what I'm playing at. Digging in the sand, looking for artifacts that probably aren't there."

"You are from Spain?" Blasko confirmed.

"Yes, though there are those who wouldn't consider a Gitano really Spanish."

"You must have worked very hard to get where you are," Blasko said with more than a little admiration in his voice.

"I was fortunate to have received an opportunity to study at the University of Seville. Now I'm an academic and I should be digging through library stacks. I came to this country to do research into the great gold fleets of the 1500s.

I was reviewing log books that a collector had donated to the library in Arkham, Massachusetts."

This caught Josephine's attention. "Do you know a man named Franklin Carter?"

Jamila's eyes became hooded. "What do you know of Franklin?"

"So you *do* know him."

"I've never met him, but I corresponded with him several times. He… helped me with my research. But what does he have to do with this?"

Josephine weighed the pros and cons of telling the truth. Finally, she said, "He was the one who sent the letters to everyone."

"Ahhh, that makes sense. I wondered who would have known that I was in America. Is this all some sort of joke that he is playing on us?"

"No. The information in the letters is real, or at least it came from an older source than Franklin Carter."

"How do *you* know Franklin?" Jamila asked again.

"He's my cousin," Josephine said.

"Is he here?" Jamila looked around the room as though she expected Carter to step out of the shadows.

"That's not important right now," Blasko deflected. "Who do you think is the killer?"

"Donavan. He is a disgusting man." She turned her head as though she was looking for somewhere to spit.

"Y'all had an affair?" Josephine asked and saw Jamila grit her teeth.

"He is a pig!"

"What happened?"

"A real man can handle a real woman. We… met and there was an… attraction. Yes, I admit it. But he was jealous of me."

"You mean he was jealous of other men being around you?"

Jamila made a face. "No! That would be what a real man does. No, no, he was jealous because I am a celebrated scholar and he is just an assistant professor at a provincial university."

Blasko looked puzzled. "Exactly how long have you all been on the island?"

"Two veeeeery long weeks."

"So, in two weeks, you all met, had an affair, he became jealous of your scholarship and then you dropped him." Blasko raised his eyebrows at the amount of drama packed into such a short time.

"Exactly. I hate him."

"He didn't mention you," Blasko said and was rewarded with a furious Jamila, who stood up and kicked her chair away from the table.

"How dare he! Ignore *me*? I should teach him a lesson he'll never forget. First he belittles my manuscript on the voyages of Hernán Cortés and now he pretends that he wasn't passionate for me." This time she actually did spit.

"Where were you yesterday morning around the time I was attacked?" Josephine asked, looking to steer the conversation in a more useful direction.

"When the letter was stolen? I was in the dining room eating my breakfast. Remember, I saw you come back to the hotel."

"There were witnesses who saw you at breakfast?"

"Maybe. I don't know. That strange girl who assists Mrs. Lachlan served me. When I finished, I left through the French doors onto the porch."

Blasko and Josephine had agreed not to ask where everyone was when Brock had been killed, as the answer would have been the same for everyone—asleep in their rooms. After a few more questions, they let Jamila go with the promise to send in Captain Hume.

"She certainly has the hot blood needed to kill someone," Josephine observed.

"She could be very dangerous in the heat of the moment," Blasko agreed.

The door opened again and Captain Hume entered,

looking entirely worn out.

"Can I get you something?" Josephine asked with concern.

"Had a brandy after dinner. Best not have any more." He sat down across from them. "Reminds me of the old boards of inquiry I used to run. Bring them in and question them." The old man seemed lost in the past.

"Captain, tell us more about your background," Blasko asked.

"A life spent abroad. Mostly in service. Either in the military or to the Foreign Office."

"But you were involved in some archeological digs in the Middle East, correct?"

"Quite right. I served in the Royal Marines in the South Pacific. Got interested in anthropology and archeology, so I retired and helped the Syrians dig up some of their own relics. British government didn't like it. A former Royal Marine mucking about in the Middle East while they were trying to sort out the borders after the war. Received a reprimand for bad judgment. Reduced my retirement pay to a lieutenant's. Didn't help that I got a bucketful of publicity. Especially over here in the States. It was just a year or so before the discovery of King Tutankhamun's tomb. Of course, that overshadowed anything I'd been a part of. Just as well."

"And you received a letter…" Blasko let it hang, knowing that the captain didn't need any encouragement to talk.

"Precisely. About a month ago. Surprised me. List of Syrian artifacts from a rather obscure cult. Obscure to most, at any rate. However, there was a direct connection to the discoveries I'd helped with in Syria."

"You came here as soon as you got the letter?"

"I'm not sure what this has to do with anything."

"We suspect that Brock wasn't who he said he was. Therefore, we thought it might be prudent to discover whether anyone else is here under false pretenses." Blasko leaned back in his chair and gave Hume a slight smile as he explained his line of questioning. The captain seemed to become more and more agitated as Blasko spoke.

"See here, now. I won't have my honor questioned. I'm Captain Reginald Hume, late of His Majesty's general staff and a decorated member of the Imperial Camel Corps."

His face became red and puffy, and Josephine half expected to see him snap to attention and click his heels. He reminded her a bit of Colonel Etheridge.

"I meant no disrespect, Captain. You said you've conducted investigations in the past, so you understand the need to be thorough," Blasko explained, still leaning back.

"Well, of course. A man just doesn't take kindly to being asked... I'm tired... Long day on that blasted island."

Josephine frowned at Blasko and raised her eyebrows

"I'm sorry, Captain," Blasko said, not sounding sorry at all. "We know you are a loyal subject of His Majesty the King. Tell me, did you ever suspect that Mr. Brock wasn't who he said he was?"

"Never. A man's word... I mean, he presented himself as Wallace Brock from the University of Chicago, and there was no reason to question him."

"Do you feel like you're any closer to finding the treasure?" Josephine asked.

"No, blast it! I talked with Zhao this evening. There are several areas on the island that we still need to search, but nothing we looked at today yielded any clues." He was still breathing heavily from his earlier outrage.

"You need to get some rest," Josephine said. "We'll talk more tomorrow." She stood up and walked him to the door. "Maybe you should take the day off."

"And let the others go on without me? I will not! I came this far."

"Why are you really here?" Josephine asked once they were alone outside the room. Of course, the captain had no way of knowing that Blasko's unnaturally good hearing would pick up every word they said.

"I need this," the old man confessed. "The humiliation I

suffered from the demotion. I am not a wealthy man. The cut in my pay… I have a daughter. I want to leave her something, even if it's just the memory of a father who did everything he could to restore our honor and fortune."

Without another word, he headed back to his room.

CHAPTER TWENTY

"You were a little rough on him," Josephine said when she came back into the room.

"I didn't ask him anything that I haven't asked everyone else. The man is unsteady on his feet, literally and figuratively."

"I doubt he's our killer."

"Why? Because he's getting old? Mark my words, Josie, the old lions are the most dangerous. They have no fear of death, but a great horror at the thought of running out of time."

"Says the man who will never run out of time."

"There will come a day," Blasko said darkly, and Josephine felt a quick rush of fear. But before she could say anything else, the door opened and Neith walked in.

She looked the least tired of the group. She'd taken time to apply fresh makeup and wore a sleek white dress with a gold necklace and bracelets. Josephine was impressed with her elegance. *Why pull out the stops now?* she wondered.

"What a delight to have you join us," Blasko said with a smile, standing and giving her a slight bow.

Of course, that's *the reason for the fancy dress and doodads.* Josephine frowned.

"I enjoyed our talk the other night on the verandah." Neith stepped up to the table and extended her hand to Blasko, who took it and touched it lightly with his lips. Not once did she even glance at Josephine, who felt a snarl rising in her throat.

"Have a seat," Josephine said brusquely. Neith looked at her, then turned back to Blasko and slowly lowered herself to the chair across from them.

"I do not know what I could possibly tell you about the horrible death of Mr. Brock."

"How well did you know him?" Josephine asked before Blasko could say anything.

"Not as well as some," she said coyly, wagging her finger in the universal naughty sign.

"What do you mean by that?" Josephine tossed at her.

Neith turned and faced her, her smile fading. "I think you know what I'm talking about. He was a crude man. Not amusing like our Mr. Donavan. Rough. Others might like that sort, but I do not."

"Do you mean Miss Molina?" Blasko asked. "But I thought she was… interested in Donavan."

"Oh yes. Yes, at first it was Donavan, but then she went after Brock." Facing Blasko again, Neith's smile returned.

"How far did the attraction go?" Josephine asked.

Neith shrugged, never taking her eyes off of Blasko. "Who's to say?"

"Make a guess," Josephine said with a bluntness that caused both Blasko and Neith to stare at her. "Did you ever see Jamila go into Brock's room? Ever see them kiss or hold hands?"

"I saw her rub her hand down his lapel when they were talking in the moonlight in front of the hotel three nights ago."

"Were you jealous?" Josephine wanted to make a dent in the woman's flirty veneer.

"Jealous?" Neith said with a sharp-edged double meaning that caused Josephine's blood pressure to rise even more.

Blasko was looking back and forth between the two women with a mildly shocked expression on his face.

Stop this, Josephine said to herself before her mouth spewed, "Were you jealous of Jamila's attention to Brock?"

"No. I was truthful when I said that Brock was crude. I like my men suave." She flicked her eyes in Blasko's direction, who cleared his throat and looked over at Josephine as if to say, *What can I do?*

"Tell us about your background," Josephine said, forcing a smile that didn't fool anyone.

"You said that you are here to study the Timucua mounds," Blasko reminded Neith.

A crooked smile appeared on her face. "That may not be the whole truth."

"You received a letter like everyone else, didn't you?" Josephine interjected.

"The Egyptian Museum in Cairo did. I… found it and here I am."

"What do you mean you *found* it?" Josephine asked.

Neith rolled her eyes and sighed dramatically. "I open the mail for the director of the museum. Sometimes I read the letters."

"You're his secretary?" Josephine leaned forward.

"My father was a clerk at the museum. He taught me a great deal about Egyptian history and artifacts. More than some of the college-educated people who work at the museum. I recognized several of the items listed in the letter as pieces that had gone missing before the turn of the century. My father kept records of items which were stolen or lost."

"So you just decided to come over here and recover them?" Josephine sounded suspicious.

"That's right. I wanted to prove that I can be more than a secretary." For the first time, Neith looked humble, turning her eyes to look out the window at the stars. Josephine was surprised to feel a pang of sympathy for her.

"Who do you think killed Brock?"

"Jamila. Women can be very dangerous." Her smile returned.

"Motive?" Josephine asked.

"Love. Sex. Men and women mix and good things, or very bad things, can happen. This time a bad thing happened."

"What about the murder of the man who attacked me?"

"What about it? I don't think that was one of us. You say he was murdered and then the body disappeared. Why would one of us move the body after you saw it? What could we do with the body? You think one of us brought the dead man back up to the hotel and put him in our room? Search us, then."

"You have a point," Blasko admitted, and Josephine had to agree that the disappearing body didn't fit with one of the other guests being the killer. Could there have been two murderers?

"You didn't have to flirt with her," Josephine told Blasko when Neith had gone.

"I wasn't flirting. I was just being polite," he answered, unable to hide a smirk that made Josephine narrow her eyes.

"She was certainly flirting with you."

"Are you surprised?" The smirk grew more prominent.

"You cad," Josephine said, only half in jest.

There was a soft knock on the door before Zhao entered.

"Have a seat." Blasko waved toward the chair.

"How close do you think you were to finding the treasure today?" Josephine asked once he was across from them.

"Close. I'm sure that I read the information in your uncle's letter correctly. If I only had the other half…" He bowed his head.

"You know, some folks think you were being less than honest today."

"Captain Hume believes that if he could see your half of the letter, he could figure out where the treasure is hidden," Zhao said.

"You saw everything that was in the letter. Have you

given him all of that information?" Josephine asked.

"No. We agreed that I'd share it only as needed, in case one of the others has the second half so they won't be able to take the treasure for themselves."

"What if *you* have the other half of the letter?"

"Everyone is watching me very closely. I couldn't use it without all the others knowing."

"Unless you just hold out until all the others give up and go home," Josephine said.

"They are very tenacious. I don't believe that all of them would ever leave unless I do. As you said, they are already suspicious of me."

"Were you ever suspicious of Wallace Brock?"

"Suspicious? Why would I be? He was like the rest. Interested in the treasure and looking over his shoulder, as they say."

"How did you come to be here?" Blasko asked.

"I am an expert in some... esoteric Chinese subcultures."

"Subcultures?"

"You might call them cults. There were strange idols that they worshiped. The descriptions in the letter that was sent to my university in Hong Kong were reminiscent of items I uncovered in the mountains near Tibet. The department head recognized the relationship and forwarded the letter to me." He spread his arms. "As you see, I am here."

"Who do you think killed Brock?" Josephine asked.

"Maybe he died by accident like the sheriff said."

"Unlikely." Josephine shook her head.

"Yes, you are probably right. I don't know, and I don't really care. I am concerned for my life since obtaining the secrets in your letter, but I don't have any thoughts about pursuing justice for Mr. Brock. During the short time that I got to know him, I never got the impression that he cared anything for me," Zhao said bluntly.

"But you are here answering our questions."

"I am a man of honor. We made a deal."

They let Zhao go.

"We didn't learn much," Josephine said, frowning.

"Perhaps. But I believe that one of them is responsible for Brock's death."

"Several of them are here under somewhat odd circumstances—stealing letters or running off with what should be someone else's job."

"Hardly motives for murder."

"No. I think we know what the motive is. The pot of gold at the end of the rainbow. What we have is a whole group of people who are willing to be deceptive and who want, or even *need*, to find those artifacts."

"True. The trouble with the two murders is that the whole means, motive and opportunity method is useless. They all have the means and opportunity. On top of that, they all have the same motive. Gold."

"So how do we catch a killer if we can't use the usual investigative methods?"

Blasko looked thoughtful for a few minutes, then took Josephine's hands in his. "Don't go to the island with them tomorrow."

"You don't have to worry. I won't leave you unprotected again."

"I'm not worried about myself. But when they return to the island, I want to go. We need to talk them into waiting until tomorrow evening."

"That's going to be a hard sell."

"They're tired. The heat will be miserable during the day."

"Only Neith looked like she escaped getting sunburned," Josephine agreed. "Why do you want to go?"

"I have a plan... or at least the beginnings of a plan. But I'll need to be there."

"Maybe they'll go for it. Like you said, they were all looking pretty bushed."

"How did they get out to the island today? Which boat did they take?"

"I think they used the one Donavan rented. Remember,

he offered to take me for a ride in it," Josephine said and watched a small flash of red appear in Blasko's green eyes. She found it very satisfying after his performance with Neith.

"Do you know which one it is?"

"Maybe. I watched them load up and leave this morning."

"Point it out to me and I'll try to buy us a little insurance in case we can't persuade them to go along with our plan."

"What's *your* plan?"

"Not now." He stood and pulled her up with him. "Walk out on the balcony with me."

The moon was almost directly overhead and shone enough light on the town for even Josephine to be able to see the boats at the dock.

"It's the boat on the far left with the stripe down the side," Josephine said, pointing. "Do you know anything about boats?"

"Not a thing. However, having owned a car for more than six months, I've learned that it doesn't take much for an engine to fail."

Josephine chuckled. "Well, don't do anything that will leave them stuck out in the Gulf, and remember that whatever you do has to be fixed by dusk, otherwise none of us will be going out to the island."

"Yes, you're right," Blasko said in a way that suggested he clearly hadn't thought it all through.

"Are you sure you know what you're doing?" Josephine asked doubtfully.

"Of course. Let's go try to talk them into going tomorrow evening."

Blasko rapped on Captain Hume's door, which was opened by an unhappy-looking Donavan. Inside there were blankets and bedrolls spread around the floor, while the treasure hunters sat sprawled here and there, sipping various cocktails.

"Care to join us? We're all hoping that we can drink enough to get a sound night's sleep," Hume said with a tired smile.

"I'm not drinking so much that one of you all can slip out without me noticing," Donavan groused.

"I would very much like to go out to the island with you tomorrow," Blasko told them. "However, as you know I have a rather severe allergy to sunlight. It would be most convenient if you could wait until dusk to leave for the island."

For a moment everyone just stared at Blasko, their faces stunned.

"Are you out of your ever lovin' mind?" Donavan broke the silence.

"Actually, if you think about it, you might do better if you avoided the heat of the day," Josephine argued.

"I can see not leaving until the afternoon," Jamila said.

"Yeah, but not dusk. We don't have enough lanterns or flashlights. 'Sides, you can't get the big picture at night," Donavan said.

"I agree with Mr. Donavan. Darkness would hamper our efforts," Neith said.

"Not that we had much luck today," Hume admitted.

"You were all mighty sunburned," Josephine pointed out.

"We'll leave at three. I'm sorry, Baron, but we can't wait until dusk," Donavan said, taking on the air of leadership, if not the actual authority.

There was a little more back and forth, but the decision had been made.

Back on the balcony, Blasko looked at Josephine and said, "Plan B it is."

Josephine embraced him, then remembered his wound. She touched the spot on his chest gently and asked, "Are you well enough to go out tonight?"

"I'm fine. I'm more concerned for you. You might have been hurt, or worse, this afternoon. When Anton comes back, let him do his job."

"I shouldn't have brought us here."

"There is a purpose to it all. We just don't always see it."

He pulled away from her. "I'm going to see Carter."

"Do you think there's anything that can be done to help him?"

"I honestly don't know."

He leaned down to kiss her, then swung his leg over the balcony railing.

"You *do* know that the hotel has a door?" she reminded him.

Blasko just waved and climbed down the side of the building with an unnatural grace.

CHAPTER TWENTY-ONE

Blasko rapped on the door of the cabin and was surprised when it was opened by a sober Carter. The bag was still on his arm.

"You're back?"

"Josephine said she'd seen you."

"Thanks for letting her know that I'm turning into a human octopus." Carter's words dripped with sarcasm.

"I thought someone should check on you. But since we're talking about Josephine, we still haven't addressed the matter of that book you sent to her." Blasko stepped in close to Carter and shut the door behind him. His attitude was menacing.

"Josephine needs to know what you are."

"She has always known."

"She knows what you told her. I'm not sure you fully understand your own situation."

"You mean to tell me that there is something about vampirism I don't already know. Me? I've lived with this for hundreds of years, yet you are going to educate *me*?" Blasko said with derision.

"You can learn a few things from books," Carter said, backing away from him.

"I agree. But books are written by men, and men lie for their own purposes. You think you can tell the difference between a printed truth and a lie?"

"I know a—" Carter was about to say that he knew a monster when he saw one. Instead, he reached with his good hand and felt the hideous thing that lurked inside the bag. "Maybe I've been a bit… judgmental in the past."

Blasko advanced on Carter again. "Don't get between Josephine and me. You are her cousin, and maybe you even mean to be her friend. But if you want to be *our* friend, you had best respect who we both are. Is that clear?"

"I suppose I can see your side." Carter's bag of tentacles grew even more agitated. He tried to restrain them with his other hand. "I have my own monster to deal with."

The hopelessness in his voice reached through Blasko's anger and the vampire relaxed. "I have a plan for catching a murderer and you're a big part of it," he told Carter. "Once that's done, I give you my word I will do everything I can to help you save yourself from that thing."

"Including looking into the *Necronomicon* and any other grimoires that we may find?"

"Yes. But you will have to do what I tell you."

"Do I have any other options?"

Blasko spent the next hour going over his plan with a reluctant Carter. Shortly after midnight, they had settled all the details to their mutual satisfaction.

"There's one other part of the plan that I need your assistance with," Blasko said.

"What?"

"We need to sabotage the boat that the treasure hunters are using so they can't go out until dark."

"I don't know much about diesel engines."

"You know more than I do. We will wait until the moon sets. The docks will be shrouded in darkness. With my eyesight, I can see to work on it, but I'll need you there to offer advice." Blasko had a hard time admitting that he ever needed help with anything, but he couldn't convince himself that he had the slightest clue how to disable an engine.

"We'll need some tools," Carter said.

Blasko realized that he hadn't thought even that far ahead, and patted himself on the back for thinking to ask for Carter's help.

"There is a box under the sink in your kitchen. That's where I found the… ah… instrument to conduct your surgery. I'll meet you back here when the moon sets."

"Where are you going now?"

"To stir the pot a little," Blasko said with a grin that would cast a chill on any man's heart.

"I don't think—" Carter started, but stopped when Blasko raised his hand.

"Trust me."

His tone left Carter with no doubt whatsoever that what Blasko had in mind was dangerous and stupid. However, Blasko's stern expression convinced him that there was nothing he could say to stop the vampire from whatever reckless enterprise he had in mind.

Back outside, Blasko headed with a determined step toward The Dragon. The "R" on the sign was still burned out and Blasko remembered the shrine to a god named Dagon that he'd seen on the boat last night. He doubted that it was a coincidence.

Several of the odd locals were standing around outside the bar. Startled, they stopped talking when Blasko approached. He ignored them, not breaking his stride as he stepped onto the curb and up the coquina stone steps into the bar.

There were half a dozen customers inside. The bartender was a bald man who towered over the cypress bar. He looked up and almost dropped the glass he was polishing when he saw Blasko. There was an odd green glow to the lighting in the bar, but the corners were dark enough to hide the features of the men seated in the booths.

"What do you want?" the bartender managed to say after recovering from his shock.

"A drink. Isn't that your *raison d'être?*"

"What the hell are you talking about? I want you out of here." The angry man reached for something hidden under the bar. With lightening speed, Blasko moved to the counter and reached over, clasping the bartender's hand in an iron grip.

"Leave your hands where I can see them," Blasko ordered. He could sense movement behind him. "And if I feel so much as a finger touch me, I will separate your arm from your body. Tell them to go back to their seats. I am only here for a glass of wine and a friendly chat."

"Back away from him," the bartender said, trying not to cry out from the crushing pain as Blasko tightened his grip. "No one's going to talk to you, mister."

"Then it's going to be a lopsided conversation." Blasko released the bartender's arm as he heard the men behind him return to their booths.

"I was involved in a fight down at the docks last night. I won't argue about why, but both parties came away with some nasty wounds. Maybe I was at fault." Blasko shrugged and looked around the room at the men lurking in the shadows. "Either way, the man's sons tried to exact revenge on me this afternoon. Fair enough. But a woman that I care for very much was also in the room. If she'd been hurt, then we would not be talking. As it is, I say that we're even. Any man who doesn't feel that way needs only to send a message up to the hotel with a date and time at night for us to meet. Is that understood?"

There was a thick silence in the room. Blasko heard a small scuffle as a young man hidden in the darkness started to move, but the man sitting with him put up a restraining hand.

"Mister, I think you're out of your depth," the bartender said, rubbing his arm.

"Give me a decent red wine."

"We got ale."

"That will do." The drink would do nothing for Blasko

except to wet his throat, but he knew that standing at the bar and drinking the ale would punctuate the message he wanted to send.

With an ill will, the bartender poured Blasko an ale.

"One more thing. This was the second time that my lady has been involved in an altercation with a man from this island. If there is a third time, I will not worry about who gets hurt. I will storm through this town until there is not an able-bodied man left to stand at this bar."

"Bold words," said a man in the back of the room.

With a speed and accuracy that stunned everyone, Blasko hurled the glass he was holding at the darkness and hit the man square in the forehead, sending him backward against the wall, squealing in pain.

Again the bartender made a move for whatever weapon he kept below the counter, but as soon as he saw Blasko spin toward him, he fell back against the wall with his hands up. Blasko turned back toward the others as he heard movement from that direction, freezing the men in their advance. They shrank away as he faced them. Their malformed, fishlike faces gave Blasko a moment's hesitation, but he held his ground. Even in the darkness, he could tell that these men were the very young and the very old ones of the island.

"You better not be here when the fishermen come in," the bartender hissed.

"Tell them what I said." Blasko pulled a gold coin from his coat pocket and tossed it onto the bar before doing his best to saunter out. The men who'd been watching from the door scuttled away from him.

With one ear trained behind him, Blasko walked away to wait in the darkness until it was time to return to Carter's place. The energy he had expended had left him tired, and the wound in his chest was aching. It hadn't healed as quickly as he'd led Josephine to believe.

Finding a spot where he could watch part of the town without being observed, Blasko settled down by an old live oak tree to rest. He observed a few figures moving about, including several near The Dragon. He could imagine the conversations among the locals and the consternation that would result. Would they come after him? Or would they decide that the cost of a confrontation wasn't worth the price?

He and the town were both experiencing the classic dilemma of the predator—what price are you willing to pay to protect your territory? For Blasko, the territory in question was his and Josephine's lives, and there was no price too high. For the strange villagers, the question would be: what was the cost of ignoring him compared to the cost of confronting him? Blasko's objective at the bar had been to convince them that he was capable of inflicting a high price for any further attacks on him or Josephine.

Blasko wished that the blood of the locals wasn't tainted with whatever poison had mutated them into fishlike creatures that had to hide in the dark. If he could draw strength from them, he'd be in a much better position to protect Josephine. As it was, one show of strength had forced him to rest, and he knew that he couldn't admit his weakness to Josephine. She would insist that he feed from her again, and too much of that would not be prudent.

Watching the docks, Blasko became confident that he and Carter could get down there and do what they needed to do without being detected. Eventually he pushed himself up from the ground and started back toward the rented cottage.

"I've got the tools," Blasko said, retrieving the metal box from underneath Carter's kitchen sink.

Carter looked nervous and his bagged tentacles undulated erratically. "How am I going to see anything in the dark?" He swatted at his mutated arm and added, "The changes go halfway past my elbow now."

"We'll get it fixed..." Blasko said, not able to keep the doubt out of his voice. "Somehow. And don't worry about seeing. I'll just ask you questions about what I see. Any attempt on our part to use a lantern or a flashlight would be seen from a thousand yards away in the dark."

"You don't know a thing about engines and you're going to describe the parts to me, and I don't know much more than you. This should work great."

"Don't worry so much." Blasko said, reaching out and grabbing Carter's arm to push him out the door. When he realized that he'd touched the mutated arm, he jerked his hand back reflexively. "Sorry."

"It creeps me out too," Carter said, following Blasko into the street.

The vampire guided Carter through the dark streets and down to the docks. As they got closer to the water, Blasko noticed that Carter was jerking about oddly.

"What's wrong?" he whispered.

"The damned tentacles are flailing about. I don't know what the hell's going on," a frustrated Carter hissed back. Blasko saw that he was trying to control the mutated arm and not having much luck. "It's like the damned thing is getting excited."

"We're getting close to the docks and the water."

"Cripes!" Carter clinched the arm to his side as best he could. "I've got to take the bag off."

He pulled it off and Blasko watched in horrified fascination as the tentacles reached out toward the water of their own accord. Forcing himself to look away, Blasko pulled Carter onward toward the dock.

Before stepping out onto the dock, Blasko took another good look up and down, checking out every boat. He didn't want to run into another stab-happy sailor tonight. Seeing nothing, he guided the twitching Carter onto the dock. They moved as quickly and silently as they could down to the boat that Josephine had indicated.

They climbed on board, which was complicated by Carter's tentacles trying to get into the water. Blasko pulled Carter down onto the deck behind the gunwale.

"The hatch for the engine must be here somewhere,"

Blasko said, looking for a ring or handle to pull on. When he found it, he lifted the hatch. Even his eyes had to adjust to the almost-total blackness under the deck.

"I can see wires and lots of metal things. Looks a bit like my automobile's engine… but different."

"That's helpful," Carter sighed. "Okay, I've been thinking about this. You need to take a piece or two off. Try to find something that isn't too obvious. That way, when they haven't been able to get the boat to start, you can present yourself as an expert and fix it by replacing the parts you remove."

As he spoke, Blasko could hear strange sucking and smacking sounds that he realized were the suckers on Carter's tentacles, clutching and unclutching the deck. Repressing a shudder, he said doubtfully, "Do you think that will work?"

"Just remember what you take off and how to put it back."

"But will anyone believe that I am an expert on boat engines?"

"They will when you fix it."

The plan sounded reasonable the way Carter laid it out, so Blasko started looking for parts he could remove. "I found a wire that I can take off if I have one of those things."

"What things?"

"A screwdriver, I think."

"We're going to have to review a few terms if you're going to sound convincing this evening," Carter said, trying to open the toolbox with one hand while wrestling with his tentacles, which were still trying to drag him toward the water.

After forty-five minutes, Blasko had managed to remove a couple of wires and opened a valve whose proper placement he had carefully committed to memory.

"There are probably easier ways to delay them," Carter said, trying to bag his arm again as they snuck back toward his cottage.

"I didn't hear you making any suggestions." Blasko was worn out from the evening's activities, but the thought of closing himself off in his coffin and letting the day's events play out was unappealing. He had no choice.

Back at the hotel, he looked in on Josephine to let her know he'd returned.

"What did you do to the boat?" she asked.

"I have no idea, but I think I can repair it. Carter gave me some lessons on how to sound like a mechanic."

"Franklin? I wouldn't think him an expert either."

"Compared to me?" Blasko asked with his eyebrows raised.

"I take your point."

CHAPTER TWENTY-TWO

Josephine was alone at breakfast the next morning. She spent a few hours in Blasko's room with a book, then finally heard movement down the hall around noon. She opened the door to see several of the treasure hunters emerge from Captain Hume's room, looking like they'd had a hard night's rest. Eric Donavan half waved at her as he stumbled down the stairs, looking for something to eat. Neith walked to her own room with a frown planted on her face.

"Spending the night all together was abysmal," she said to Josephine before entering her room and closing the door loudly.

As the day worn on, Josephine heard more and more commotion as the other guests rambled about the hotel, obviously restless to return to the hunt.

At two, the door to Blasko's room opened and a weary Anton came in, carrying an envelope.

"I have the response. It is from both of the gentlemen. Your Mr. Bobby wanted me to tell you something too. He says that he would have come himself, except that there has been a fire. He had to stay and help, but if you don't return by the day after tomorrow, he will come down here."

"You made good time," Josephine told Anton gratefully,

receiving a small smile from the little man. "You've earned a pass for all the times you've annoyed me." Instead of causing the smile to disappear, her comment made it grow a bit larger.

"Thank you, miss. Here."

She took the envelope and tore it open, settling back into her chair to read.

They had discovered that Neith had left Cairo without telling anyone where she was going. At one point, there had been speculation that she'd thrown herself into the Nile. Her colleagues hadn't been that excited to hear she was alive.

Donavan proved to be as he had presented himself. He was well liked at the university, but they weren't that concerned that he was gone.

The part about Captain Hume was interesting. He had been accused of going native when he left his ship in the South Pacific. The current commander of his regiment in the Royal Marines had compared his behavior to something out of Conrad's *Heart of Darkness*. They had discharged him as a captain rather than court martial him because they didn't want the scandal on record. There had been mixed opinions in his regiment about whether that was the right decision. As to his actions in the Middle East after his discharge, what Hume had told them was fairly accurate.

Jamila was respected at her university, though she had made enemies because of her ambition.

Bobby and Etheridge hadn't been able to come up with any information on Elliot Zhao. They had a couple of calls in with the overseas operator to Hong Kong, but they had decided that it was more important to send Anton back than to wait on calls that might never come in.

Josephine was reading the report and wondering how any of this was going to help them solve the murders when she came to the last part concerning Wallace Brock. Here there was some enlightenment... but also more questions.

There had been two Brocks—brothers. Wallace Brock was a professor at the University of Chicago. In early May, he had received a letter and took it to his dean. The letter had arrived at a time when Wallace was already preparing to go on sabbatical, so he just ran it by the dean and, in short order, was on a train headed to Florida.

His brother, Sergeant Manfred Brock of the Chicago Police Department, had come to the university a week later, upset that he couldn't contact his brother or even confirm that he'd arrived safely on Cedar Island. According to Manfred's lieutenant, he had requested a leave of absence to go to Florida to look for his brother. That was the last anyone has heard from either one of the Brocks.

"I have to tell you what happened to the baron yesterday," Josephine told Anton when she was done with the letter. He had been hovering close by while she read. Now she spared none of the details of what had happened, including the appearance of the attackers.

"I will guard him with my life," Anton said without any sense of exaggeration or irony.

"I'm going down to see what the other guests are doing. If they leave for the island, I might go with them."

"Is that wise? I think the baron would be very upset if you do that."

"I suspect you're right, but I want to keep an eye on them." Josephine handed him the envelope with the information he'd brought back from Sumter. "If I'm not here when the baron wakes up, give this to him."

She went back to her room and dressed in an oversized long-sleeved shirt and pants, the toughest and most practical clothes she had with her. From her suitcase she also retrieved a belt and holster that she'd had made a couple of months earlier. Life with Blasko had taught her that sometimes it paid to be armed. She'd had it designed so that the holster rested just under the waistband inside her pants, and would be hidden by her blouse. She placed the revolver in the holster, then examined the effect in the mirror. If you knew what you were looking for, it was possible to tell that she might be hiding something, but otherwise it was concealed to her satisfaction.

In the entry hall, she found Jamila smoking a cigarette and looking irritated.

"We should have gone down to the docks half an hour ago. These people have no discipline," she complained

"I'd like to go with you this time."

"Whenever that will be." Jamila nodded. "One more. Why not?"

By four o'clock, they were finally walking toward the docks. Josephine looked around at the others. They all wore a look that was a mix of desperation, hope and resignation. She looked down the street toward Carter's little cabin and wondered how he was doing. The thought of his tentacles caused her stomach to roll.

At the boat, Donavan hopped on board with practiced dexterity. Everyone else clamored aboard behind him. Josephine hoped whatever Blasko had done would keep them there until dark. She looked at her watch. It was still almost four hours until sunset.

Donavan went into the wheelhouse and came out five minutes later, looking flustered. "You all need to move toward the front. I need to look at the engine."

"Something wrong?" Captain Hume asked.

"Won't know till I look."

A few minutes later, he had the hatch open and was tinkering around in the engine compartment.

"Go in the wheelhouse and turn the key when I tell you," he yelled at the captain.

So it went for the next two hours as Donavan and Hume tried to figure out what was wrong.

"You need to go get the guy you rented this from." Hume tossed the rag he'd been holding for Donavan down on the deck.

"This is ridiculous." Jamila was pouting in a chair she'd dragged out of the cabin. The others were lying about the boat in various states of repose and irritation.

Josephine looked at her watch again. There were still two

hours until sunset. "The baron had a yacht on the Black Sea," she made up on the spot. "I think he might be able to fix it. Maybe if we all go up to dinner, when we're done he can come back down with us and have a look at it."

"I'm going to go see if that guy, Enoch something, who I rented this tub from can get it fixed," Donavan said.

"Of course. If he can't, then the baron can take a look," Hume said to Josephine.

Josephine just hoped that Enoch wouldn't be able to figure out what Blasko and Carter had done to disable the engine.

"I agree with Josephine. We should get something to eat." Jamila stood up. "I'll leave my bag here."

"I think that dinner sounds like a good idea," Zhao said, walking back from the bow of the boat with Neith close behind.

Perfect! Josephine thought. *If we go up for dinner at the hotel, we won't be ready to come back to the boat until the sun is almost down. It won't matter if Enoch fixes the boat or not. I just hope Dragomir can fix whatever he broke.*

Two hours later, everyone except Donavan had eaten and was getting ready to walk back down to the boat.

"Are you going on the dig in that outfit?" Neith asked Blasko as she saw him coming down the stairs wearing his usual Edwardian attire.

"I am not planning on doing any digging." Blasko smiled. "But I do need to go get another member of our party."

"Who's that?" Jamila asked suspiciously.

"A man who can help us," Blasko said vaguely.

"Don't take long," Zhao warned. "Miss Nicolson said that you know something about boats. We might need you to fix a small problem."

"I'll meet you there momentarily," Blasko told him, winking at Josephine as he walked past her and out the door.

Outside, the western sky was still a light blue, providing enough light to see by as the group headed back to the docks. As they got closer, Josephine could see Donavan and one of the locals standing at the stern of the boat, looking down into the engine compartment. Even from a hundred yards away, she could tell that they weren't happy.

"Have you found the trouble?" Hume asked as they approached.

"Aye, there's wires missing," Enoch said. Josephine recognized him as the strange sailor she had encountered the day before.

"Are you saying that someone took them?" Hume pressed.

"Looks like someone doesn't want us to go out to the island today." Donavan looked around at everyone with a grim expression on his face.

"Who would do this?" Neith asked.

"I assume it was whoever has the rest of the let—" Donavan stopped talking when he realized that Enoch was standing close beside him. "It doesn't matter who. We're stuck until we can get new wiring."

"I can rig something up tomorrow with the help of some of the boys. But not until then," Enoch said.

Blasko and Carter chose that moment to arrive. Donavan noticed them first, then everyone else turned to see what he was looking at. Josephine had to admit that the two men made a strange pair. Both were overdressed for an outing on a boat, with Carter hiding his burlap-covered arm under a trench coat. Only because she knew where to look, Josephine could see that the sack was making some very strange undulations.

"Have you had any luck with the boat?" Blasko called out to them. Carter had his head down and looked like he was trying to hide behind Blasko.

Enoch's face took a darker turn when he saw Blasko. "Reckon I'll be going now. We'll get this fixed up tomorrow," he said to Donavan, stepping quickly over the gunwale and onto the dock. He glared at Blasko and Carter, passing by them both without a word.

"The old guy doesn't seem to care for you," Donavan

observed.

"Had a drink at the bar with the locals last night. I guess I offended some of them."

"Who's that with you?" Hume asked.

"We aren't splitting this pie any more than we already have," Donavan said.

"Are you talking about the pie you haven't managed to find yet? Because this man is… uniquely qualified to help with the search," Blasko said.

"If he has some useful knowledge, I don't see why we wouldn't want him along," Zhao reasoned.

"You're supposed to have the information we need from that letter." Donavan glared at Zhao.

"The baron's right. We need to get this done as quickly as possible. You saw the look on that old fisherman. I'm sure there are all types of rumors flying around by now. Do you want the locals horning in on this?" Hume said.

"I agree. If we aren't careful, we'll be dividing our find up a dozen ways," Neith said, seconding Hume.

"Including a share to the state," Josephine said.

"She's right." Zhao nodded.

"We're all agreed then," Blasko said, pushing Carter into the boat.

"What's this special knowledge and why the hell does he have a bag over his hand?" Donavan asked, having noticed what Carter was trying to hide.

"It looks like there are serpents in there." Neith sounded uncomfortable.

Carter refused to look up and used his good arm to keep his left pinned to his side.

"Let's look at the motor first. I'd rather not talk details until we're away from the dock," Blasko said.

"We aren't going anywhere unless you can make a part for the engine," Donavan said.

"I may as well take a look," Blasko responded good-naturedly. He'd hidden the wires up the sleeve of his coat.

"Suit yourself. Here, I'll take your coat," Donavan said,

reaching out. "We've already lit the lantern, but you can't get it too close to the engine. There's oil on the bilge water. Don't know how flammable it is, but best not to find out. Hume, get the flashlight from the wheelhouse."

"I'll keep my coat on, thank you. I've got pretty fair night vision, so I'll just put my head down there and see what I can do." Blasko was already down on his knees by the hatch to the engine compartment.

With half his body hanging down into the dark hole, Blasko pulled the wires out of his sleeve and tried to remember where they belonged.

"Here's the light." Hume handed down the heavy flashlight. Blasko took it, even though the light was more of a hindrance to him than a help.

After a few false starts, he thought he'd gotten the wires into the right places and had remembered to close the open valve. "That should do it," he said, pulling himself out of the compartment.

"You couldn't have fixed it without the missing wires," Donavan said.

"I found them under the water," Blasko said, glad for the four inches of dirty bilge water under the engine.

"I felt around and didn't find them." Donavan wasn't convinced.

"I'll see if it will start," Hume said, moving toward the wheelhouse. Sure enough, the engine kicked over after several tries and settled down to a steady, deep-throated diesel thumping.

"I don't believe for a minute that you found those wires in the bilge water," Donavan whispered to Blasko.

Blasko gave Donavan a cold smile. "And I don't believe that you will ever find the treasure without my help."

Donavan frowned and went to the wheelhouse.

Hume helped to cast the boat from the dock and, within minutes, they were puttering out into the Gulf as the last inkling of daylight passed from the sky.

CHAPTER TWENTY-THREE

When they were about a mile off the coast, Donavan pulled back on the throttle and let the engine idle before switching on all of the boat's lights.

"Before we get any farther from shore, I want to know why we're taking this man with us," he said, leaving the wheelhouse and joining the rest of the group at the stern.

A gentle swell rocked the boat as everyone's eyes went to Blasko and Carter.

"This is Franklin Carter. He is going to help us find the treasure."

Josephine saw Jamila's eyes widen, but she kept her mouth shut.

"How can he help?" Hume asked.

"And why in heaven's name does he have a bag on his arm?" Neith rolled her eyes.

"He's—"

Carter stopped him by placing his good hand on Blasko's arm.

"I'll tell them. I've got some ties to this place. I'm a part of all that's going on here," he said, trying to suppress his northern accent.

"What kind of ties?" Donavan asked skeptically.

Carter and Blasko had agreed that the show he was about to put on would be the best way to convince the group that he could lead them to the treasure. He held up his mutated arm and yanked off the bag with a flourish.

Jamila had been standing next to Carter. Now she jumped away so fast that she almost fell into the water. Neith let out a brief scream, while Hume and Zhao both stood motionless with looks of astonishment on their faces.

"Bloody hell!" Donavan exclaimed. "That can't be real."

He stepped closer for a moment, but as soon as the glare of the boat's lights helped him verify that the flailing tentacles on the end of Carter's arm were indeed real, he moved back as far as he could.

"Anyone still doubt my *bona fides*?" Carter waved his tentacles around.

Jamila turned and threw up over the side of the boat.

"What does that prove other than that you're a freak?" Donavan asked, turning his head partly away so that he didn't have to look directly at the wriggling appendages.

"My father witnessed Peter Nicolson burying the treasure," Carter lied. "I can lead you there."

"If you've known where the gold is all these years, why didn't you dig it up yourself?" Donavan was trying to maintain his composure, but it wasn't easy.

"What would I do with the gold?" Carter was trying hard to act like a man who was so deformed that he was close to madness. After the last couple of days, he had a lot of material to draw from. His biggest fear was that he might act the part too well. "Find some girl to marry me? Buy a car to drive to the theatre?"

"Okay, then, why are you willing to help us now?"

"I've promised to take him to a surgeon that I know," Blasko spoke up. To everyone except Josephine, this made perfect sense. Only she knew that no surgeon in the world could remove the mutation.

"Well, he's here now," Hume grumbled.

"If he finds the treasure, we'll cut him in for a share. But if we find it with the information we already have, I say he's out of luck." Donavan was grinding his teeth as he spoke.

"I'll agree to that. Because I know that I can find it." Carter tried to look smug, but he was having a hard time controlling his tentacles. It didn't really matter what expression he had on his face since no one wanted to look at him.

"Those are obscene." Jamila shook her head and went toward the bow of the boat. Zhao and Neith followed her. Donavan went into the wheelhouse to set the boat back on course for the small island.

As the boat drew near to it, Blasko stared out at the sandy island. The moon was providing more than enough light for him to make out details. There were a couple of mounds made from piles of oyster shells left by the Timucua tribe hundreds of years before the first conquistadors walked the sands of Florida. Most of the island's waterline was covered with mangroves, while here and there were a few sandy beaches. Donavan steered the boat close to one of the larger sandy landing spots.

"We have to use the raft to get ashore," Hume told Blasko, Josephine and Carter as Donavan dropped the anchor.

Blasko looked concerned as he watched Donavan and Zhao take a four-man raft from the side of the wheelhouse and drop it off the side of the boat, as everyone else came back from the bow.

"What's wrong?" Even in the dark, Josephine could tell that Blasko was worried about something.

He shook his head, frowning.

"What?" she whispered.

He turned and started toward the bow with Josephine at his heels.

"The bottoms of my shoes are lined with gold coins and a little of my native earth," he said, looking toward the stern to make sure no one else could hear him.

"That can't be comfortable," Josephine said, not grasping

his concern.

"I told you that I don't do well on boats. The running water… The gold and earth has helped, but…"

"Are you worried about the smaller raft?"

"What I was taught is that the gold must be between me and running water. It's not unbearable standing here on deck. But if I have to get in a raft, sitting so close to the water…" He shrugged.

"That seems like a bit of a stretch. I mean, it's not like your whole body is balanced over the gold in your shoes. Your elbows and arms have—"

"We're sending the first group over!" Donavan shouted from the stern.

Blasko waved to let him know that they'd heard. "You have a point. I just don't feel like being wrong and bursting into flame, turning into dust or dropping down into the bowels of hell. Or maybe all three."

"Do you think that could happen? Really?"

"You can trust me when I tell you that the danger of sunlight is not a myth," Blasko snapped, then composed himself. "Nothing for it now."

"I'm sure you'll be fine," Josephine said, though his obvious concern made her doubt her own confidence.

Blasko pulled her close and gave her a long and tender kiss. Then he stood back and said, his accent growing stronger with emotion, "If I am reduced to a skeleton on the way to shore, know that I love you, Josephine Nicolson."

Bemused and a little stunned, Josephine watched as he turned and made his way back to the stern where Carter and Hume were waiting.

When Donavan returned from dropping off the first group, he held the raft to the stern of the boat as Josephine and Carter climbed in. Blasko gingerly lowered himself into the small raft, tucking his feet up under his body as best he could. When Donavan shoved off, she was sure she saw Blasko hold his breath. Josephine gripped his hand in encouragement. They were halfway across the hundred-yard gap between the boat and the shore before Blasko relaxed.

"What am I supposed to do now?" Carter asked once they were on land and Donavan had returned to the boat for the last time to fetch Captain Hume.

"When everyone is together, we can suggest that you and I go off alone. I read the part of the letter that Josephine still has. Where it was torn, I thought I could make out a reference to the east side of the island. So we'll start there. The killer can't afford—"

"I want to know the rest of your plan," Josephine interrupted.

"If it works, it will happen fast."

"As the cheese in your trap, I hope it doesn't happen so fast that you don't see it coming," Carter groused.

"Whoever killed the others and has the missing half of the letter probably already knows where the gold is. I'm sure they're just trying to make the search a little harder so no one will realize who they are. But he or she can't afford to let *us* find it, or they lose more of their share," Blasko said.

"If he knows where the treasure is, then he'll know if we're heading in the right direction," Carter said.

"I guess it's worth a shot." Josephine frowned. She didn't like it, though she had to admit that a trap seemed the only way to catch this killer. When all the suspects shared a motive, the means and the opportunity, what other choice did they have?

"You stay with the main party and keep an eye on things. Carter and I will go off on our own." Blasko noticed that the others were getting their equipment ready and looked like they would soon be setting out.

"What do I do if—"

"Just keep an eye on them. If one of them leaves to come after us, that's probably our killer," Blasko said quickly as the group headed their way.

Josephine had more questions about Blasko's plan, but Donavan was already within hearing distance. She decided that all she could do was go along with it. With her right hand, she reached down and felt for the revolver that was still secure under her shirt.

"We're lucky that, with the moon and clear skies, we hardly need to use our lanterns," Donavan said.

"We've already searched the mound to the north. I believe we should try the other mound," Zhao said.

"What good was that letter if you're just guessing?" Donavan's hands were balled up into fists.

"We found the island," Zhao argued. "Almost everything after the description of the island was missing." He looked around as though he expected to see one of the others holding the missing half of the letter.

"If this is the right island. We haven't proven that yet," Neith pointed out.

"The directions were clear as far—" Zhao started to defend himself.

"Fine, fine," Donavan said, cutting him off. "What about our new expert?" He looked at Carter.

"We're going off on our own," Blasko said.

"Oh no. No! We stick together. That was part of the rules we agreed on." Jamila's attitude had changed from boredom to utter fury.

"We will inform you if and when we find anything," Blasko said.

"But why not stick together?" Donavan took up Jamila's cause.

Carter held out his hand and, even in the limited light of the moon, the rest of the party flinched away from it.

"It is even creepier in the dark," Jamila said with a shiver.

"I don't see how—" Donavan started before Hume chimed in.

"Let them go off alone. They can't go anywhere. You secured the boat, and we'll have the raft in sight if we're working on the other mound."

"Yes, let them do what they want. I don't believe he knows anything more than we do," Neith added.

"But if he *does* know where—"

"He needs to think and look for the landmarks he remembers. Having all of you tagging along behind us won't help," Blasko pointed out.

"I was just a boy when I witnessed the gold being buried," Carter said.

"Yeah, I meant to ask you about that—" Donavan started.

Blasko cut him off. "Enough! We are wasting time talking."

"Fine! We'll check back with you in two hours," Donavan said.

After a bit more back and forth, the parties split up. Blasko and Carter headed for the east side of the island while everyone else went toward the larger of the two mounds.

Blasko stopped once they were out of sight of the others.

"What are you doing?" Carter asked as Blasko sat down in the sand and took off one of his shoes.

"Getting a little salt."

"What?" Carter, exasperated, fought to control his tentacled arm as he watched Blasko pry a few gold coins from the bottom of his shoe.

"Salting the mine. Isn't that what you call it? We can show them these gold coins as proof that we found the treasure."

"A few gold coins? That doesn't seem very convincing."

"These people are so keyed up that the mere sight of gold will send them into a frenzy."

"We only want to catch the killer, right?"

"Yes, yes. And this is just like the smell of cheese to get him to fully commit to the trap."

"I think you're mixing your salted mine and mousetrap metaphors. In my opinion, we're either wasting our time or you're going to get us all killed." Carter slapped at his arm. "And at this point, I think I wouldn't mind being killed."

"I told you that I'll help you get rid of that... thing."

"You chopped the damned thing off, but here we are."

"Let's worry about finding our killer right now. Which

involves you looking around like you know what you're doing," Blasko reminded him, pocketing the coins and putting his shoe back on.

For the next hour, they traipsed around the east end of the island, plowing through the sand.

"This is insane. Besides, my arm is going crazy," Carter complained.

"Fine. We'll start making our way back toward the others." Blasko was beginning to doubt his own plan.

They'd gone about a hundred yards when they saw Captain Hume approaching them across a small dune. He had a Webley revolver in his hand and was pointing it at them.

"There you are. I've been looking for you. Damned difficult in all this sand. Reminds me of Syria."

CHAPTER TWENTY-FOUR

"Our killer," Blasko said with satisfaction.

"Great. Now that he's caught us, what do we do with him?" Carter said acidly.

"Stand still, Baron. I think we all know what you are, and if you think I haven't taken precautions, you're wrong. I cast a couple of silver bullets as soon as you arrived with your 'sunlight allergy.' Ha! That might fool the rubes, but not someone who's studied the world's dark underbelly."

"Why can't you just share the treasure?" Blasko said, ignoring the reference to his condition. As for the silver bullets, while he doubted their effect on werewolves, he wasn't so sure about his own ability to withstand them and he hoped he wouldn't find out tonight. Regular bullets were painful and damaging enough.

"The gold is only a small part of what's hidden here. I'm more interested in the documents. Now shut up before I shoot you just for the pleasure of the experience." He turned to Carter. "You with the squid for a hand, where is the treasure?"

"I'm sure you're going to find this very amusing, but I don't have a clue. At least not much of one. This was all about catching you."

"The hell you say. I should have known. Get down on the ground." Hume jabbed the gun at them for emphasis. "Doesn't matter 'cause we actually found it yesterday."

"You've got the other half of the letter," Blasko said, carefully lowering himself to the sand while trying to keep an eye on their captor.

"Of course I do."

"Maybe you found part of the gold, but you didn't find all of it," Blasko said, moving his hand toward his pocket.

"Don't move," Hume said. "What are you talking about?"

"I've got some of the gold to prove it."

"I don't believe you."

"It's in my pocket."

"Okay, but if you come up with anything other than gold in your hand, you're both dead."

Blasko reached into his pocket and pulled out the gold coins. *At least they're helping to stall the captain*, Blasko thought. He held the coins out awkwardly from his position on the ground.

"Toss them over here."

Blasko complied and Hume picked them up and looked them over as best he could in the dark.

"Nonsense. These are Romanian. We found the real gold. All of the coins are from an earlier period. Mostly Spanish and English." He put Blasko's coins in his pocket.

"You found the treasure, but you haven't dug it up?" Blasko didn't see any point in arguing about the coins.

"I will when I have time. But now I think we're going to have to take care of everyone." Hume stretched out his arm, pointing the gun at Carter. "And I'll start with this abomination."

"Don't!" Blasko said. "You don't want to alert the others with the gunshot."

"I don't mind. Go ahead and shoot me!" Carter yelled as his tentacled hand dug and squirmed in the sand.

"I'd be glad to do that for you."

"Stop!" Josephine yelled from behind the captain.

"Let me guess who this is," he said, turning toward her.

"Drop your gun or I will shoot you dead," Josephine commanded with an icy tone that would have made Al Capone proud. The revolver was steady in her hand.

"Of course, my dear." Hume let his gun fall to the ground. "Now let me get a good look at you."

Blasko pulled his Colt .45 from his shoulder holster, glad that he'd thought to put in on before leaving the hotel. "Don't you move," he commanded. He didn't know what tricks the captain might have up his sleeve, but he didn't want to run the risk of something happening to Josephine.

"No need to worry. I'm at your mercy." Hume turned back to Blasko while Josephine advanced closer.

"He has the other half of the letter," Blasko told her.

"Not on me. Heavens no," Hume said with a smile.

"You killed that man to get it," Josephine accused him.

"Yes, I did. You're very fortunate. I would have killed *you* if he hadn't intervened."

"What did you do to Mitzi Alexander, the postmistress?" Josephine asked, starting to piece it all together.

"I had planned on killing you both together, but that thief was lurking around outside and by the time I realized what was happening, he'd attacked you."

"How did you… Oh. You were the person she mentioned," Josephine said, remembering Mitzi talking about someone who'd recently come into her life.

"It was pathetic, really. I showed her a little bit of interest, figuring that the island postmistress would know all the gossip, and next thing I knew she was throwing herself at me. The best part was that she felt the need to unburden herself by telling me about her last lover, your Uncle Peter. Twenty years between men. Very sad. One was an idiot and the other a killer. Can't say she had a lot of luck in the love department."

"She told you about the letter?" Josephine asked.

"Hinted at it, though she did tell me that he'd found a

treasure. When you arrived, I began to put two and two together." He seemed more than willing to talk. "After you were attacked and I'd disposed of the evidence, I had to kill Mitzi. I did feel a little twinge of regret."

"And what about Wallace Brock?"

"Funny story. I was the first person he met on the island. Talk about serendipity. At the time, I thought we were the only two people who had received the letters, so I disposed of him before he even had a chance to check into the hotel."

"You're a monster!" Josephine growled.

"Ha! Take a closer look at your companions before you start hurling words like that around. You might damage that glass house you live in."

"Josephine! He said *we*," Blasko yelled, remembering the pronoun the captain had used earlier.

"He did," said a woman's voice from behind Josephine. "Don't move."

Neith walked slowly up behind Josephine, and Blasko could see her finger tightening around the trigger of the Luger she held in her hand.

"Josie, don't move! She's got a gun," Blasko warned.

"Thank you, Baron," Neith said. "Now if you and your girlfriend will both drop your guns, we can get on with this."

"What did you do with the others?" Hume asked her as he bent over to pick his Webley up out of the sand.

"Tied up. I saw this one follow you off into the dunes and decided that we had no choice."

"Perfect. We just need to dig up the hoard and get rid of all the dead weight."

"What about Manfred Brock?" Blasko asked, trying to stall.

"You mean the other one? I must say, it was quite a shock when he walked through the door. They looked remarkably alike."

"We don't have time for this," Neith said.

"Nonsense. I want to wait until sunrise to see what happens to this fool when the first rays strike his skin. So there's plenty of time. Where was I? Oh yes. I had to keep calm and move forward with my plans until I could figure out how to dispose of the second Mr. Brock. Once it was clear that the sheriff doesn't care what happens on Cedar Island, it was very easy to have Neith seduce her way into Brock's room so she could hit him over the head. Then together we drowned him."

"What do you want to do with *him*?" Neith pointed her gun at Carter.

"I think we'll turn him over to our aquatic friends. I would bet they will find his mutation very interesting. Trying to pass yourself off as a local—what a crude attempt at deception," Captain Hume scolded.

"We should get back to the others before one of them worms their way out of the ropes," Neith warned.

"You've got a point. Get up!" he said to Carter, who was still kneeling in the sand.

Neith glared at Blasko and trained her Luger squarely back on Josephine. "I tell you now, if you make any move or attempt to escape, I will shoot this woman full of holes."

"And if any harm comes to her, I will pull your limbs from your body and feed you to the sharks," Blasko promised with a smile.

"Brave words for a vampire who's going to be just so much dust come morning," Neith hissed.

"And I thought we were getting along so well the other night."

She spat at him and, to everyone's surprise, Josephine turned toward her and returned the favor. Neith whipped up her hand holding the pistol and slapped it across Josephine's face, knocking her down. Enraged, Blasko lunged toward Neith, but Hume stepped between them.

"May the gods destroy your house and the house of those who gave you birth!" Neith screamed at Josephine.

"Don't even think about it," Hume said to Josephine, pointing his own gun at her when he noticed that she was starting to move her legs with the intention of sweeping

Neith off her feet. "Enough of this foolishness! Stand up, all of you. And if there are any more delays, Miss Nicolson will die with a bullet through her head. Is that understood?"

Soon they were walking through the moonlit dunes on their way to the beach where they had come ashore. As they drew closer to the beach, Blasko could see the other three treasure hunters stretched out in the sand with their hands and feet tied and gags in their mouths.

"What's your plan?" he asked Captain Hume.

"For the others, I'm thinking they might have a boating accident. As for you, we'll just let you bask in the dawn of a new day. You have Neith to thank for filling me in on your unusual nature. She recognized you for what you are right away. Clever girl. I met her father when I was working in Syria. When I expressed interest in some of the more esoteric cults, he was very helpful in obtaining obscure books and documents from the Egyptian Museum's collections."

"You aren't here for the gold, are you?" Carter asked.

"The gold is a wonderful perk. But you're right, it's the books in the cache that are the real prize."

"How did you get a copy of the letter?" Carter turned to look at Hume, who was walking behind them with the gun pointed at their backs.

"What's it to you?"

"I know I didn't send you one."

"Ah! I wondered what part you really played in this. The… octopus appendage threw me. So you're the letter writer. Yes, you have the look of an antiquarian about you. For your enlightenment, you sent a letter to the British Museum. In that particular letter, you included Nicolson's descriptions of various grimoires. A friend of mine at the museum recognized them as books that I would be very interested in. He subsequently sold me the letter for a hefty price, but I think it will be more than worth the cost."

As they reached the others, Blasko could smell blood. Looking at the bound group, he noticed that Zhao was unconscious, the back of his head matted with blood.

"Get down on the ground next to them," Neith ordered.

When they hesitated, Neith struck Blasko in the back of the head with her pistol. He only turned and smiled at her, blood dripping onto his shoulder from a cut on his scalp.

"You are a tough one. I can respect that. Fine. I will put a sizable dent in your girlfriend's skull instead," Neith threatened, moving behind Josephine. Blasko dropped instantly to his knees, followed by Josephine and Carter.

Neith pulled a long rope and a knife from her bag while Captain Hume gathered up a couple of shovels. She cut off a length and tossed it at Josephine. "You tie up the mutant."

Josephine was cursing herself for not having realized that Captain Hume was involved in the murders. It seemed so obvious now. When she'd copied their names out of the hotel's ledger, his had been first by a couple of days. When she'd seen in Bobby's letter that Wallace Brock had gone missing, she should have guessed that the first of the guests would have had an opportunity to get rid of him. Not to mention the clue Mitzi had unknowingly dropped about her gentleman caller. All of this roiled around in her mind as she tried to tie Carter's good hand to his groping tentacles, all while trying not to touch the creepy things herself.

"Make the knot tight," Neith said, standing over her. Josephine thought about kicking the woman's legs out from under her, but what good would that do? More than likely, it would just get them all shot here on the beach. Except for Blasko. The captain seemed perversely interested in watching him die in the morning sun.

Once Blasko and Josephine were also tied up, the captain told Neith, "You will need to stay and watch them. I will take Donavan and Jamila with me."

"Is that wise?"

"We need to move the treasure tonight and go somewhere we can lie low for a while. I can use their help."

Captain Hume cut Donavan's and Jamila's hands loose, then had them untie each other's legs and retie them with about two feet of rope connecting their feet together. Donavan's eyes blazed while his jaw worked over the rag stuffed in his mouth. Jamila stared down at the ground as though scared to meet her captor's eyes.

"Now you're hobbled. Try to run and I'll shoot you dead." Hume pointed toward one of the mounds. "March."

Josephine watched as they went off, shuffling through the sand. Lying next to the wounded Zhao, she was worried about him. He hadn't moved or made a sound.

"You can't kill me," Carter said, twisting around so that he could face Neith.

"Shut up unless you want to be gagged."

Carter's movement had left him half lying against Josephine, not flat on the ground but rather leaning onto her. Josephine felt an odd movement between them and started to flinch away when she realized that his tentacles were reaching for her. As she tried to squirm away from him, Carter pressed his elbow against her side. It was clear that he wanted her to stay where she was.

"I just… don't want to die. For a while, I did want to die, but I don't now," Carter babbled. "I could be useful. I have a copy of the *Necronomicon*."

Neith looked at him. "You know something of the Old Ones and their books?"

"I flatter myself that I'm a scholar of dark lore."

Josephine could feel the tentacles grasping at the ropes around her wrists while Carter talked to Neith.

"Maybe you could be of use to us," Neith wondered aloud.

"I can. I swear," Carter said, squirming about to keep eye contact with the Egyptian woman.

As Carter moved, Josephine felt him poke her in the side with his good hand. She shifted as though he was making her uncomfortable, while actually turning to give him better access to her hands and the ties that bound them.

"You don't want that charlatan. *I'm* the man you need," Blasko piped up.

Josephine raised her head to see him looking over at her and Carter. He had obviously guessed what was going on and was helping Carter stall for time.

"Baron, I don't think I could save you if I wanted to. Captain Hume has been looking forward to staking you out in the sunlight ever since I told him what you are."

"You've met another vampire?" Blasko asked, and Josephine was sure that there was more than just an attempt at diversion in his question.

"Oh yes," Neith said.

"Where?"

"It was years ago. She was… interesting."

"You seem to have come out of the meeting in one piece."

"We had an understanding."

"Is she still alive?"

Josephine felt the tentacles working in concert with Carter's fingers to untie her bindings. She was glad that Blasko had managed to gain Neith's full attention.

"She's still undead, if that's what you mean," Neith said, smiling at Blasko.

"Why don't you let Hume burn her alive instead of me?" Blasko asked, changing tack in the verbal sparring.

"No. You are going to be the sacrificial lamb. I think Dagon will be pleased."

"Who?"

"Dagon, the eldritch god from our distant past, come back to rise above the waves and bring forth his warriors. All hail!" Neith started to sway back and forth as she spoke, and the whites of her eyes shone in the moonlight.

Josephine felt her hands go free. She didn't even resent the tentacles she felt running over her wrist as they pulled the rope away. With Neith focused on Blasko and half in a trance, Carter scooted around close enough to whisper to Josephine.

"We have to get our feet free very quickly. I think I can do that by bending backward and using my tentacles. When

I'm free, I'll go straight at her. Untie yourself, then come help me subdue her before she can fire the gun or yell for help."

Blasko was watching them and sincerely hoped that he was right about what they were doing. Suddenly, Neith seemed to come out of her reverie and Blasko grabbed for her attention again.

"Your Dagon sounds like the twin of a monster we sent back to the pits of hell last year."

"You know not of what you speak," Neith said, drawn back into the *tête-à-tête* with Blasko.

"I know a half-ass god when I hear of one." Blasko was well aware of the effect his words would have on Neith.

"Monster! Blasphemer!" she snarled, running forward and kicking at him. Blasko tried to dodge the blows while keeping Carter in his peripheral vision. As soon as he saw Carter crouch to spring, Blasko swung his feet and swept Neith's legs out from under her.

As she hit the ground, Carter charged at her. Everything happened quickly as Carter threw himself on top of Neith, swinging his tentacled appendage in her face. He needn't have worried about her crying for help, as the suckers closed over her mouth and prevented her from making any sound. As her eyes grew wide in panic, Carter realized that he needed to shift one tentacle away from her nose so she could breathe.

Her hand holding the gun flung out toward Blasko, who rolled onto the gun and pinned it to the sand beneath him. Reflexively, she pulled the trigger. Smothered by Blasko's body, it made little sound. The bullet barely grazed his side and buried itself in the sand.

"Help me hold her!" Carter barked as Josephine joined him.

Blasko rolled off of Neith's hand, then bit into the wrist that held the gun. She heaved and flopped against the pain, finally releasing her hold on the gun so Blasko could shove it away from her.

With Neith restrained, Blasko concentrated on freeing himself. He pulled and struggled with all his strength at the bonds holding his hands. Sawing his arms back and forth with no regard for the rope tearing into his wrists, he pulled them loose, then quickly untied his legs. Blood from his wrists dripped over his fingers as he loosened the rope and flung it aside. Then he grabbed the Luger from the sand and bent over Neith.

Placing the muzzle of the gun a foot from her head, he said, "Stop struggling or I will shoot you. Blink if you understand me."

Her eyes remained fixed and angry. She flailed at him with the arm he'd bit, throwing blood everywhere.

"Don't shoot her," Carter said, and used one of his tentacles to again close off her nose, this time on purpose.

Neith struggled as she slowly lost oxygen. Just before she would have passed out, she started to blink furiously. Carter pulled the tentacle away from her nose and she inhaled deeply.

Josephine ran to Zhao and pulled the rag out of his mouth, touching him gently to make sure he was still alive. Reassured, she came back beside Carter.

"You know you will die if you make a sound?" Josephine asked Neith, who blinked once in answer to the question. "Franklin, take your tentacles away."

Carter pulled them away slowly. As soon as Josephine had the chance, she crammed the rag into Neith's mouth.

Blasko stuffed the gun through his belt and picked up enough rope to tie up Neith. Once she was bound, they went over to Zhao.

"He's alive, but I'd say he has a concussion," Blasko said. "Getting him to a doctor has to be a priority."

They all looked at the boat floating a hundred yards off shore.

"Can you row?" Blasko asked Carter.

"Probably not well." He held up his tentacles.

"Then I'll need to be the ferryman. I'll take Zhao and

Josephine first. You stay here with Neith."

"We could all go and leave her here," Carter suggested.

"There's still Donavan and Jamila to think about," Josephine reminded him.

"Exactly," Blasko said. "I'll come back once you're all off the island. I can deal with the good captain. What I don't want is to have to worry about Neith too."

Carter nodded.

Blasko and Carter carried Zhao to the raft. Once he and Josephine were onboard, Blasko pushed the raft into waist-deep water, ignoring his own discomfort, then he climbed in and began to row hard for the boat.

They were halfway there when the moonlight illuminated three of the mutated fishmen from Cedar Island climbing up the side of the boat.

CHAPTER TWENTY-FIVE

"Look," Blasko told Josephine.

"Two of them look like the ones who tried to kill you." Josephine's voice was raw with tension.

"Damn it! We have to turn around." Blasko swung the raft about and rowed back toward the beach, where Carter stood looking confused.

"There are some of the locals on the boat!" Blasko yelled when they were fifty feet from shore.

Suddenly they were bumped from below and the raft rocked violently. Before they could react, the raft was bumped again and they were thrown into the water.

The creatures surrounded them in the water. Josephine had gone in closest to the shore, but she hesitated for a moment until she saw Blasko's head bob to the surface.

"Swim!" he yelled at her as one of the creatures grabbed onto him with its awkward webbed hands. Blasko took hold of the arm and, with as much leverage as he could muster in the water, he twisted it back until he heard a sickening snap. The creature howled in pain and fell away from him.

Rapidly losing strength in the water, Blasko dove down in search of Zhao. His hand brushed the man's shirt and he grabbed it, twisting to get a good grip before pushing off the bottom toward land. He surfaced as the water became shallow enough to walk. Hearing the monsters surging through the water behind him, he didn't look back. Josephine and Carter waded out to help him.

They all made it to shore only to see two of the creatures pull themselves out of the water behind them. Blasko felt for the pistol he'd taken from Neith, but it was gone, lost when the raft capsized.

"Give it up, Baron," said Captain Hume from behind him. He was pointing a gun at all of them. "Don't worry about our friends from the sea. Or, I should say, *my* friends from the sea. Move back toward me slowly, or I'll be forced to shoot one of your companions. Not even sure myself which one I'd kill first."

The captain's callous tone left no doubt that he was sincere. Blasko backed away, still looking at the creatures. Fresh out of the water, they looked even more like fish-human hybrids than the men he'd met in the bar.

"You attacked our father," the one on the right said in a voice that sounded like he was trying to swallow water while he spoke. Blasko could see odd marks on their necks, below where their ears should have been. He guessed that they were gills.

"Your father attacked me first!" Blasko yelled to them.

"Don't care," the other one mumbled in the same waterlogged voice.

"These are the Marsh brothers," Captain Hume said, as if making a formal introduction.

"Do you have them?" the brother on the right asked him.

"First introduce yourself to the vampire standing before you. He is a marvel. And you have only about five hours left to get to know him."

"We kill him."

"That's a little rude. Baron, that one is Jasper. The one on the left is Silas. Trust me, boys, he will suffer much more if we stake him out on the sand so he can experience the sunrise."

"Do you have the journals?" Jasper asked again.

"Everything is there. We still need to carry it down here to the beach."

"Must hurry," Silas said menacingly.

"Why? We have all of these hooligans rounded up. Which reminds me." Captain Hume stepped over and pulled the rag out of Neith's mouth.

"About time!" she yelled.

"Careful. Now that the Marsh brothers are here, I'm no longer sure that you are necessary to my plans."

"I wouldn't try that," Neith warned. "You aren't half the scholar I am."

"There's some truth there. Fine." He bent down and untied her. She glared at him the whole time.

"Did they help you with the murders?" Blasko asked.

"Funny thing about that. When I killed Wallace Brock, I took him out in a small boat in the middle of the night to get rid of him. That's when I met these two. Once I explained that I was familiar with their ancestors and cousins on the other side of the world, we talked and learned that we had some compatible goals. We were all—"

"What the hell are they?" Josephine interrupted.

"They are hybrids. Their great-great-grandfather, Obed Marsh, mated with the Deep Ones, dwellers from the depths. At least that's what one tribe in the South Pacific calls them. I was there at Kanaky where the natives live in harmony with the Deep Ones. Obed Marsh visited the islands in the early 1800s and learned some of their secrets. He brought wealth and the Deep Ones to Innsmouth, Massachusetts."

"This is the corruption I was talking about," Carter said, pointing with his good hand at them.

"Show them your other arm. They'll be amused," Hume said.

"The hell with you!"

"Do it." Hume pointed the gun at Josephine. Reluctantly, Carter held up his arm.

The Marshes were more than interested. They slouched toward him in an oddly effective shuffle, eager to examine the tentacles.

"You have been touched by Dagon! The great elder," Jasper proclaimed.

"Told you they'd like those tentacles." Hume laughed. "Don't get too friendly with him, boys. Robert Olmstead is a relative of the Carters."

"*Distant* relative," Carter mumbled.

"What are you getting out of this?" Blasko asked the captain.

"Riches and eternal life."

"Trust me. Eternal life is overrated."

"The books I found will give me powers that are hard to comprehend. All will be mine when I take the Oath of Dagon."

"Remember your promise to us!" Jasper burbled angrily.

"You'll get your gold."

"You promised them gold?" Blasko asked.

"More than that. The journals of Obed Marsh chronicle the deals he made for the gold trinkets he melted down at the Innsmouth refinery. With the journals, they can reconstruct the network he'd formed with the Deep Ones. The other fools around here have only been after fish! Pathetic use of a relationship that could net them a fortune and immense power."

"We will rebuild our family's fortune!" Silas was shaking, but whether with anger or excitement, Blasko couldn't tell.

"One thing I don't understand is why you killed the one who attacked me," Josephine said.

Captain Hume ignored her. "Enough talk. Now that you all are here, we can kill these interlopers and be done. Everyone except the vampire."

"I kill her." Silas Marsh was obviously still angry at Josephine for interrupting their attack on Blasko.

"Touch her and I will pull you apart with my bare hands," Blasko said with an intensity that made even a creature such as Silas pause.

"I don't fear you," he said, never blinking his bulging black eyes.

"More the fool you," Blasko warned.

The creature hissed and moved toward Josephine. Carter, standing next to her, stepped in to stop Silas's advance. He extended his tentacled arm and Silas hesitated.

"Go on. Kill her," Jasper urged.

Silas reached out and swatted Carter to the side. Carter stumbled and almost went to the ground. As he regained his balance, it brought him close enough to Captain Hume that he would be able to get inside his gun arm before the man could pull the trigger. Glancing quickly at Blasko to make sure the vampire was aware of what was about to happen, Carter charged forward. Unfortunately, Hume saw the move coming and swung his gun in closer to his body. Even as Carter grabbed the captain's arm with his tentacles, he was still able to shoot Carter in the leg as they both fell to the sand.

Blasko took advantage of the confusion and flew at Silas, who stopped his attack on Josephine to meet the assault. What Silas hadn't counted on was Josephine. Once he turned away from her, she ran at him and grabbed his face with her nails. They sank deep into the wet, scaly skin of his face. Blasko slammed into him from behind and all three of them hit the ground.

Silas was howling at the pain from Josephine's nails. Jasper ran to his brother's aide and was able to batter Blasko into a defensive retreat, while Silas managed to get Josephine under some control. Blasko struggled and landed a stunning blow to Jasper, who fell back away from him.

Carter, ignoring the fiery pain in his leg, used the same tactic that had worked so well on Neith to smother the captain with his tentacles. Hume flailed desperately as he lost oxygen, finally releasing his hold on the gun.

Neith, who'd been stunned by the turn of events, came out of her temporary paralysis and ran to Hume's aid. She grabbed the gun he'd dropped and placed it against Carter's temple.

"Let him go or I will kill you!" she screamed in Carter's face.

Feeling the barrel of the gun against his head and hearing the truth in her voice, Carter released his hold. Hume kicked at Carter as he fought his way to a standing position.

"Stop fighting or Carter dies!" Neith shouted to the others. Josephine and Blasko slowly gave up their struggles against the Marsh brothers. Silas and Jasper pulled both of them to the ground and squatted on top of them, nasty wet grins on their faces.

Blasko was at a loss what to do. If he attacked the creatures, then Carter would die. If he did nothing, the monsters would kill Josephine. Even if by some miracle he was able to fight them off, Carter would still die and then Neith would turn the gun on him.

For a moment nothing happened. They were all too exhausted from the fighting. Then Blasko saw Silas's mouth open, revealing rows of sharp teeth that he lowered toward Josephine. Blasko's body tensed as he prepared to throw Jasper off his back and lunge at Silas, Carter's life be damned.

"Stop!" yelled a voice, coming loud and clear from the dunes behind them. It sounded almost like a movie director yelling "*Cut!*" and had the same effect. Everyone looked around to see who had spoken and what power they had to enforce the command.

Josephine couldn't believe what she was seeing. Lined up on the shallow dunes and holding lanterns were a dozen more creatures. Some of them were wearing fishermen's clothes, while others weren't wearing anything at all. They had Donavan and Jamila with them, though both looked as if they were in some sort of daze. In the middle of the group stood the man who'd shouted. She recognized Enoch, the fisherman who had creeped her out the day before and who had rented the boat to Donavan. He was holding a shotgun to his shoulder, pointed at the Marsh brothers.

"Silas, Jasper, let them go," he ordered.

The Marsh brothers turned as one and started back toward the surf. Hume and Neith followed close behind them, heading for the raft.

Blasko, Josephine and Carter stared in disbelief at the surprise retreat. As they watched, a dozen more heads rose out of the water. The creatures moved slowly and steadily into the shallows, causing the four fugitives to stop.

"We've taken the rest of your crew, Jasper. Everyone needs to just give up 'cause we got you dead to rights," Enoch said, walking toward them.

Blasko and Josephine got to their feet and Blasko went to check on Carter, who waved him off. After a brief examination, he'd realized that the bullet had only dug a channel along his thigh, not penetrating his leg. He stood up slowly and limped over to Blasko and Josephine, and the three of them faced Enoch.

"I met you the other day," Josephine said, brushing nervously at the sand on her clothes.

"You were scared of me." Enoch walked toward her, but Blasko and Carter moved in to block his path.

"If I meant you harm, there would be nothing you could do to prevent it," Enoch said. "I've come to stop this coup. It is a desecration of all that we believe."

"And exactly what is that?" Blasko asked.

"We are servants of the True Order of Dagon."

"From Innsmouth," Carter said.

"Yes and no. My father was on the ship that brought the gold and documents to this place. He and Hiram Sargent sabotaged it. When it sank, they brought the treasure here and hid it."

"According to the story my uncle heard, the ship went down in a storm." Josephine looked at the man carefully, trying to determine his motives.

"There was a storm, but the ship could have weathered it. My father and his friend took the opportunity to end another of Obed Marsh's mad dreams. Obed built that ship, the *Sumatra Princess*, in order to bring men and supplies, as well as gold and sacred documents, to Cedar Island as part of a colonization scheme."

"Why?" asked Carter, fascinated.

"He knew that, sooner or later, Innsmouth was going to be cleansed by the people of Arkham. It was only a matter of time before someone noticed that the decay and rot were more than just the result of the financial collapse of a seaside town."

"Why did your father try to stop him?"

"My family and a few others in Innsmouth never bought into Obed's avarice. My grandmother was a Kanaky Islander. She knew about the Deep Ones. That they had to be controlled. Instead, Obed thought he could join with them to gain gold and power. His Esoteric Order of Dagon was a nasty attempt to force the shore-huggers to breed with and accept the Deep Ones and Obed's hybrids. When he talked of expanding his empire by colonizing an island in Florida, my father saw it as an opportunity to take down some of Obed's ego and escape his control."

"So your father and his friend took over the island for themselves," Carter said.

"No! They moved here with the intent of living in harmony with the people here. And we have."

"Obed never came looking for his gold or papers?" Carter pushed.

"Word reached him about the wreck and that all hands were lost along with the ship. Some of Obed's own people thought that his idea to colonize an island in Florida was folly. Even if Obed had wanted to, he would have been hard pressed to mount a search effort. Since the whole escapade was an embarrassment to him, he was more than willing to let it go."

"You seem to have done well enough on the island," Blasko observed.

"My father inherited a great deal of my grandmother's

knowledge. He could call the Deep Ones and had runes and spells to control them. He taught others. The True Order of Dagon was founded with the purpose to live in harmony with the Deep Ones *and* the shore dwellers."

"What happened to all that harmony?" Blasko pointed at the Marsh brothers to make his point.

"After the raids on Innsmouth, some of the survivors came here, including those two. Over the last few years, most of them have become part of the community. But there are those who long for the old days in Innsmouth and aren't willing to drop the ways of the Esoteric Order of Dagon. They saw the chance to find old Obed's gold and journals as the opportunity to return to their wickedness."

"Who killed my uncle?" Josephine asked.

"An event I deeply regret. One of our people found out that he had discovered the treasure and panicked. I can't tell you that it was an accident, but it wasn't planned and the person regretted it."

"Regretted it? Is that all?"

"If we are discovered, every member of our order knows that we would be rounded up and killed or put into asylums. Exactly what happened to those in Innsmouth. The man who killed your uncle was punished."

"How?"

"Hideously," was all Enoch would say. His words sent a chill up Josephine's spine and ended any curiosity she still had.

"What about the man who tried to steal the letter?"

"Elijah had been watching Mitzi, our postmistress, ever since Captain Hume had taken an interest in her. He overheard the conversation you had with her, and decided on his own to get the letter sooner rather than later. A decision I would have approved. Remember, it's worth our lives not to be discovered. If a great treasure hoard had been found here, we would have been exposed to the eyes of the world."

"Captain Hume killed Elijah," Josephine said.

"I didn't have a choice," Hume barked out in his defense.

"He was my nephew." Enoch looked over at the others. "We knew it was one of them, but we didn't know which. We disposed of the body, as we've always done with our kind."

"You can't let an outsider get a good look at one of your dead," Blasko agreed. Everyone grew silent for a moment, then he asked, "What about us?"

"We can't let you have the gold, and we need some of the books that are in the cache."

"What for?"

"That is the good news for you and your friends. There are spells that we can use to cloak Cedar Island from the outside world. It will be a long process, but when it's done, we will be safe from you and yours."

"What about the people on the island who aren't members of the True Order of Dagon?"

"As we work our spells, they will eventually want to move away. Once off the island, they will only remember their lives, but not the truth of our existence. With time, the island will disappear off of maps and everyone who's been here will forget the island ever existed."

"Even us?" Josephine asked.

"You and the baron… I see his blood in you. No, I think you will always remember."

"And the other treasure hunters?"

"Captain Hume and Neith stay. The others… I think they can be made to forget and want nothing more than to return to their old lives."

"You promise a great deal," Carter said.

"Do you wish your arm returned to normal?" Enoch asked.

Carter looked stunned at the prospect. "You can do that? Yes, please," he whispered.

"I think it's rather remarkable as it is, but if you want it to return to its natural state, we can do that."

A small part of Josephine's mind wanted to know what

they planned to do with Hume, Neith and the Marshes, but the more rational part told her that knowing would only lead to scars on her psyche and nightmares when she slept.

Blasko looked at the sky, knowing that dawn was rapidly approaching. "We need to return to Cedar Island. Would you help us get the others to the boat?"

Once everyone was on the rented boat, Enoch handed Josephine a small bottle from his pocket.

"Give them all this tonic when you put them to bed. When they wake, their memories will already be fading. As for the young Asian, I think he will survive if he's tended to. A member of our order has some medical knowledge. I'll send him to the hotel later this morning." Then he turned to Carter. "Wait for me in your cabin. We have a lot of work to do."

They returned to the hotel half an hour before dawn. Josephine sent Blasko to his coffin, while Anton helped her put the three treasure hunters to bed. Anton offered to watch over Zhao until the promised help arrived.

"I'll sleep in the baron's room," Josephine told Anton. While she was confident that they were no longer in any danger, she was sure that she would sleep better being close to him.

At noon, Josephine heard a soft but determined knocking on Blasko's door. She tried to ignore it, but whoever it was wasn't going away. She got up and hurriedly draped a blanket over Blasko's coffin to hide it. When she opened the door, she saw a nervous-looking Bobby Tucker standing in the hallway.

"Why are you in the baron's room?" he asked.

Amused that this was his first question, she opened the door wider so that he could see the bed. Josephine didn't want Bobby getting any crazy ideas.

"He's… sleeping elsewhere," she said evasively, hoping Bobby wouldn't ask any more questions about Blasko.

"What are you doing here? Anton said you wouldn't come for a few more days."

"I couldn't wait. I was worried about what y'all had gotten yourselves into this time."

"She's not in her—" Grace said, coming out of Josephine's room and seeing her standing in Blasko's door wearing her robe. "What you doing in there?" she asked with more than a hint of reproach.

"I was getting some much-needed rest until y'all showed up." Josephine hadn't meant to sound so ungrateful. "I'm sorry. I appreciate that you're here, but we had a tough night. I'd like to get a few more hours' sleep."

After a little more convincing, they let her go back to bed.

Later, she joined Bobby for a drink in the dining room. Looking down at his glass of whiskey, Bobby said, "I won't ask why you were in your cousin's room." There was more sadness than anger in his voice.

Josephine thought about ignoring his comment, but she cared about Bobby and realized he deserved more, especially after driving all that way to check on her.

"Bobby, I want to be honest with you. Dragomir and—"

"I know. I can see it in the way you look at each other. Are you really cousins?"

"No. It's a… long story."

"If it affects you, I'd like to hear it."

"I know you would." She took his hand. "I don't have a dearer friend in the world than you, but the story involves secrets that aren't mine alone."

"I'm not stupid. After everything we've been through, I've sort of figured out that Blasko isn't like… other people."

"I will tell you someday. Just not today."

"Are you coming home now?"

"We'll leave as soon as the sun sets." She squeezed his hand, then let it go.

EPILOGUE

Blasko sat in the parlor trying to read Dashiell Hammett's *The Glass Key*, which had arrived in the mail that day. However, he was finding it hard to concentrate over the sound of Josephine's footsteps as she walked from one end of the room to the other, varying her destination just enough so that he couldn't accuse her of pacing. With a heavy sigh, he put the book down on the end table.

"What's wrong?" he asked, anticipating that it had something to do with their strange experiences on Cedar Island the week before. They'd both been a little restless since their return.

Josephine stopped and looked out the open window, then finished the gin and lime she'd mixed a few minutes earlier. "You don't want to talk about it."

Resisting the urge to sigh again, Blasko stood up and walked over to her. The weather had improved a little that week and a light summer breeze came through the window, blowing a lock of hair across her face. He reached out and tenderly brushed it away. "Tell me."

"It's about what you said on the boat." Josephine leaned against him and he wrapped his arms around her. "Did you really mean it?"

"Yes, I meant it. Josie, I think I've loved you from the first moment I saw you in my old fortress—you were so fearless and strong… and maybe a little reckless." His lips ran softly over her hair as he held her in a firm embrace. "At first I thought what I felt was just a part of our blood bond, and that's why I tried to deny it. Now I know that it is so much more… But still I worry. I would give anything to avoid the pain I will feel as I watch you grow old. Or, worse, feeling your envy and anger as you grow more feeble while I remain the same."

She looked up at him and he could see the love in her eyes. "So where does that leave us?" she asked.

"You know what the choices are. Do you think you could live as I do?"

The bluntness of the question made her pause. "I don't know," she finally whispered into his shoulder.

"Would I have chosen to be like this, knowing what I do now? No… never. What's been done to me can never be undone. I won't let it happen to you."

"Even if I ask you to do it?"

"I told you what it is like. What if I changed you, but then you came to hate me… or yourself? How could either of us live with that?"

"Maybe you could become… human again. I'm sorry, I know that sounds awful. I don't mean that you aren't human now…" Josephine shook her head and tears fell onto Blasko's shirt as she clung to him.

"Years ago I searched for a way out of this… condition. I never found anything to give me the faintest glimmer of hope."

"Maybe Franklin can help. He told us how Enoch used the old books to undo his deformity and now he's recovering."

Blasko eased back from her and gave her a small smile, pulling a handkerchief out of his pocket to wipe away her tears. "And I would have enjoyed watching the process, especially once he realized he had to take the Oath of the

True Order of Dagon. But remember that the corruption had only reached his shoulder. What I suffer from took me over body and soul centuries ago."

"But we could search for a way," Josephine insisted. When he didn't respond, she pressed him. "Promise me that you won't give up. It might be useless, but we have to try."

Blasko had never seen her plead for anything and it took him by surprise. For a moment he couldn't speak, but then he said, "We'll search together," and sealed the promise with a kiss.

After Josephine had gone to bed, Blasko walked down the stairs to his basement apartment, where he found Anton petting and talking to Poe, the resident black cat.

"Why don't you take him upstairs and feed him?" Blasko suggested. Anton nodded and carried the cat, happily cradled in his arms, up the stairs. Blasko locked the door behind him.

In his bedchamber, Blasko went over to the bier that held his coffin and shifted it enough to open the lid of a compartment he'd cut into the floor beneath it. The space held several items he valued, along with the *Necronomicon* that he'd taken from Carter.

He heard a squeaking overhead and looked up to see Vasile hanging upside down between the floor joists, looking down at him. The bat seemed anxious at the sight of the book and flew over to the small hole in the wall near the ceiling that allowed him to fly outside.

"The book scares me too," Blasko admitted.

He heard more squeaking near the hole and saw a second bat stick its face into the room and nuzzle Vasile. "I am happy for you, my friend. We all need love."

With great trepidation, Blasko carried the book into his parlor and settled into his favorite chair. For a few minutes he just sat and looked down at the strange leather binding. At last, he sighed and opened the cover, beginning his search of the accursed volume.

Baron Blasko and Josephine return in:

DUST
The Baron Blasko Mysteries–Book 5

Cover design by Corvid Design
Cover illustration ©2020 Duncan Eagleson

AUTHOR'S NOTE

Fans of H.P. Lovecraft will have noticed the influence of his short story "The Shadow Over Innsmouth." If you're not familiar with Lovecraft, be sure to check it out. It's a very accessible introduction to the author and the mythos he created.

ABOUT THE AUTHOR

A. E. Howe lives and writes on a farm in the wilds of North Florida with his wife, horses and more cats than he can count. He received a degree in English Education from the University of Georgia and is a produced screenwriter and playwright. His first published book was *Broken State*. The Larry Macklin Mysteries is his first series and he released a new series, the Baron Blasko Mysteries, in summer 2018. The first book in the Macklin series, *November's Past*, was awarded two silver medals in the 2017 President's Book Awards, presented by the Florida Authors & Publishers Association; the ninth book, *July's Trials*, was awarded two silver medals in 2018. Howe is a member of the Mystery Writers of America, and was co-host of the "Guns of Hollywood" podcast for four years on the Firearms Radio Network. When not writing, Howe enjoys riding, competitive shooting and working on the farm.

www.ingramcontent.com/pod-product-compliance
Lightning Source LLC
Chambersburg PA
CBHW061541210726
48287CB00006B/2037